Ruby
Book 1

Daughters of the Dagger
Series

Elizabeth Rose

Cover created by Elizabeth Rose Krejcik

ISBN -10: 1500813737
ISBN-13: 978-1500813734

Books by Elizabeth Rose:

♛ (Legacy of the Blade Series)
♛ Prequel
♛ Lord of the Blade – Book 1
♛ Lady Renegade – Book 2
♛ Lord of Illusion – Book 3
♛ Lady of the Mist – Book 4

♗ (Daughters of the Dagger Series)
♗ Prequel
♗ Ruby – Book 1
♗ Sapphire – Book 2
♗ Amber – Book 3
♗ Amethyst – Book 4

♟ (MadMan MacKeefe Series)
♟ Onyx – Book 1
♟ Aidan – Book 2
♟ Ian – Book 3

❋ (Elemental Series)
❋ The Dragon and the DreamWalker – Book 1: Fire
❋ The Duke and the Dryad – Book 2: Earth
❋ The Sword and the Sylph – Book 3: Air
❋ The Sheik and the Siren –Book 4: Water

♘ (Greek Myth Fantasy)
♘ Kyros' Secret
♘ The Oracle of Delphi
♘ Thief of Olympus
♘ The Pandora Curse

And More!
Visit http://elizabethrosenovels.com
to read excerpts, and to view video book trailers.

Prequel

One

England, 1335

Mirabelle de Burgh slipped four gold coins from the pouch at her waist and slid them quickly across the table toward the old hag with the clouded eyes. She hoped this was the old blind woman she'd been searching for, and that the cordwainer's wife in the high part of town had been telling the truth and not just idle gossip. If this was only the product of wagging tongues and not superstition as she hoped, then she'd just seen the last of her coins. Being on Grope Lane, she was already surprised that she hadn't been accosted.

She pulled the hood of her cloak higher and glanced nervously down the dark, narrow street that wasn't really more than an alley. She knew she shouldn't be in this questionable part of town, and especially not unescorted. This is where the beggars, the thieves and the tarts all saw to make their living.

Elizabeth Rose

Grope Lane was scattered with litter and rotten fruit as well as discarded bones from rancid meat and old fish. Pots filled with urine were being dumped out of overhead windows constantly, and she had to walk a crooked path on her way here just to keep from being splashed.

Pigs roamed freely amongst the crowd as well as stray, mangy dogs. Women in gowns that exposed most of their breasts as well as their legs leaned lazily in front of the pub as well as in every shadowed doorway. And though she was hidden beneath her cloak and covered from head to foot, Mirabelle knew every filthy, despicable man in that alleyway had his eyes fastened on her at that moment.

A shiver coursed through her and as she'd put the coins on the table, she couldn't help but notice her own hand shaking. She risked everything by sneaking away from her husband and coming here to begin with, but she'd done it out of naught more than desperation.

The odor clinging to the heavy air filled her nostrils and twisted her stomach, making her want to wretch. She felt lightheaded and knew she needed to get away from here quickly before she swooned. Her husband, Talbot, Earl of Blackpool, wouldn't be happy that she'd stolen his coins to begin with, let alone spent them on something he would consider blasphemy – the work of the devil. But that's not the way she saw it at all. This was merely acting on a superstition in order to help them, and nothing else.

She had to hurry, as Talbot would be finished at the blacksmith's soon and realize she was no longer waiting for her shoes to be repaired at the cordwainer's. She looked back to the old blind woman sitting behind the table, only hoping she truly had the daggers even tho though her table top was empty.

Mirabelle believed the superstition that if one bought a dagger from a blind woman, she was sure to conceive a child anon. Ever since her marriage to the earl two years prior, she had not been able to bear him an heir. He wanted a son desperately, and she was determined to give him one, no matter what she had to do to achieve it.

"Hurry," she said the to the woman, glancing back toward the main street. "I'll take as many daggers as my money will buy."

The old woman reached out her bony fingers, patting the table, feeling around the surface. Then she picked up a coin in her hand. She ran her thumb over it and tested the weight in her palm to make sure 'twas gold. Then she brought it to her face and sniffed it and her tongue lashed out and she tasted it as well. When the woman was satisfied that it was gold indeed, she reached under the table and pulled out a tray with five of the most beautiful and expensive looking daggers Mirabelle had ever seen in her life.

Each was an etched metal with an intricate design that ran over the two-toned hilt and down the blade. The top had a knobbed grip that reminded her of a crown. And in the center of each hilt was mounted a large oval gemstone, each being of a different type and of various colors. Her heart beat wildly. She wanted them all. She wanted a child for each of the daggers.

"I'll take them all," she said, scooping them into a pile.

The old woman's hand shot out and covered hers. Mirabelle felt as if she'd been struck with a hot iron rod as the woman's bony finger tapped the top of her hand. She pulled her hand back and held it against her chest, not liking the way it felt.

"You only have enough gold for four," the woman told her. "So choose carefully. And remember, if you name each of your children after the stone in the hilt, they will be sure to find true love in this lifetime."

"True love? Really?" She looked back down the alley, searching for her husband. Thankfully he was not in sight. She'd once been married to a cruel man who had beaten and hurt her, and she was just lucky when the earl killed him and claimed her as his bride. The moment he'd saved her from the wretched man, she'd known he was her true love. She was so happy now, and she wanted her children to be happy as well. And most of all, she wanted to let the earl know she was a good wife, by giving him the sons he wanted and deserved.

She had no choice. She had to buy these daggers and assure herself of not only conceiving a child but sealing her children's fate of true love as well. She was so excited she could barely stand it.

"I want all boys," she announced. "I haven't been able to conceive a baby for my husband and I don't want his eye wandering. He wants sons more than anything, and when we married I promised him I would give him many."

The old woman nodded slightly. "The purchase of each dagger ensures you will get what you want."

"All right then," she said opening the large bag attached to her waist belt. "I will choose now." She ran her hand over the beautiful daggers and surveyed the precious stones twinkling in a stray beam of sunlight that happened to shine down through the tall, two storey, top-heavy buildings around her. "But please, can you tell me the name of each stone so I will know what to name my children in order for them to attain their true love?"

"The dark red stone is a ruby," the blind woman told her, reaching out and somehow knowing just by the feel of it, which one it was. She held it up to her. "This is one of the hardest stones and also the most precious. This child will be very courageous and strong, as well as have a heart and a mind of their own."

"I like that," she said anxiously picking up the dagger with the purple stone and handing it to the old woman. "What is this one, please?"

The old woman ran her fingers across the stone, seeming to be in deep thought. "This is amethyst. The child of this stone will center around perfection as well as have a positive outlook on life and a strong spirit. This stone also ensures business affairs to prosper." The woman put down the dagger and told her about the others without picking them up. "The golden stone is amber. The fire within it has the power to purify and heal, though it is the most delicate of all the stones. This is also the most virtuous and said to bring good luck to warriors."

"Aye, that sounds wonderful," she said, listening intently. "And what about the blue stone?"

"The blue stone is sapphire," the woman told her. "This is the stone of awakening and this child will know prosperity and abundance in more ways than one. And the child will find joy, though it may not be in such a virtuous form as with the amber. Never-the-less, joy will be found in other ways."

"Prosperous, yes," she said, devouring what she was hearing, even if she knew her husband would object to having sons named after these stones. But she'd convince him. Her children's fate would be formed because of it.

"Quickly," she said, glancing at the beggars and dirty men eying her from the other end of the street. "Tell me about the last stone. The black one."

"You might not want to consider this one," said the old woman, reaching out to take it away.

"Nay, please," she said, laying her hand on top of the woman's, causing her to release it and replace her hand back under the table. "I want to know."

"That is onyx," said the old woman. "It is the most powerful of all the stones, and this child will be unstoppable."

"Oh, I want that," she said.

"But . . ." the old woman held up a finger. "Because of the orange line down the middle, there is much duality involved. So much, so that one may think this child has gone mad. This one will be wild with no boundaries at all. And they will also follow their path alone, for this is not like the other stones. I don't advise you to choose it, but the decision must be yours." The old woman held her hands on her lap and waited for Mirabelle's answer.

Once more she scanned the gems, knowing this was taking much too long. She liked everything the woman said, but she needed to choose quickly. She ended up taking the old woman's advice and taking all but the black onyx.

"All right, I have chosen and will put the blades into my pouch," she told the blind woman.

"Four only," she reminded her.

"Of course," she said, scooping up the ruby, sapphire, amethyst and amber ones and placing them into her pouch with nimble fingers. Mirabelle was very aware of her surroundings, knowing she had to guard these well. She pulled the drawstring closed and once more looked at the dagger with the onyx stone.

Black. The color of death, she told herself. She feared it, yet it called to her at the same time. The old woman had said this child would be the most powerful of all the other stones. She wanted to give her husband a powerful son who could someday be a great leader and ruler. She struggled with her decision, not wanting to leave any of them behind, but not having enough gold to buy them all. Still, she knew she had to have it.

"Thank you," she said to the old hag, turning to go. But something made her stop and look at the black-stoned dagger once more. She just couldn't leave it. And there was no way she'd be able to ask her husband for the money. There was only one thing to do. She couldn't even believe she was considering the illicit thought in her head, but she had to steal it.

Knowing the old woman was blind, she took advantage of her by slipping the fifth dagger beneath the folds of her cape. The woman sat still, staring into the air, and Mirabelle let out a breath of relief that she'd succeeded. She turned quickly to leave, but smashed into the chest of a beggar boy standing right behind her. The dagger with the black stone slipped from her grip and clattered to the cobbled stones of the alleyway at her feet. She gasped and looked down. The stone had cracked right up the crooked orange line, leaving the stone damaged, though it still remained mounted in the hilt

"Do ye have a coin ta spare, milady?" asked the young boy, holding out his dirty hand.

"Nay! Leave me alone," she cried, backing away from him, noticing the old woman making her way around the table and bending down and patting the ground, retrieving the dagger with the black stone.

"You tried to steal from me," the blind hag accused her.

"Nay, I . . . just knocked it from the table, that's all," she lied, feeling the panic in her chest growing, threatening to choke her.

"A bite of food perhaps?" asked the boy, his gaunt hand snaking out toward her once again, and she reached out and pushed it away with two fingers, not wanting to touch him.

"I said nay, now leave me already."

"Please, my lady will ye help a poor boy?"

"Nay! Now go away," she warned him, shooing him with her hand. She noticed the whores and dirtied men looking over and venturing closer.

"But you must have somethin' te give me?" the boy tried one last time.

"How many times do I have to tell you, no? Now leave me and I never want to see you again," she shouted.

The boy hung his head low, disappointed. He left, wandering down the alley searching the street for any bit of discarded food.

"You tried to steal a dagger and you broke the stone in the process." The old woman stood and held up the dagger in two hands for her to see.

"Nay, I didn't. Truly," she said, thinking the woman was going to make her pay for it or make her trade one of the daggers in her pouch. She couldn't allow that. She clutched the bag to her chest protectively, not wanting to give up any of her promised children, and started away.

"You also pushed away a boy," the old woman told her. "Not once, but four times. Because of these things, you will pay for your actions."

She stopped and turned abruptly. "What are you saying?" she asked. "I told you, I have no more money. I cannot pay."

"By denying that boy, you have pushed every boy child from your life. Because you dismissed him four times, each of your four daggers will now bring you only girls."

"No, tell me that is not true. Please."

"And you will pay for this dagger you broke, tho 'twill not be with coin."

"I tell you, I didn't try to steal it," she tried one last time to convince her.

"You lie. You think because I am blind you can take from me whatever you want without paying. But now you will pay. And 'twill be in ways you've never imagined. Because of your greediness and deceitfulness, you will lose not only a boy child but also your true love in exchange for your actions today."

"Nay, I don't want to lose my true love. My husband means everything to me. Please don't say he is going to die because of me."

"Who said he was going to die? Besides, it was your actions that caused this, so you will be the one to pay."

"What?" she asked, suddenly realizing that if her husband wasn't going to die, then the old hag must have meant her. It was bad enough her actions had ruined her chance to ever give her husband the son he'd always wanted, but now she was going to lose her life in the process. She would never be able to live out her life with her true love after all. What had she done? In her desperation she had become greedy and deceitful. She had never acted this way before. And now, she had ruined everything. She could

8

never tell her husband what she'd done, or he would never love her again.

She felt the alleyway becoming smaller as the smelly, deceitful thieves, beggars and whores closed in around her. They reached out and touched her cloak, and she suddenly felt like she was no better than them.

She clutched the bag with the daggers tightly, holding it to her chest. Dread filled her, and her heart raced. She had to get out of there and back to her husband. Her head pounded and she no longer knew who she was. Holding her pouch protectively, she pushed her way through the devilish crowd, and ran down the alley as fast as she could. She never wanted to see that blind hag or even think about her words of doom ever again. She was going to have children now, and that was all that mattered, even if they weren't boys. But she couldn't get the vision of that dagger with the broken black stone out of her mind. Neither would she ever forget the voice of the hag warning her not to choose it in the first place. This was going to haunt her for the rest of her life.

Two

"Push, my lady, push," shouted the midwife.

Mirabelle gritted her teeth and pushed with all her might. Even the pain of birthing this baby could not dampen the joy in her soul. Her husband waited just outside the chamber door, pacing back and forth. He had high hopes the baby would be a son, but she knew differently.

"I see the baby's head," called out the midwife, and the rest of the servants scurried around, preparing coverings and a basin of water to cleanse the baby once 'twas born. One last push, and Mirabelle knew by the instant cry that her baby had now entered into this world.

"'Tis a girl," announced the midwife proudly. "A beautiful baby girl." She finished the preparations and laid the child on Mirabelle's chest. The midwife had wrapped the baby in a swaddling cloth, so when Mirabelle's husband rushed into the chamber, he didn't know if 'twas a girl or a boy.

"Do I have a son?" he asked, with hope in his eyes, but Mirabelle just shook her head. Her heart broke at his disappointment, but she reached out and touched his hand to comfort her true love.

Ruby

"Perhaps next time," she told him, knowing it was a lie. Still, she needed to give him hope. A hope of which no man should ever be deprived.

"I am still elated," he told her, kissing her on her head and rubbing his hand over the baby's back. "I will love any child you bear me, even if 'tis not a boy."

"Do you really mean that?" she asked, hoping he did, and praying the outcome may be different in the future, but she knew it wouldn't.

"Of course, my love," he told her with a smile that didn't reach his eyes.

She should have told him her secret right then and there, but she just couldn't. She'd just birthed a baby, and it was a joyous day, so she would not ruin it with idle chatter of silly superstitions that he wouldn't believe anyway. Perhaps he was right in not believing in them, and she should think the same. After all, this was just their first child, and perhaps the blind old hag had naught to do with her having a daughter instead of a son. But still, she reminded herself, the dagger did bring on conception just as the old hag had promised. And so quickly, too, as it had not yet been a year since her purchase. She'd just have to wait and see what would happen next before she worried more.

"What shall we name her?" asked Talbot, taking the baby into his arms. She realized he was going to make a wonderful father.

"I think she's a gem," said Mirabelle, remembering the hidden daggers that lay at the back of her wardrobe in a wooden box with a lid. She'd never showed them to him, but she would. Some day. Just not today. She went over the types of gems in her mind, remembering she was supposed to name her children after the stones in order to insure they'd find their true love. "Ruby is a pretty name, don't you agree?" she asked.

"Ruby?" His brow creased as if he thought it odd. Odd indeed, as it was not one of the more popular or common names of the time. Matter of fact, they didn't know anyone named Ruby.

"Don't you like the name?" she asked, holding her breath waiting for her husband's answer.

"I'm not sure," he said. "'Tis . . . different. But if you like it, my love, then Ruby shall be our first-born's name."

Mirabelle felt relief wash through her and she was once again able to breathe. It had been easy this time to convince him, as 'twas but their first child and her husband was playing to her wishes. But, she reminded herself, it may not be as easy with the naming of their next child. And it was only going to be a matter of time before she'd have to tell him of her deceit and deception.

Three

'Twas less than a year later, and as promised by the old hag after her purchase of the daggers, Mirabelle had birthed her second child. She sat up in bed, holding on to the newborn, her heart pumping rapidly as her husband entered the room with their first-born child, Ruby, in his arms. He hurried to the bed and sat on the edge, peering over Mirabelle's shoulder in order to see their new baby.

"Is it a boy?" he asked excitedly. "Tell me, wife, have you given me the son I want so desperately to be my heir?"

She just smiled and handed him the baby bundled in a tight cloth. Little Ruby looked on with curious brown eyes. Her blond hair was so pale it almost looked white.

"It is a son?" he shouted taking the baby in his hands, his smile widening from ear to ear. She wanted to lie and tell him he was right, and hopefully she'd believe it too. But nothing could change the course of events she'd set in motion the day she'd turned away the beggar boy. So, instead she just shook her head sullenly, her heart breaking as she watched the smile disappear quickly from his face.

"Another daughter?" he asked, trying to feign a smile. "Well, that's wonderful, too."

"It is," she said. "And since she is another gem, I think we should name her after a stone as well."

"I don't think so," he said with a shake of his head. "I would like a common name this time. Perhaps Gwyneth or Matilda."

She felt her pulse rising and knew she had to do something quickly to change his mind. And there was naught else but the obvious, she was afraid. She reached under the pillow where she had hidden the wooden box with the daggers and brought it forth.

"What is that?" her husband asked, his eyes narrowing as he surveyed it.

"'Tis . . . a present," she said, trying to think quickly of what she would tell him.

"What kind of present?" he asked. "And from whom?"

"Tis a present for our children," she answered. "From . . . from my cousin Lady Clarista," she lied.

"Lady Clarista?" he asked. "That is your English cousin who married that damned Scotsman named Ian MacKeefe, isn't it? I hate the Scots and don't want anything from that bloodthirsty cutthroat."

"'Tis not from him, but from Clarista only," she tried to convince him. "Look, she saved her money for a long time in order to give us these beautiful daggers for our children." She held up the dagger with the dark red stone. "See? She sent a dagger with a ruby in it since we named our first born, Ruby. I think it is a wonderful gift."

"She did?" Still holding the new baby, he looked curiously at the box. "Well, why did she send more than one dagger, if we hadn't yet had more children?"

"Why, because she knew I was pregnant," she said, pulling another blade from the box with the dark blue stone. "This is a sapphire. So we will name our new baby, Sapphire."

"This all seems a bit odd," he said, and she knew he was doubting her concocted story. "I know how tight the strings are on a Scotsman's pouch, and ol' Ian MacKeefe would never allow his wife to spend so much on such expensive gifts – especially for a baby."

"Well, as I said, she bought them, not him."

"With what? She would have to steal his gold to afford jeweled daggers. And any woman who would steal gold from her husband deserves to be beaten."

She slammed shut the lid on the box quickly before he could see the other two daggers. She'd never expected him to say that. "You don't really believe that, do you?" she asked, feeling anxiety course through her. "After all, you saved me from my first husband who was an ogre and beat me every day," she said.

"You are right, my love," he answered. "I am happy for the gift and if you want to name our second born, Sapphire, that is fine. But just tell that addlepated cousin of yours not to send any more jeweled daggers as gifts for any future children. If MacKeefe discovers what she's done it'll cause a blood feud between our families. I don't fancy another war, as this country has seen enough. Besides, I know our next born will be a boy and I would never consider naming my son after a damned gemstone."

"Of course not," she said, knowing for a fact that he would never have to do that. Because in her heart, though she wanted a son as well, she knew she'd never bear a boy. And she only had herself to blame for that. Her heart ached, wondering what lie she was going to have to tell her husband when the next daughter came along, as well as another jeweled dagger.

Elizabeth Rose

Four

The twins, Amethyst and Amber were born a year and a half later. To Mirabelle's relief, her husband had been away fighting for the king and not present at the time. This enabled her to name them after the gemstones and also to have the last two daggers already present by the time he returned home.

Of course he was not happy that she named them after gemstones – especially two more of them – and even less happy that she'd told them her cousin, Clarista, had sent two more daggers as presents.

Her husband had threatened to send a missive up to the Highlands to tell The MacKeefe himself just what his wife had been buying with his coin, but Mirabelle pleaded with him not to do it. She was able to distract him, as he enjoyed having two more children. He'd loved every one of their daughters, but as the years passed she could see the hope in his eyes diminishing of ever having a son.

And then the day came that surprised her more than anyone else. When the twins were already three years old and she and her husband had both accepted the fact that they would have no more children in this lifetime, the unexpected happened. She was pregnant once again.

Her husband paced the floor inside the bedchamber this time, certain the baby would be a boy, and not wanting to miss it by waiting outside the door as was proper. All her children were present on this occasion, being entertained by the nursemaid as she kept the girls occupied in the corner of the bedchamber, showing them their jeweled daggers.

Though the girls were still young, Mirabelle decided they should have their daggers even at this early age. She wanted them to know they were named from a gemstone, and had told them the qualities of each stone and what they'd meant. That part may be forgotten through the years, but 'twas important they remember that their mother was the one who gave them the opportunity to find true love.

She'd told them they would all find their true love and the daggers would prove it, but they were young and they didn't understand. Neither did she explain further, afraid her husband would hear and start asking questions.

But now, she lay in pain – more pain than she'd ever known birthing any of her daughters. She didn't expect this, and neither did she expect to bear another child in this lifetime, so she didn't understand it at all.

The one thing she really feared, was the part of the old hag telling her she would die. She'd thought she'd escaped her awful accusations, but today proved that the blind woman would have her revenge after all.

"What's the matter, sweetheart?" Talbot came to the bedside and held her hand. "You seem to be in so much pain. Was it like this when you birthed our daughters?"

She bit back the cry that threatened to spill from her lips, batting away the tears wanting to consume her.

"Nay, this is different, husband. This pregnancy is . . . more severe than all the rest."

"Then mayhap it's a boy," he said, and once more she saw that hope in his eyes. She was about to tell him that he was wrong or she didn't know, until she suddenly remembered the words of the blind woman on that day so long ago.

Because of your greediness and deceitfulness, you will not only lose a boy child but also your true love in exchange for your actions today.

She hadn't really realized until now that what the old woman meant was that she would birth a son and lose it, as well as lose her own life in the process.

"Aye, 'tis a boy," she reassured him with a sad smile. "But 'twill not live, my dear husband, and neither will I."

"Do not speak such utter nonsense," he told her. "You are going to be fine. So, do you really think it is a boy this time?"

"Yes, I am positive," she told him, gripping his hand and letting out a loud scream as the baby started to come.

"How can you say that?" he asked. "We thought the rest were boys as well."

"Nay," she said with tears in her eyes, bearing down so as not to have her children in the room frightened by her screams of pain. "I knew all along we would have four girls, and I am sorry I never told you."

"Be still, wife. You are not thinking with a clear mind."

"Nay!" she screamed this time as she felt the size of the baby ripping her body apart. 'Twas almost as if she were birthing the son of the devil himself. "I deceived you and lied to you my true love, and now because of it you shall lose your only son and I shall die as well."

His face turned stone-like and the hope she'd seen there earlier now changed to darkened grief. "This has something to do with those cursed daggers, doesn't it?" he asked. "Wife, you need to tell me the truth right now."

"I'm sorry," she screamed, tears flowing down her cheeks. "I wanted to birth you a son so badly, and I was afraid you'd find a mistress if I couldn't give you what you wanted."

Ruby

"What are you saying?" He stood next to the bed and she'd never seen him look so angry, as he was normally a very calm man.

"Push, my lady," interrupted the midwife. "This baby is big and it cannot seem to escape from your body."

She clenched her jaw and pushed, but unfortunately the baby would not come. She screamed out in pain as well as anguish, and when she looked over to her four daughters they were all staring at her with wide eyes of fear. She wanted naught more than to comfort them and tell them all would be fine, but she couldn't. Besides, she knew 'twould only be another lie.

"Tell me," her husband shouted, and she had the feeling he already knew she'd done something wrong and was being punished by God.

"I stole your gold coins and used them to buy daggers from a blind old hag," she shouted, trying desperately to catch her breath as the air seemed to be avoiding her lungs.

"You were the one to buy the jeweled daggers, and not your cousin, Clarista? Why? Why would you do such a thing?"

"Because I'd heard the superstition that each jeweled dagger bought from a blind hag would ensure the birth of a child."

"Push, my lady, as the baby is turning blue and you are losing too much blood." The midwife worked quickly, but Mirabelle could tell by the look of horror upon the woman's face that there was naught much more she could do to help. It wouldn't be long now before her spirit fled her body and she left her daughters and her true love forever.

She felt the fires of hell running through her and then the hot poker of that old woman's finger as if she were there pointing out the fact she'd done wrong and would now die.

"This is blasphemy!" the earl told her. "This whole thing is the work of a witch, and you have sold your soul to the devil."

"Nay, it's a superstition only," she told him. "Nothing more. Please forgive me, for I only wanted to please you."

"What did the old hag tell you?" he asked, his voice low and firm.

"That I would have a child for each bought dagger," she explained. "And if I named them after the gemstones, they would each find their true love in this lifetime."

"This is all nonsense," he said, his voice growing louder as he was trying to be heard over every one of her screams.

"But I tried to steal a fifth dagger," she told him, tears now running down her face. "The stone broke when I dropped it as I bumped into a poor beggar boy."

"What do you mean?" he asked. "What is it you are trying to tell me?"

"Bring more cloth," called out the midwife, and all the servants ran around the room frantically. Her daughter Ruby broke free from the nursemaid's hold and ran to be by her side.

"I'm sorry, my lady," said the nursemaid running over to collect her.

"Nay, let her stay," said Mirabelle, running a hand through Ruby's silvery white locks. "Bring my other children to me as well. I want to say goodbye."

"Goodbye?" asked her husband, his anger diminishing as he must have realized the severity of the situation. "Wife, stop scaring the children."

Her daughters rushed to her side, every one of them crying except for Ruby, who like her gemstone was the strongest of them all, even at only the mere age of five years old.

"Children, I want to tell you all I am so sorry, and not to be greedy or deceitful as 'twill only come back to haunt you some day."

"Mirabelle, stop it," Talbot ground out, a frantic look on his face as he realized that he might lose her in childbirth after all.

"I pushed away a beggar boy four times," she cried. "The hag told me because of this I'd pushed away the sons in my life and would only have daughters."

"Why didn't you tell me this years ago?" asked her husband, leaning his body over hers, his hand reaching out to touch her arm.

"Because I was afraid you would be angry with me," she said. "I wanted children for you so desperately that I tried to steal the last dagger, but I dropped it and the onyx stone cracked right up the orange line in it. The old woman told me I'd lose a son as well as my true love because of it."

She no longer felt the pain now. Instead, she felt the weight of the world and all her guilt being lifted from her shoulders by her confession. Now, with her soul clean, she was ready to leave this world and move on. "Goodbye, my dear daughters," she said, reaching out and kissing each one of them in turn.

Little Ruby tried to stay strong but she, too, ended up crying. Mirabelle wiped a tear from the girl's eye and forced a smile. "Take care of your father for me," she told her.

"I will," the little girl said. "I'll stay with him forever, Mama, I promise."

Then Mirabelle took her husband's hand in hers, feeling the blood draining from her body quickly. Her head dizzied and her sight blurred and she knew she was on the edge of leaving her family and her world forever.

"Take care of our daughters, my love," she told him. "Please, don't betroth them, but rather let them find their own husbands. Their true loves. I am sorry once again for what I've done and only wish now that I had told you years ago."

"Mirabelle, don't," he said, and she saw for the first time since she'd known him the tears streaming from his eyes.

"I love you . . . all," she said, feeling her world slipping from her with each shallow breath. "And my biggest regret, dear husband . . . is that I could not birth you a son."

"The baby's a boy, my lord," called out the midwife.

Talbot's head snapped around, his heart thumping wildly in his chest at hearing the midwife's announcement.

"I have a son?" he asked, not understanding why the midwife looked so forlorn. Then with the shake of her head and by the bluish tone to the baby's skin, he understood. The old blind hag had been right. They had lost a son. His only son.

"Mama, wake up," he heard one of his daughter's say from behind him, and when he turned back to his beautiful wife he realized - she was dead.

"Nay!" he cried out, getting to his feet. This couldn't be happening. The servants ran around the room in a chaotic frenzy, and the midwife just stood there with the blue baby in her hands staring at it with a frozen look of horror upon her face. He glanced down at the baby and now understood her fear. The baby had one eye of black and another of a bright orange. Though the boy was blue and didn't move, his eyes were still open and staring forward in an eerie gaze of death.

"This is the work of the devil!" he ground out, feeling his entire body shake as he spoke. His daughters cried, and the servants frantically tried to bring his wife back to life but to no avail. His heart broke to see his beloved Mirabelle lying lifeless and drained in a puddle of blood. He'd not only lost his only son but now his wife and mother of his children as well. And 'twas all because of that damned blind hag and those cursed jeweled daggers.

"'Tis no one's fault," the nursemaid reassured him, gathering up the girls and trying to pull them away from their departed mother.

He looked down at his dead wife and reached out slowly to close her eyes. Then he leaned over and kissed her on the forehead in one final goodbye. Though he would always love her, the fire of anger burned wild within his veins for what she'd done. He wanted nothing again to ever remind him of this awful day.

"'Tis those damned daggers!" he cried out, rushing across the room and collecting them up from the floor where his daughters had been coveting them earlier. His grabbed the large wooden box with the rounded lid, much like a small trunk, and put them inside.

"What are you doing with our daggers, Papa?" asked Sapphire.

"These are what killed your mother and your brother as well. I will not have these anywhere near any of you ever again."

The girls realized he'd meant to get rid of them and started crying.

"No, Papa, please," cried Ruby. "Mama gave those to us."

Though it broke his heart to take away from his girls the last remembrance of their mother, he couldn't have these evil things in his castle any longer.

He called to his henchman who stood at the door, and the soldier rushed in at his request. He handed him the box with the daggers. "Get rid of these immediately," he told him.

"What should I do with them, my lord?" asked the guard.

"I don't care, just get them out of my sight."

"Should I sell them my lord?" asked the guard peeking into the box. "They look like they will bring in a good amount of coin."

"Nay!" he shouted. "I want no coin from those cursed things and neither will anyone who lives here or who is in my service have anything to do with them ever again."

"Then, shall I bury them, my lord? Or bring them to another town on trade?"

"Just give them to the first beggar you see outside my gate and be done with it already," he told him.

"Aye, my lord." The guard turned to leave, and once again Talbot's eyes fell upon the blue baby with the devil eyes in the midwife's arms.

"Is he dead?" asked the earl.

"I believe so, my lord," said the midwife, "as he stares with his eyes open without making a sound and his skin has turned blue."

"Guard, wait!" he called out, going to the midwife and taking the dead baby from her arms.

"Take those daggers out of the box."

"My lord?"

"I need that box for a coffin."

"Are you going to bury the boy, my lord?" The guard removed the daggers from the box and put them in a pouch at his side.

"Nay. He is a demon child and neither has he been baptized. He will never be looked upon by the eyes of God. He is also the reason my wife died, as his body was too big for her to birth. Take this with you as well and throw it into the sea," he said.

He placed the baby in the box and snapped the lid down. The box had holes in the top and he swore he could see the boy's orange eye staring at him through the lid. A shiver coursed through him and he handed the small coffin to the guard.

"Now go," he told him. "And do not return here until you've done as I've instructed."

"Aye, my lord," said the guard, holding the box under his arm.

The guard rushed from the room and down the stairs of the tower. He jumped onto his horse and rode hard out the castle gate. He remembered what the earl had ordered him to do, and the first beggar he saw was a blind old woman sitting on the grass just outside the castle's gate. He dismounted and walked over to her, still holding onto the box.

"Old woman," he called, and hunkered down in front of her, laying the box at her feet as he prepared to retrieve the daggers from his pouch. He noticed she already had a jeweled dagger with a cracked black stone, turning it over and over in her hand.

"I have been instructed to give these jeweled daggers to the first beggar I see." He reached for them and as he took them from his pouch, he noticed she had opened the lid of the box. Her hands were inside as she tried to decipher its contents without sight.

"What is this?" she asked, feeling around inside the box as she could not see for herself that a dead blue baby lay within.

"'Tis the dead newborn son of the earl," he told her.

"Interesting," she said, looking up to him with her clouded eyes, all the while her hands still inside the box. He couldn't see what she was doing since the lid was up, but he knew he needed to get to the sea with the baby as instructed right away.

"Give me that," he said, pulling her hands out of the box and snapping down the lid. Then he shoved the daggers into her hands, no longer seeing the dagger with the black stone she'd been toying with when he'd first arrived.

"Four jeweled daggers?" she said, chuckling and enabling him to see her brown and broken teeth. "And why are these coming back to me now?"

He didn't understand what she meant, but had no time to waste. "The countess is dead," he told her. "And the earl blames it all on these daggers."

"Really?" She chuckled again, and he felt as if the woman was not in her right mind. "And what shall I do with these?" she asked.

"Whatever you wish," he said, putting the box under his arm and mounting his horse.

"Who are you giving the baby to?" she asked. He thought it an odd question since the baby was dead.

"I am burying it at sea," he told her. "The earl has instructed me to dump it into the ocean. I am going to climb the highest cliff right now and throw it over the edge."

"Nay, don't do that," she said.

"Why not?" asked the guard.

"Because it might wash back up to the shore and you wouldn't want the earl's daughters to see that, now would you?"

"Aye, this is true," he said in thought. "Besides, the sight of it would only upset the earl."

"'Twould be better to dump it far in the ocean."

"True, but I would need a ship for that."

"I heard a merchant speak just this day of a ship setting sail right now from the shores of Blackpool. I believe he said the ship is headed for the Highlands. You could give the captain a coin or two and have him throw it into the water when he gets out to sea."

"Yes," he said, "I will do that. Thank you."

As he rode away, the blind old hag just smiled. She held up the four daggers in front of her clouded eyes and ran her fingers over the stones.

"I will miss that dagger with the black onyx," she said. "But at least, now 'twill always be with the boy."

She smiled once again and nodded, knowing that in time each dagger would be returned to its owner and they'd find true love, just as she'd promised the countess the day she'd sold them to her. That is, they would all someday be returned to the *Daughters of the Dagger.*

Ruby

Chapter 1

England, 1355

Lady Ruby de Burgh of Blackpool steadied her lance - the old handle off a worn broom - and rode her mare full force toward the roughly made quintain she'd constructed. Leftover broken lances she'd scavenged off the knight's practice field were put to good use by her creative abilities. She'd constructed her own quintain of a tall post mounted on a wide base, anchored down with boulders. Atop it sat a cross-arm that swiveled when she hit it.

The moist earth flew in all directions as her horse thundered over the ground, bringing her closer to her target. She raised the stick, fastened her sight on the center of the painted red and white broken shield, and pulled her arm back, ready to hit it dead center.

"Ruby!" came her father's voice from somewhere behind her. It was enough to distract her and cause her to miss her mark. The broom handle smashed into the wooden arm of the quintain instead of the shield, and she lost speed. The sandbag on the opposite side of the crossbar swung around, hitting her in the center of her back.

"Ooomph!" Her breath was forced from her as the sandbag continued its revolution, but not before unseating her from her horse and landing her in the center of a huge mud puddle.

"Lady Ruby, how many times do I have to tell you to stop acting like a man!" Her father, Talbot, Earl of Blackpool, stood just outside the wooden rail of the lists. Beside him stood his steward, Severin, and also a tall handsome man she'd never seen before.

Ruby flipped her muddy, long blond braid over her shoulder and proudly got to her feet in ankle-deep mud.

"Papa, I am not acting like a man." She smoothed down her crumpled, torn and dirty gown, and tried to sound more mature than her age of twenty years.

"Then what do you call this nonsense? Riding a horse astride and performing feats of knights?"

She knew her father was only upholding his image in front of the other men, as he'd seen her practice her version of jousting many times before and had never reprimanded her. But she'd obviously embarrassed him now at a most inappropriate moment. She knew she should act the ever-obedient daughter of an earl as was proper, but the burning desire within her to act of her own accord made her speak boldly.

"The quintain is an extraordinary device that can quicken one's reflexes and sharpen the senses. I don't see why women aren't allowed to use it too."

The deep laugh of the man standing next to her father

28

only rattled her nerves. She didn't see what was so amusing. Being one of four daughters of an earl was hard enough, not to mention eyebrows always lifting because of her attraction to unladylike activities. She'd spent most her time as a child sneaking away to the armory to look at the weapons, or in the stable coaxing the stablemaster to let her ride the warhorses mounted in a man's saddle.

She'd even cut short all her hair when she was ten and dressed like a page, joining a hunting party of men off in the woods for days. That, she had to admit was a mistake. Not only had she worried as well as infuriated her father, but she'd learned more about men's desires and fantasies of coupling with a woman than she ever wanted to know. That alone was enough to scare her into never wanting a man as long as she lived.

Most girls in her position were betrothed at an early age and already married, or even fostered out to help assure alliances with other holdings. With four girls in the family, the ability to supply decent dowries - even for an earl - became quite costly.

By right, one or two of her sisters or even she, should have been sent to a convent. But luckily her father decided against it. He'd never remarried after the death of his wife, and he'd been so heartbroken to have lost her in childbirth as well as his only son, that he wanted to keep his daughters with him as long as possible to help him ease the pain. He'd also made a promise to his wife on her deathbed not to betroth any of his daughters, but to allow them to find their own true loves instead. 'Twas certainly an uncommon promise for such a powerful man to make, but then again, there was nothing common about Ruby's late mother either.

When her mother was alive, she'd seen something

special in Ruby, and told her that she had a good heart. She'd also told her she was the strongest of all her sisters and needed to watch over all of them and help protect them as well. Ruby had always been her father's favorite child, and because of this, she had never been disciplined with a heavy hand.

Since her mother's death when Ruby was only five, she tried harder than ever to make her father happy again. She'd promised her mother on her deathbed that she would always be there for her father. She would keep that promise and be near her father's side always, as she never planned on leaving.

"Ruby, come here. I'd like you to meet Lord Nyle Dacre from Sheffield."

Ruby picked up her soggy skirt and sloshed her mud soaked slippers across the damp earth till she met her father and his guest at the rail.

"You're Lord Sheffield?" she asked cocking her head, squinting from the sun breaking through the clouds. The summer breeze blew a loose strand of hair over her face and she swept it away with a muddy finger, leaving her cheek smudged in the process.

"You're Lady Ruby, first-born daughter of the Earl of Blackpool?" he rallied.

"Papa, what is the meaning of this?" she asked, feeling a sinking sensation in her chest. Sheffield's castle was far down south and far from the coast as well. He had to have travelled at least several days in order to get here, so he wasn't here on a social visit. She was sure that she wasn't going to like the reason behind his arrival, as she could feel it in her bones that it wasn't good.

"Surely you've heard of Lord Sheffield?" asked Severin,

her father's steward who had a reputation for a wagging tongue. He'd been so quiet, Ruby almost forgot he was there. But if it wasn't for Severin, she wouldn't have known all the horror stories about the infamous Lord Sheffield. Severin had been telling her tales of warriors for years - her idea of a good bedtime story. That is, unless she actually had to meet one of the men of these horrific tales. This in itself was a scary feat.

"Yes, I've heard of you," she answered directly to Lord Sheffield, ignoring Severin altogether.

"And what, my lady, have you heard?" Lord Sheffield chuckled lowly again, his dark arrogant head cocked in amusement. His long oaken hair was well past his shoulders, and the breeze lifted it gently around his sculpted face. His eyes were a dark steel grey, and though he was grinning she still felt the danger that lie beneath his controlled gestures.

Ruby felt her heart thumping loudly and hoped the man couldn't hear it too. He was handsome indeed, much taller than her father, and much younger than the gossip make him out to be. Still, he was probably close to ten years her senior. She found herself thinking of the stories Severin had told her about this dangerous man just recently. Lord Sheffield hid a thousand sins behind his cool façade, and Ruby wondered how he could look so calm after all the murders he'd committed.

His cloak was black, lined in satiny purple, and it reached all the way down to his feet. His tunic and hose were a slate gray, and the only piece of jewelry was the shiny gold ring on his finger that bore the crest of the Sheffields - a gryphon. She decided he reminded her of a gryphon as well. His narrowed eyes watched her every move and she felt as if he were a predator and she his prey.

"I've heard you've killed off two wives," Ruby answered, chin raised in challenge.

"Lady Ruby!" exclaimed Severin in surprise.

"Ruby!" echoed her father. "Lord Sheffield has had a long journey, and I advise you to watch that loose tongue of yours and pay respect or –"

"Three now, actually." Lord Sheffield met her challenge with a reply of his own. His eyes interlocked with hers in some kind of defiant battle. She felt his gaze freeze the blood in her veins, yet heat her in desire in the same instant. It wasn't lust that stirred her passion, but rather the spar of words between them. Like her, this man was not afraid to speak his mind, or worry what circumstances would develop by his actions. This was obvious by the way he wasn't trying to hide the fact he'd killed off three wives in the past few months.

Ruby liked a challenge. She lived for a challenge. But being a woman, her life was indeed dull. And though she feared the man standing in front of her, a strange part of her welcomed his arrival at their castle after all. He obviously held some strange form of power within him to be able to make her feel this way from just a mere look.

"Egads, Sheffield, why do you jest with my daughter?" scolded the earl.

"Who's jesting?" he asked, his eyes still focused on Ruby. "My third wife died only a sennight ago. Word is I poisoned her." Lord Sheffield's eyes bore into her, and he obviously waited for a reaction. She refused to give it to him, but now that she realized how dangerous a man he really was, she suddenly regretted being so forward after all.

"A sennight ago?" She tried to sound calm and nonchalant as if they were discussing the weather, but inside she felt her body shaking to be so close to a murderer. She only hoped he couldn't see through her bravado.

"Aye," he answered with a stone-like face. "That is the reason I am searching for a new bride."

"What?" she blurted out before she could stop herself. This man was amazing and not in the kindest form of the word. She wondered how he could be so hard-hearted that his dead wife's body was barely cold and already he shopped for another as if it were naught more than going to market to bring home another choice of livestock.

She backed away quickly, breaking the gaze, and the man once again chuckled lowly, doing naught to calm her nerves. She found herself wanting – needing – to know more, and before she could stop herself, she once again met with his sparring challenge of conversation.

"What about the other two?" Ruby asked anxiously. "How did they die? Did you poison them as well?"

Instead of answering, Lord Sheffield cleared his throat and looked over to the steward. "I'm sure Severin there could inform you as to the details."

"I . . . I . . . excuse me my lords, but I do think I hear the falconer calling from the mews." Severin left swiftly from the scene. Ruby watched his red head look back only once before he disappeared into a crowd of serfs from the village mingling with the merchants setting up their wares in the courtyard.

"Enough of this nonsense," the earl broke in. "Now, you've met all my daughters, Sheffield. Shall we go back to the solar so you can make your choice?"

"Choice? He means to marry one of us?" Ruby asked, hearing the slight squeak of her own voice. She knew he had said he was looking for a wife, but never had she thought he meant to find one at Blackpool Castle. There was no doubt now why he'd traveled all the way here from Sheffield. How could her father allow this, knowing what a dangerous man Lord Sheffield really was? Besides, her father had promised her dying mother that the girls could find husbands of their own choosing. Certainly, not a one of them would choose this man of free will. Whatever poor girl he chose would no doubt end up dead in a few months time at most. "Papa, you can't allow this!"

"Of course I can," said her father, and she was shocked by his decision.

"But you made a promise to Mother. Are you saying you really mean to give one of your daughters to the Lord of Death?"

"Lord of Death?" Sheffield grinned, and when he did she thought she saw a twinkle in his eye. "I haven't heard that one before, but I suppose it precedes my reputation."

"I am sure the deaths of his wives are only coincidental," said the earl. "The king himself has a close alliance with Lord Sheffield. This man is favored by King Edward and has spent time at his side in Windsor, Ruby. He has saved the king's life at battle and also been made a member of the most prestigious order of chivalry there is – the Order of the Garter. The girl Sheffield chooses should be honored to marry him and birth his heirs.

Her father looked to her with sincerity in his eyes, and she noticed the tone of admiration in his voice. He was not at all concerned with turning over one of his daughters to this wretched brute.

"I am sorry but I can no longer uphold my word to your dying mother," he continued. "I have sworn allegiance to the king and cannot deny a man he holds in such high regards.

Ruby

I'd gladly give Lord Sheffield the hand of any one of my daughters and be proud of it."

Ruby felt as if her father had betrayed them. However, she also knew he could not pass up an opportunity to have one of his daughters married to a close friend of the king. It would suit him well, and possibly bring him favors of the king also.

"Well, any girl addlepated enough to let herself be trapped with the Lord of Death deserves what she gets!" She spat out the words, ignoring the reprimanding look from her father. Still, she worried not, because while Lord Sheffield may be favored by the king, she knew she was her father's favorite. He wouldn't stop her from speaking her mind, as he held her in high regards, just like he did Lord Sheffield.

Her heart already ached for whichever of her sisters the man chose. But 'twould not be her leaving Blackpool as this man's betrothed. At least she could count on that. After all, her father knew the promise she'd made to her dying mother to watch over him and stay with him always. Ruby would be going nowhere, as she would be staying at Blackpool with him for the rest of her life.

She wondered which of her three sisters the murderer would choose as his bride. They were all proficient at the things a man considered admirable in a woman, such as knowing needlework, weaving, and how to run a household. Yes, any of them would do well in tending to a man's every needs - the ideal wife for any lord.

She, however, had never even attempted stitching or weaving a tapestry nor did she plan on trying. But put a sword in her hand instead of a needle, and she'd give any man a challenge. Thank goodness for the old knight Oakley who'd taken a liking to her and trained her with a sword in secret. And she had her father to thank for the sword she'd found one day near her favorite sitting rock, though the man would never admit to giving it to her and therefore promoting her wild ways.

Right now she only wished for her jeweled dagger her mother had given her as a child instead of the plain one at her waist. That dagger would have been better protection should she need to use it. She missed the dagger with the ruby in the hilt, from which she was named. Her sisters, Sapphire, Amethyst, and Amber had been named after the gems in the hilts of their daggers as well. However, her father had seen to disposing of the weapons the day her mother died, saying they were what caused her death. Her mother had bought them from a blind hag, as she'd heard a superstition that it would help her to conceive. And that it did. Unfortunately, her mother's greediness of trying to steal a fifth dagger had brought about the consequences of both losing her baby boy at birth and also losing her own life in the process.

She remembered the story her mother used to tell her that by naming her children after the gems, it would ensure each of them to be married to their true love. She just shook her head, knowing the Lord of Death would never be anyone's true love. Now if only they'd all had their daggers, this ill-conceived turn of events would not be happening right now.

Ruby knew she acted nothing like a lady, and no lord would ever want her for his wife. Actually, she'd counted on it. This is what would keep her safe from suitors, and allow her to keep her promise to her mother – and therefore stay with her father forever.

Not wanting to hear more, nor caring if her actions were

rude, she turned to leave. She picked up her skirt and trudged through the field toward her horse, hearing their voices behind her discussing this absurd notion. Sheffield would probably pick her younger sister, Sapphire, or mayhap even one of her youngest sisters, Amber or Amethyst - the twins.

Sapphire had the beauty in the family with her bright blue eyes and long rich mahogany hair that trailed all the way down to her waist. Not to mention she had prosperous amounts of womanly curves in all the right places. No man could keep from lusting for what Sapphire could give him, and Ruby was sure it would make Lord Sheffield very happy.

Amethyst, on the other hand, was pretty in a different sort of way. With indigo eyes and ebony hair, she too was alluring, and her mind was as lively as her high-spirited ways. She could match any man's knowledge when it came to being learned, and she always held a positive attitude even in the hardest of times.

While Amethyst was lively, her twin, Amber, was the quiet and obedient one with the virtues of a nun. She was the one, Ruby was sure, who God favored the most. Amber was meticulous and loved schedules and rules. And she showed more devotion and commitment for everything she did than any of her sisters.

Yes, all three had the qualifications a man looked for in a bride. Not to mention, their father was an earl and could provide a sizeable dowry as well. Or at least for the first and mayhap second of the girls to be married, anyway.

So, she decided, the Lord of Death would choose her sister, Sapphire. Of course, the twins were virtually inseparable, so he may choose them both - saving him time to have to find another wife after he killed off the first in another sennight or so. Ruby felt a sadness enveloping her as she was already remorseful at the loss of whichever sister he chose.

"I don't need to go back to the solar, Earl Blackpool, as I've already made my decision."

"Really?" asked the earl. "Will it be Sapphire, or perhaps one of the twins? Any of the three would make a wonderful wife for you. I am sure you will be very pleased."

Ruby noticed how her father never mentioned her name, and a smile crossed her face. This was going exactly how she'd planned. No man wanted a woman who acted the way she did and they both knew it. And no man would take her away from her father and make her act like the stuffed, flirtatious lady she was expected to be. She put her foot in the stirrup meaning to mount her horse, but stopped abruptly at the sound of Lord Sheffield's next words.

"I'll take . . . her."

She figured one of her sisters must have joined them, so turned curiously to see who it was who would be the next victim of the Lord of Death. Her body froze and she felt a shiver run up her spine when she realized he was pointing at her!

His tall, dark form was silhouetted against a suddenly cloudy sky. His cloak whipped in the wind that had seemed to pick up just since his arrival. His arm outstretched, his long finger pointed directly at her. Dark clouds passed in front of the sun and the temperature suddenly dropped as the threatening sky rumbled in the distance as if it were warning here of her doomed fate.

"Her?" Her father's jaw dropped open. "You want Ruby? Surely you are jesting, Sheffield. She knows naught of the ways of a lady, nor would she make you a good wife.

Ruby

Now let's head inside so you can choose a proper lady to marry instead, as I have three other very eligible daughters."

"I don't want a proper lady," Sheffield answered with conviction. "I want a strong woman who'll bear me many warriors. Someone who is brave and sturdy, just like I've seen by watching her trying to joust like a man, or by challenging me with her words. I've already had three proper wives and they were so frail that they died easily. No, Earl Blackpool, do not even try to change my mind. I have already decided that my next bride will be your daughter, Ruby."

Chapter 2

Ruby couldn't have heard the man correctly. Had he really just claimed that he wanted her hand in marriage? This had to be some kind of a mistake. No man was supposed to want her with the way she acted. She'd seen to that by her unruly ways. Her behavior was supposed to frighten men away, not attract them.

"My many pardons, Lord Sheffield," she said, putting on her most polite act, "but the wind has picked up and it almost sounded as tho you mentioned my name and bride in the same sentence."

"The wind has nothing to do with it. You heard me correctly."

Ruby's eyes darted to her father, and when she saw the despair on his face and the downward turn of his mouth, she knew this wasn't a lie. She was to become this man's wife, and if her father agreed, she could do nothing to stop it.

"Papa - tell him he can't have me."

"Sheffield, certainly you don't really want her." He tried to sound jovial but Ruby could hear the desperation in his tone. "I have three others from which you can choose that would suit you better."

"A nobleman never goes back on his word. You have already told me I can choose any of your daughters I wish. Would you really want this getting back to the king, Blackpool?"

"I . . . well . . . of course not. I would never want the king to think I went back on my word. I am honorable, same as you."

The earl looked over to Ruby and she saw the unspoken pain in his eyes. She knew he didn't want her to leave his side any more than she wanted to go. But he had no choice in the matter, as he would never want his name sullied in the eyes of the king, and neither would she.

She knew he couldn't ignore the fact that a marriage of convenience to such a powerful man as Lord Sheffield would make him an ally and guarantee that no battle between their lands would ever transpire. Her only saving grace would have been if he had chosen one of her sisters instead.

"I'm sorry, sweetheart," her father said to her, shaking his head regretfully. A sincere sadness reflected in his eyes. "Lord Sheffield has made his choice." Then, before she could object, they turned their backs on her and headed for the castle.

She could do naught but just stand there and stare, as any spark of hope diminished like a quick snuff of a candle on a windy day. She knew her fate now lie in that vile man's hands. She'd be taken away from Blackpool, her father, and her sisters forever. Not to mention, she would probably never live to see the rising sun of a new day.

She watched them go, biting her bottom lip to keep from shouting out. She knew she should not embarrass her father further by objecting or asking him not to keep his word. Still, she couldn't just accept a fate such as this, and allow herself to be taken without even a struggle. No, she had to try to do something to stop it.

She took off running after the men. "But Papa, I've made a promise to mother to stay with you forever," she tried in one last futile attempt.

"And I've made a promise to Lord Sheffield," came her father's reply.

She ran ahead of them, planting herself directly in front of the men, causing them to stop. She put her hands on her hips as she spoke. "What good is that promise if I wind up dead by my new husband's own hand?"

"I can see I'll have my work cut out in taming your daughter, Blackpool," said Lord Sheffield with a shake of his head. "Though I want a strong bride to bear me warriors, I will not let her forget to whom she answers now."

The men stepped around her and continued on route toward the castle.

"I'm afraid she knows naught of what's expected of a lady," her father apologized. "I'm to blame for that. I should have raised her properly instead of letting her run wild."

"There's nothing wrong with the way I act." Ruby ran up behind Lord Sheffield, accidentally stepping on the back of his trailing cloak. It ripped near the hem and he stopped suddenly, stiffening as if she had struck him. Then with a reserved coolness to his movement, he turned slowly to face her.

The suggestion of annoyance burned in his eyes as they suddenly darkened dangerously. His mouth was a firm line and a muscle twitched in his clenched jaw. She could already picture him killing her off in the first day. She'd have to make sure she slept with her dagger under her pillow for protection - and as far away from him as possible.

He surveyed the torn cloak, making a big show of taking it off and folding it neatly into a small square. That enabled her to see his broad shoulders that had been hidden under the cloak as well as his long legs. It was almost amusing to see such a rugged warrior placing so much importance on the folding of a torn and dirtied garment. Then his large, battle-scarred hands shot forward and he handed her his cloak. Instinctively, she reached for it and the exchange was made between them.

"Your first job, wife, will be to mend my cloak."

She suddenly realized her mistake of accepting anything from the Lord of Death. "I don't know how to sew." She shifted his cloak to one hand and flipped her long blond braid behind her with the other. She raised her chin in defiance.

"Then I'll teach you."

"What? You know how to sew?" She narrowed her eyes as she tried to decide whether or not he was lying. "Sewing is a woman's chore, not a knight's."

"So surprised are you that a man could know a woman's skills? Don't you practice a man's activities and think naught of it?"

"Why yes, but -"

"I have much to teach you, bride. But first I must come to terms with your father of our deal. I hope your dowry includes bolts of satin and thread as well. You're going to need it. I won't have my wife running around in torn skirts covered with mud."

"Ruby," her father answered wearily. "Go to your chamber at once. Wash your face and hands and dress properly. Have your handmaiden pack your trunk. I'll tell Severin to send up a page for it as soon as you are ready."

"I'm leaving? Now?" Panic threatened to choke her and she felt her throat tighten with every word. "What about the three weeks of posting the wedding banns, as is proper?"

"I'm sorry," said her father, "but the deal was that Lord Sheffield take his betrothed with him today. When and where the actual ceremony takes place will be his decision now."

"And if I may point out," Lord Sheffield said to Ruby, "you do not seem to be the kind of girl who does anything that's proper. So what does it matter to you if we follow procedure or not?"

"It matters to me! Papa, you're really going to let him do this?"

Her father just stared at her and she swore his eyes seemed a bit glassy. The only time she had seen anything near this was when he'd shed tears at the death of her mother. Then he nodded his head slightly, and without a word to her, he turned and gave his attention to Lord Sheffield instead. "Will you be staying for the midday meal?"

"Nay. I'll be leaving as soon as we seal our agreement," came the man's low and controlled answer. "I'd like to get back as soon as possible, as it is a good journey and 'tis already well into the morning hours."

"Then I'll have the cook send some food for your journey home."

Ruby watched the men walk to the castle, discussing her wedding to this dark lord as naught more than an exchange of goods, and excluding her completely. She was close to tears, but she wouldn't show it. She knew her father had no choice in the matter. He had given his word and it was final. Still, she longed for a hug or a reassuring word from him, trying to convince her all would be fine though they both knew otherwise.

She'd go with Lord Sheffield, only to save face for her father in the eyes of the king, and to seal a deal that would protect her father's lands. But there was no way she'd marry him. She'd escape as soon as she could. If she did this, it could not bring ill fate to her father if he knew naught about it. She'd avoid her marriage and at the same time she'd escape her death.

She looked down at her fingers clutching her husband-to-be's cloak. She ran a hand over the top of the fine silk, wondering what it felt like to be this cloth and pressed up against the man's body. She wasn't blind, and realized he was more handsome than any man she'd ever seen. She also knew he was more dangerous and somehow this intrigued her.

Three wives this man had already taken to his bed, and she would be just another. She reminded herself that marriage obviously meant nothing to him as he disposed of wives quickly. Within a sennight of his last wife's death he was already looking for another. She had no doubt she would do something to anger him and be naught more than his next victim.

She longed for the true love promised to her by the superstition of her missing jeweled dagger. If only she had that as a last thread of hope, but she didn't.

He may be the most attractive man she'd ever met, but yet she loathed him more than anyone she'd ever known. He said he wanted a strong woman - not frail like his last three wives who died so easily. What did this mean? Did he want her to put up a fight when he decided to kill her off? Well, if a fight is what he wanted, then a fight he would get. She'd bring all her weapons in her trunk. Her sword, her dagger, and anything else she could find along the way. She wouldn't go to her demise without trying to save her life in the process.

This man was not her true love, and if she had to leave her home and her family, she at least wanted something in return. She wanted him not, and the sooner he knew this, the better.

She let go of his cloak, letting it slip through her fingers and fall to the ground in a crumpled heap. The neatly folded rich cape of such a domineering, powerful man now lay in the mud of the same earth that now covered each and every one of his late wives, naught more than discarded trash. She smiled slightly, lifting her skirt and stepping forward directly onto the center of his cloak as she headed up to her chamber to prepare for her departure with the Lord of Death.

Chapter 3

Lord Nyle paced impatiently in the courtyard, already aggravated that his future bride would be causing them to travel well into the night before they even stopped to make camp. He stood next to his squire, Locke, who held the reins of his horse under his right, gnarled and twisted arm, while he petted the horse's nose with his good left hand. A stableboy from Blackpool Castle stood waiting with a light brown palfrey for Ruby which had a lady's saddle mounted on top.

"What did the lady say?" asked Locke curiously.

Locke had been his squire for the last five years. The boy had always been loyal to Nyle, and it did not go unnoticed. When Locke lost the use of his right arm in battle protecting him, Nyle knew he would never make it to knighthood. While he could still use the arm slightly, 'twas twisted and damaged and his fingers were curled and gnarled.

He could not hold a weapon in his right hand. He should have been dismissed from his position of squire, but Nyle wouldn't hear of it. Even with one arm hanging basically useless at his side, Locke was still able to protect him, and could hold his own in any fight. Nyle had seen to that when he taught the boy to wield a sword left-handed, as he, himself, had dominance of his left hand. Many people feared him for this fact alone, saying he was spawned from the devil. They'd called Locke his cursed minion. No man wielded a sword with his left hand, but now, there were two of them. The fear that ran rampant when he and Locke entered a castle's courtyard was almost enough to make him laugh aloud.

"What lady?" Nyle continued his pacing.

"Lady Ruby. Your future wife," Locke reminded him.

"She's no lady. She's the furthest thing from a lady I've ever seen. It's deplorable the way she's been brought up - raised more like a squire than the daughter of an earl."

"It sounds as if you disapprove of Lady Ruby."

"Of course I do. You know I like my women feminine, obedient, and very willing. There's nothing - nothing at all about this Ruby that fits the description of a lady."

"Then why did you choose her for you bride, my lord?" asked Locke, bewildered.

Why indeed? Nyle just shook his head. It was more of an impulsive decision. Mayhap he'd done it just to spite the little shrew. Or mayhap he'd done it because he'd admired the way she stood up to him and met his words in challenge. But truly, he'd chosen her because he was starting to doubt his wives' deaths were accidents after all, and he knew that once he was married, whoever was stalking him would be after him again. That is, out to kill his wife.

He needed to catch this assassin and find out who he was, and this was his best bait yet. A woman who knew how to handle herself and could defend herself in his absence was just what he needed.

"Just between us, Locke, this girl is going to be my lure to catch the murderer who I have decided resides within the very walls of my castle."

"What? Are you saying you are going to use her as a pawn?"

"I don't have a choice. You can see as well as everyone else that I have been made a fool of by this traitor whom I cannot seem to catch."

"I am remorseful for your losses, my lord, but do you think it wise to put Lady Ruby right in the path of danger?"

"Danger? Hah! Whoever this assassin is who is trying to make me look incompetent in the eyes of my king, will have his hands full with this one. I sincerely doubt I'll have to sleep with one eye open, as if anything is amiss I'll be alerted by her open mouth."

This woman excited him in a strange way. She had a mind and tongue of her own. These traits in a woman were unheard of and could only bring trouble to the union of their marriage, but for some reason she still stirred his loins. He'd always been attracted to trouble like a thirsty horse drawn to water. He knew he needed Lady Ruby as much as she needed him.

He needed a wife for more reasons than one, and she needed a man who would be able to put her in her place. His secret mission back in Sheffield was about to be put into motion, and it required him to have a strong wife to help him keep it safe. He was on a hushed mission for King Edward III, and determined to succeed no matter what happened.

However, by the happenings of the past few months, things were not going as planned. He was supposed to have married already, and have a wife before this mission could continue, but luck hadn't been on his side. It almost seemed as if someone had been trying to stop the mission before it began. But all hope was restored once he saw the shrew. With Ruby as his wife, the cur trying to get to him by killing off his wives would be doomed. He almost felt pity for the man in an odd sort of way. Ruby would slow the murderer down long enough for Nyle to stab his own sword through the bastard's heart, but not before he caught the assassin and brought him before the king to confess.

Being the only living son of the late William Sheffield, Nyle was desperately in need of an heir to keep the lands in the family's name. But his past three wives had all died on their wedding days, before he'd even had the chance to consummate the marriages. That was not good for any man's morale.

Still, Nyle had not married the women with a goal to conceive, as that would have just been a bonus. He'd married on orders of the king, as he needed a wife or King Edward would never even consider him a candidate to watch over his bastard child. He needed a wife in order to carry out the guise that the child was theirs.

Tibbar was the one-year-old boy's name, and Nyle had been the one to name him. He'd taken a special interest in the boy while living in Windsor Castle. Because of his fondness of the child and the child's fondness toward Nyle, the king believed he was the best fit to protect him. But when Nyle's father passed away unexpectedly several months ago, he returned to inherit his father's estate and lands at Sheffield.

Nyle had been at the king's right hand in service for the past five years. He'd been there to help save the king at the

Ruby

Battle of Winchelsea when the king's ship, the Cog Thomas was rammed by a Castilian vessel and sank to the bottom of the channel. But through all his dangerous missions, Nyle had to say he'd never been entrusted to do anything like what this mission entailed.

King Edward liked his ladies, and having had a dozen children of his own, he felt the queen would not be happy to know he'd taken a mistress. After all, his newest son, Thomas, was only born six months ago, yet the king had a secret mistress - one that Nyle knew only too well. When the king found his mistress, Lady Jocelyn, in bed with another man, he'd had the man executed, taken the baby, and banished his mistress from his kingdom.

Now the king wanted Nyle to take over the care of his bastard baby, but it seemed as if someone didn't like that idea and was trying to stop him. Three dead wives were proof of what someone would do to keep the baby out of Sheffield. Nyle hadn't loved any of his wives, but he still swore he'd do whatever it took to avenge their needless deaths.

"M'lord?" He heard a small voice and looked down to see two small girls beside him. Their hair was tangled and their faces dirty, and a horrid thought suddenly ran rampant through his brain. He pictured himself the father of all girls. Girls with dirty faces and torn clothes who thought nothing of acting like men. What had he done? Mayhap he shouldn't have chosen Lady Ruby after all.

"M'lord," repeated the little girl. "We found this while playing and wondered if 'twas yours?"

He was surprised to see his cloak in their filthy little hands. His garment was covered with a muddy footprint and the tear in the hem had grown larger. Looking closer, he could see that the footprint looked an awful lot like the muddy slipper worn by his newly betrothed.

"Why, yes. Yes, I thank you." He looked over to his squire. "Locke, take my cloak from the girls and put it in the travel bag."

"Your cloak?" Locke looked at the dirty, torn garment as he took it from the children with one hand.

"Don't mention this to anyone," Nyle muttered to his squire as he took two coins from his pocket and handed them to the girls. The girls' eyes lit up as they palmed their treasures.

"Thank you m'lord," they called as they ran off to play. Once again, Nyle pictured himself with two little girls such as this and just shuddered. After all - one filthy, mouthy, untamed wench was going to be more than he wanted to handle.

"My daughter shall be ready in a moment," said the earl coming to see Nyle off.

"I thank you for your generous dowry," said Nyle, looking at the cart loaded down with silks, spices, grains, weapons, jewelry, and a box of coins. There were crates with chickens and one of his best stallions for breeding also included in the deal. The cart was hitched to a travelling horse and one of the earl's men sat at the ready to deliver it to his home.

"My daughter will have her handmaid along to assist her."

Nyle doubted Lady Ruby needed anyone's help, let alone a handmaid. "I'm sure she'll manage fine without one. I have my own servants in Sheffield to assist her once we arrive."

"I won't go without her!" came Ruby's voice from the

stairs of the great hall.

Nyle's eyes darted upward toward her voice, intending to reprimand her for overstepping him, but he swallowed his words when he saw the beautiful woman standing at the top of the stairs.

If he hadn't recognized her voice, he would have thought her to be someone else. Dressed in a satin cream-colored gown with long dangling tippets lined in gold trim, stood his betrothed, glaring down at him. A handmaid was straightening the long train of her gown that trailed out a full body's length behind her. A rare color and an odd choice for a gown since he knew how much she liked to wallow in the mud. He'd no doubt the gown would be filthy in no time.

Still, she was surprisingly clean, especially since he'd just witnessed her filthy, muddy body not long ago. Her hair was wet as if had just been washed, and 'twas also plaited in a long strand that hung over her shoulder, halfway to her waist. She reached one slim hand around it and used her long fingers to flip the braid carelessly to her back in her signature act of defiance. While her tresses seemed to be a dirty blond earlier, he could see now that her hair was so light it almost looked like glowing white spun silk. Her eyes were golden orbs of sunlight, shining a tawny brown.

And while most ladies strived for a fair, pale complexion, her face held a smooth golden tone to it, which looked as if 'twas kissed by the sun from her days on the practice field. She was adorned with a glittering ruby ring on her right hand, and an ornate neckpiece boasting several rubies there as well. They winked in the sunlight as she surveyed him.

A kitchen servant appeared with a bundle in his hands that Nyle guessed to be food, and two pages dragged along her clothing trunks and loaded them into the wagon. Her sisters ran out to hug her and wish her luck. The twins wiped the tears from their eyes with the back of their hands and Sapphire pulled her closer protectively as she eyed him up. Then she whispered something into Ruby's ear and kissed her once more before releasing her.

Ruby said goodbye to each of her sisters in turn, but yet kept her composure and did not cry, but nor did she smile. She just maintained that stone-like expression upon her face and he wondered how long the little spitfire would be able to keep it up. Not long, he bet, knowing that as soon as they left the castle she'd probably be showing her true colors again.

"Is that you, Lady Ruby?" he questioned, walking to the stairs, delightfully surprised at her sudden transformation.

"Who did you think I was? One of your dead wives come back to haunt you?"

If he'd had any doubt at all as to her identity, her sharp tongue brought him back to his senses. It was the shrew. Even with the nice outer packaging, he'd already seen what truly lie underneath. Like a wormy apple, her appearance couldn't disguise the bitterness inside, and 'twas no secret she wasn't the fresh and docile image she was now portraying herself to be.

"Thank you, Papa for the ring and necklace."

She fingered the short necklace around her throat, his eyes following her actions. He marveled at the beauty of her long neck and the line of silken white skin that peeked out ever so slightly from under the neckline of her gown. 'Twas a true contrast to the skin that had seen the sun, and he found himself wanting to inspect just where those lines stopped and started. Once again this led him to believe there were two sides to this complex woman and he longed to find out more.

Ruby

"'Twas your mother's jewelry, Ruby," the earl told her. "She would have wanted you to have it. I bought it for her right after you were born. I gave her gemstone jewelry to celebrate the birth of each of our daughters." He smiled and wrapped his arms around the twins who were standing on each side of him.

"You look beautiful, Ruby," called out her sister Amethyst, reaching out and giving her another hug.

"I'll miss you," said the girl's twin, Amber, wiping a tear from her eye.

"I will too," added her sister, Sapphire. "But you are so lucky that you will be married and someday soon have children as well."

Nyle half-expected her to have a reaction to that comment, but she didn't say a word.

She reached out and again embraced each of her sisters in a hug, then threw herself into her father's arms and buried her face in his chest, obviously not wanting to go. The earl kissed her atop the head and ran a loving hand over her hair.

Nyle felt a tinge of jealousy that Ruby had such a close relationship with her father. Nyle had always been at arms with his belated father. He had a twin brother at one time who was now dead, as well as a sister still alive and married in Scotland. But his father had planned to have his brother, Nigel, inherit his dwellings, tho Nyle had been the first born of the twins. Now, none of that mattered, as his entire family except for his sister had died and he had inherited everything after all.

Nyle ran his thumb over the gold signet ring on his finger – the ring that had once been his father's and was now his. He wished they could have made amends before he'd left this world, and realized now that he'd been wrong in staying away at Windsor and avoiding his father for the past five years. But he had other things to think about now, and the first one was standing right in front of him.

"'Tis time to depart." Nyle held out his hand to assist Ruby down the stairs, intending to help her mount her horse as well.

She only glared at him, and ignored his proffered hand and descended the stairs on her own. Her handmaid held up the train of her gown, and stood next to her as she prepared to mount her horse. Ruby put her foot in the stirrup and hopped on by herself expertly, causing Nyle to just smile. Why had he thought she'd ever need help to mount? Once her leg was wrapped securely around the saddle horn, the handmaid splayed her gown out over the back of the horse. It was quite a sight to see, and so opposite the girl he'd just met an hour ago.

He could have sworn he saw a tear in her eye as she turned the horse and headed toward the gate. Nyle pulled himself up into the saddle of his own steed, already perturbed that she was the one leading the way when her place was behind him.

"Take good care of her," came the earl's final words. "You harm her in any way and I'll deal with you personally, Sheffield."

Nyle gave a slight nod to the earl, and turned his horse and headed for the gate. He didn't doubt for a moment the earl would have his men ready for combat if Ruby died. And with the luck he'd been having lately, he only prayed she wouldn't end up dead. Rumors said he was responsible for his wives' deaths, though he'd never harmed a one. He knew with his reputation, if Ruby wound up dead too, he'd never be able to convince a soul of his innocence.

He watched her charge out of the gate, passing up the cart with the dowry and spooking its horse in the process. The driver was securing the trunks with rope in the cart and was knocked to the ground as the horse reared and took off at full gallop, spilling the dowry everywhere along the way.

"Damn her!" shouted Nyle.

Chickens squawked and flew out of the smashed cages as she passed. Children scrambled after the spilled goods, and the horse broke loose sending the remaining items on the cart straight into a nearby pond.

"Locke, retrieve my dowry at once," called out Nyle, gritting his teeth and shaking his head. "I'm going after the girl, so say a prayer while you're at it."

"A prayer, my lord?" Locke lifted his lithe body onto his horse to go after the goods.

"Aye. For when I catch up with her, she'll need all the prayers she can get, because I am going to kill her!"

Chapter 4

Ruby charged her horse through the woods, looking over her shoulder sporadically to see Lord Nyle chasing her, the darkened anger on his face making her go even faster. She hadn't meant to spill the dowry in the lake and scatter it over the courtyard. She'd only meant to show Lord Nyle she could ride a horse. She wasn't a proper lady but she could ride a horse mounted in a lady's saddle faster than any man riding astride.

She had hoped he would change his mind about marrying her, but obviously she'd only infuriated him. She wouldn't stop now if her life depended on it. She was sure by the scowl on the man's face he would kill her if he ever caught up with her. She'd managed to lose him once or twice in the woods, hiding and taking unmarked trails that were hard to decipher in the thicket. But even though she knew the area like the back of her hand, he was experienced at tracking and before long was always right behind her. She had no idea what happened to his entourage, the dowry or her handmaiden, but right now neither did she care.

She felt no different than an innocent deer being hunted down by a wolf. He the hunter, she the hunted, she rode for her life for what seemed like hours, never stopping for fear he'd find her. She always stayed just ahead of him and took turns down paths that weren't fit for riding. Now, as her horse tired, she knew she had no choice but to stop.

Looking over her shoulder once again, she neither saw nor heard any sign that he'd followed her into the deepest part of the woods. Ruby had no idea where she was anymore, but it was getting darker by the minute, and in the damp night air she shivered. She stopped her horse near a stream, and dropped herself to the ground. She fell to her knees in the dirt. Parched, she eagerly scooped water up into her mouth, managing to spill most of it down the front of her bodice.

Though the summer was well into its season, the air of the night was still sharp at times. She drank her fill and leaned back wearily against the trunk of a tree, closing her eyes for a mere second to try to regain her breath.

Then she heard it. The snap of a twig, a low growl. She quickly pulled her dagger from her waist belt and shot to her feet. Her horse became spooked, and when she reached out to catch its loose rein it reared up, knocking her blade from her hand and running off before she could still it.

One more growl, and then she heard the sound of feet pattering closer toward her. She frantically dove to the ground, searching with her hands in the underbrush for her dagger, but it was too dark and she couldn't find it. Two shiny eyes glowed at her from the midst of the dark woods, and she picked up the train of her gown and backed against the tree, wondering just what it was that was stalking her, and wishing for her sword which was still on the cart with her dowry.

"Who's there?" she asked, hearing the tremble in her voice, wanting to continue searching the ground for her dagger, but not wanting to put herself in harm's way to do it. Then she realized it wasn't who but what. An animal came into the clearing and in the light of the moon, she could see its sharp teeth and furry coat. A wolf, head low but eyes riveted upon her, stalked toward her. She screamed, knowing her only escape was above her. She managed to reach a low branch, pulling herself upward, then climbing yet one branch higher. Looking down, she frantically pulled up her long train after her. She cursed the fact she wore this binding gown, making it impossible to climb the way she used to as a child. She tried to move her gown from under her foot and slipped, causing her to have to grab onto the branch, her feet now dangling dangerously beneath her.

She hung from her hands, lifting her feet higher, trying to wrap her knees around the branch. The skirt tangled around her and kept her from succeeding. She looked down once more and saw the wolf getting closer. If she dropped now, she'd end up right in its jaws.

"No!" she screamed. "Leave me alone."

Then the sound of hoofbeats led her to believe her horse had returned to her rescue. But when she saw Lord Sheffield heading toward her, she knew her odds had worsened. She'd much rather be thrown to the wolves than thrown into the arms of the Lord of Death.

He sprang from his horse, dagger in hand, tying his steed

to a tree, though the animal tried to run from the wolf.

"Kill it!" she screamed, her legs kicking wildly, her fingers slipping on the branch with every move she made.

He walked toward the wolf, dagger at the ready, but made no motion to lunge for it.

"Kill it!" she screamed once more.

Instead, he waved his hands and scared the wolf away. He stood beneath her now, looking up her skirt, as she had managed to lift her legs around the branch. An embarrassing position to be sure, and she despised him even more.

"Come down from there at once," he commanded.

She wanted to deny him, but couldn't. Her fingers were raw, her palms sweaty. Her grip slipped and she fell, landing atop him. In a tangle of satin and limbs, she lay prone atop his body on the cold, hard ground.

She pushed upward, realizing she was now in the position of coupling. Her bodice was low cut and the tops of her breasts were just under his nose. His frown deepened and his eyes glanced at her cleavage so close to his face he could have reached out and bit her. She felt more fearful of him now than she did of the wolf.

In one motion he had her on her back, his hands holding hers above her head, but pinned to the ground. His short blade lay at her side.

"Woman, you try my patience!" he spat. "You will get off the ground immediately and abide by my word from now on. And don't ever try such a stunt again. I've wasted most the day hunting you down, and I'll not waste another minute with this nonsense."

She struggled for breath, eyeing the dagger, wondering if she could get to it before he used it on her.

"I beg your pardon, Lord Sheffield, but I cannot remove

myself from the ground when you are resting atop me."

He moved then, and she rolled over quickly in one motion and reached for the dagger. His hand shot out and clamped around her wrist. The heat of his palm warmed her and the mere strength of his fingers wrapped around her, let her know she had no hope of escaping him now.

"Don't even think of it," he warned her.

She released the dagger and in return he released her wrist slowly, his fingers brushing her skin lightly as he did so. Whether he meant to do it purposely or not, she felt an odd tingle dance across her skin. She jerked away from him, eyeing the back of her hand, scooting across the ground.

"I'm surprised you haven't used that dagger yet," she said, rubbing her wrist and watching him closer.

"On you or the wolf?"

She didn't answer. The thought of either was frightening indeed.

He picked up the blade and her eyes widened. Then he replaced it in his belt and in one swift motion, yanked her to her feet.

"My lord!" she gasped, crashing into his strong, hard chest. "That is no way to treat a lady."

"You are no lady, Ruby, and we both know it."

She pushed away from him, meaning to run, but a wolf howled from somewhere in the distance, and she froze her actions.

"Are you ready to come with me now to Sheffield?"

She hugged her arms around her body trying to protect herself from not only him but also the night chill. "'Tis already dark, my lord, and I haven't a horse, as it seems to have wandered off."

The wolf howled again in the night, and instinctively she

took a step closer to him. She noticed the corner of his mouth raise in amusement.

"I see," he said, nodding slightly and surveying the area around them. "My horse needs rest anyway, so we'll camp here for the night and head to Sheffield Castle first thing in the morning."

"What?" She looked up in surprise, but he was already removing things from his travel bag. "We can't stay here. 'Tis not safe. There are wolves in these woods."

"The wolves aren't going to hurt you."

"How can you be so sure?"

He threw down a blanket, and gathered up twigs and branches for a fire, quickly putting them into a pile.

"The animal is curious, that's all. You leave it alone and it will do the same to you."

"I don't believe it. They are vile beasts that would rip out your throat as you sleep."

He was hunkered down lighting a fire and looked up slowly at that comment. "Some say the same about me. So fast to judge are you, when you know naught of either the wolf nor myself."

The firelight lit up his face, his dark oaken hair gleaming with a soft sheen. His perusing eyes drank her in, holding within them a secret expression of which she found hard to decipher. Suddenly, in the soft light of the flickering fire she saw an odd gentleness she hadn't noticed before. While she thought the flames would only make him seem more of the devil she thought him to be, instead they kissed his skin in a brilliant warmth that almost made her forget she was alone in the depths of the forest on a dark night and betrothed to a very dangerous man.

He got to his feet, towering over her small frame and

brushed past her to retrieve something from his travel bag. She remained silent, licking her dry lips as she saw him bring forth a flask made from the stomach of a goat, that was probably filled with wine or ale. Next, he removed from the bag a large hunk of bread. He noticed her watching him and looked her way, and she quickly lowered her lashes, pretending to be searching the ground for her dagger instead of having to meet his gaze. He settled himself on the blanket and with a nod of his head he motioned for her to sit beside him. She hesitated, and he looked up to her and raised a questioning brow.

"Ah, Ruby, I can see you fear me. Now don't you think if I wanted you dead, you'd already be?"

Those words should have comforted her? They did nothing of the sort. Still, she was cold and hungry, and with one more nod of his head, she followed his command and sat. He handed her some bread and she shoved it into her mouth eagerly until her mouth was full, as she was starving, not having eaten at all this day.

He slowed his chewing when he saw her eating, and his penetrating stare burned through her as if he hadn't ever seen anyone eat before.

"What is it?" she asked. "Why do you look at me that way? It makes me uncomfortable," she admitted.

"You have so much to learn about being a lady. You are to eat and drink daintily. Do you understand?" There was a bitter edge of cynicism to his words and also a demanding tone to his voice.

"I don't want to be a lady."

"That, my dear, is obvious. But you will become a lady soon, as we are about to take our wedding vows."

"Then I see no rush, as I have no intention of ever saying

those vows. She grabbed the wine from him and raised it to her lips, spilling some in the process, but jerking backwards, managing not to stain her gown.

"Egads, you are incorrigible. Have you never wondered how it felt to be one of the female species?"

That comment was like a dagger to her heart. While she had no intention of being a lady, she was indeed a female! Couldn't he see that? She pushed the wine toward him and curled up into a ball, resting her head on her knees.

"I wish to sleep now, my lord."

"Aye," he agreed. "We have a long day ahead of us tomorrow. And though we have been headed in the right direction all day, we will still have to ride hard to make up for lost time."

She had no sooner closed her eyes, then she found herself drifting off to sleep. In the midst of her slumber, she heard the words of Lord Nyle of Sheffield vowing he'd make her a lady if it was the last thing he ever did.

Chapter 5

The sun poked its rays through the trees, and Nyle lay wide awake atop the blanket like he'd done most the night, watching over Lady Ruby to ensure her safety. He couldn't risk losing another wife, now that he was almost certain their deaths had not been accidents after all. The assassin could be on the prowl in these very woods and following them.

Now he almost regretted letting her wander through the woods for hours yesterday, letting her think he could not catch her. But since she'd been heading in the right direction, he'd let her continue. He'd done it purposely, hoping she'd get disoriented and frightened, just to teach her a lesson. It worked wonderfully, especially with that little perk of a wolf showing up just at the right time. Now, after that little episode, he figured she'd be less apt to cause trouble.

He'd waited until she'd fallen asleep last night, then he'd found her dagger in the underbrush and also collected her horse that he'd seen grazing not far from their encampment. There was no way he was going to lose any more of his dowry.

Ruby rested her head against his chest, snuggled in

deeply beneath the crook of his arm. If she knew what she did, she'd most likely run from him in horror. This woman hated him, of that there was no doubt in his mind. But then again, he hadn't really given her any reason not to. He could have told her he wasn't the cold-hearted murderer she saw him to be, but instead he'd kept his stories to himself.

That's one thing his father had always told him, was to keep your personal doings to yourself. And though he'd fought with his father about things that didn't matter, that was one thing they'd both agreed on. Nyle liked his privacy and that's why the rumors about him cut him deep to the bone. Instead of setting people straight, he'd let them think what they wanted, and kept his life as private as he could, and that wasn't easy in these days and times.

He didn't care what she thought of him, he tried to convince himself. He didn't need her to be fond of him, he just needed her as his wife. King Edward would be sending a messenger soon to tell him where and when to meet him. He wouldn't disappoint his sovereign by not doing what he asked. He nearly had a wife now as the king instructed. And though he'd lost three in the process, he didn't plan on divulging that information to King Edward, or at least, not just yet.

If Edward knew someone was trying to stop Nyle from taking guardianship of the his bastard, and they'd even resorted to murder, the king would never leave the boy in his care. He had watched over Tibbar since the king first sired the boy, and he had become very fond of the child during the past year.

Nyle almost felt like a father to the child since the king kept the baby and banished the boy's mother, his mistress - Lady Jocelyn. But then again, thought Nyle, he may feel like the boy's father because there was a very good chance he just might be.

Ruby shifted and nuzzled her nose into his chest. Though her gown was dirty and damp, her hair still smelled clean and he found himself rubbing his cheek against it. He'd never allowed himself to enjoy any of his wives, and he certainly knew before he'd even married them that he would never love them. Actually, he hadn't been married to any of them for more than a day before they were murdered, so it hadn't mattered. Still, he'd made up his mind to never love a woman again, after what he'd been through in the past.

Nyle had once fallen in love with a woman. That is, Lady Jocelyn of the king's court. Skin soft as satin, blond hair fine as down, he'd courted her in secret, wishing for her feminine beauty in his hands, her curvy body clinging to his, making passionate love. By day he'd serve the king loyally, but by night, he'd find himself in Jocelyn's company. And one night they'd made love, he not knowing that things were going to change from then on. The next night he'd come back to her bedchamber only to find the king himself already in her bed.

Though it pained him immensely to know he could never again be with the woman he loved, he stayed on in the king's service though he realized she was the king's mistress and had never told him. Had he known, he never would have touched her. He had risked his life staying, but he couldn't bring himself to leave. He was loyal to his king and stayed in his service, even after Jocelyn birthed a baby and claimed it to be the king's bastard. He just kept his secrets to himself and said nothing.

Jocelyn proved to have never loved him in return, and

Ruby

also to be quite the little trollop. And when the king found her bed already occupied with another man one night, she was banished from his dwellings and the man was executed. Jocelyn cared naught for the baby, never even holding it or paying it any attention, she must have meant to roil the king before she left. She told him the baby might not be his, but could very well be another man's instead. Nyle wasn't sure if she meant him or yet another, but didn't want to stay to find his head at the blade of an axe next, should she decide to talk. He had tried to leave but the king insisted he stay and protect his baby named Tibbar, as the boy had taken a liking to him.

The only saving grace was when Nyle's father passed away and he returned to Sheffield to claim the castle and his lands. If only King Edward had let him be. But now, months later, the king decided his wife was starting to ask questions about the child, and until Edward could discover if the boy was actually his, he needed to find somewhere else for little Tibbar to go. He ordered Nyle to take a wife, and maintain guardianship of the child for now and raise little Tibbar in a guise as if the baby were his own.

If only he had been asked to go fight instead, how simple that would have been. Of course he couldn't deny his king, and because of it he accepted the secret mission.

Ruby yawned and stretched, looking upward directly into his eyes. How innocent she looked with her soft brown eyes smiling up at him. For some reason, even though his past lover had bright blue eyes and was far from innocent, he found himself thinking of his beloved Jocelyn.

Suddenly, Ruby realized just where she was and sat up quickly. She jumped to her feet and backed away.

"How dare you touch me, you cur!"

69

The shrew was back, and in a way he was glad, as it brought him to his senses. He took to his feet, bringing the blanket with him.

"'Twas you who touched me, sweetheart. Matter of fact, you seemed to like it."

"I'm appalled," she bit off. "How could you think I like curling up to a . . . a . . . murderer?"

He had about all he could take of this little chit. He dropped the blanket to the ground and grabbed her by the shoulders.

"I am not a murderer," he shouted. "You will stop calling me that anon."

The heel of her soft slipper came down upon his foot, probably hurting her more than him. She wiggled in his hold, trying to be free. He locked his arms around her waist to keep her from moving.

"I despise you," she said, not surprising him in the least by the tone of venom in her words. "You've taken me away from my home and my father. You've demanded I be your wife and have threatened to make me into a lady."

"Despise me if you will, but I demand you respect me as well."

Her arms came up over her head and she slipped down out of his hold, leaving him empty handed. Picking up her skirt, she ran for the horse, but he headed her off and brought her to the ground.

"You little shrew! You will not try to escape me again."

His body over hers, she had no way to move. Her hair had come loose from her braid as she'd slept, and it now fanned out around her. Nyle found himself needing to know how it felt, and reached out and touched the soft locks with his fingers. She panted heavily from beneath him and her breasts about popped from her bodice each time she tried to catch her breath. In her lady attire she reminded him of his fragile Jocelyn. He had to know if her lips tasted as sweet and soft as well.

Without thinking, he leaned forward and placed his mouth over hers. Her eyes opened wide, and the little wench actually bit his lip. He jumped up, feeling the blood she'd drawn, tasting the metallic flavor on his tongue.

"What is the matter with you?" he snapped, his hand going to his mouth. "You've wounded me."

She sat up and glared. "How dare you think to take your pleasures right here, rutting in the dirt like an animal."

"My pleasures?" He laughed at the thought. "Believe me, Lady Ruby, I would never attach the word pleasure to the likes of you."

"Oh no?" She stood and faced him defiantly. "Then why did you kiss me?"

Suddenly, he realized his memories of another woman had caused him to kiss her, when he had no intentions of ever loving her. Or did he? Something about Ruby seemed to awaken a part of his soul that he thought was dead. Had she brought feelings out of him he'd hidden away for years for another woman, or was he just always attracted to women he knew he could or should never have?

Her feelings were clear that she despised him. To him, this was a challenge he had to take. He wanted her as a wife and mother to a child that he thought could possibly be his. He wanted her to bear him strong male heirs, and he knew she could. But to love her was something he knew he was incapable of doing. He could never open his heart to love again, because his heart had a dagger stabbing through it that could never be removed.

"I kissed you only because you are my wife and 'tis my right."

"I am not your wife, and neither will I ever be."

"You have been given to me by the earl of Blackpool. We have made a deal and it cannot be broken."

"I am no man's deal, my lord. I will not marry you, neither will I be your lady. I am Lady Ruby of Blackpool, and I will return to my father's side as soon as I am able."

"So you are saying you plan on escaping?

"I will do whatever it takes."

"And I will do whatever it takes to keep you at my side. Now get on the horse, as it is time to leave."

"My horse has returned," she said happily, first noticing it, and heading toward the animal, intending to mount it.

"Not that one," he instructed. "This one." He pointed to his own horse.

She looked at him curiously, and then just shook her head. "Nay. I will ride my own horse, not yours."

"I cannot allow that, as I have no more time nor patience to be chasing you through the woods again. We will ride together to my castle where we will take the vows of marriage as soon as we arrive. Now fasten your dagger at your waist for protection, and this time try not to drop it," he said, handing her the blade. "And don't even think of trying to use it on me, or you'll see a side of me you'll wish you hadn't."

* * *

Ruby arrived at Sheffield after riding hard all day. She was bedraggled and dirty, sitting in front of Lord Nyle, his arms wrapped around her, not for her protection, but because he thought she might try to escape. She'd never been so humiliated in all her life.

His people cheered him on as they crossed the drawbridge and made their way into the castle courtyard. His entourage had already returned to the castle before them. Lord Sheffield's minion, or squire with the twisted arm, greeted them at the portcullis with a slight bow. She felt like she was entering the devil's lair. Heavily guarded, she surveyed the amount of soldiers atop the battlements and the small army of knights with weapons they'd passed at the gatehouse. She'd have a hell of a time slipping away with all these eyes watching her.

Lord Sheffield dismounted and reached up to help her down. She noticed the dried blood on his lip and prided herself for biting him when he came to seek his pleasures. She ignored his offer of guidance, and slipped off the horse herself in one swift move. She looked around his home, noticing the grandeur of the keep and the courtyard, even larger than her father's estate. But her father was an earl. Shouldn't his dwellings best this one? Obviously her betrothed was well liked by the king and rewarded greatly. Either that, or the demon lord probably claimed his riches from each of the three wives he'd murdered. She wondered how much of a dowry they'd each left behind.

He had an orchard inside the inner bailey as well as a stable, a bakehouse, and his own blacksmith right inside his walls. There was a well and small herb garden next to what looked to be the kitchen, and across the knight's practice yard she could see the kennels for his hounds and the mews for his birds of prey.

There were many people occupying his courtyard that was lined with the finest of cobbled stones. An alewife walked by followed by a man carrying a barrel over his shoulder. Several children chased a stray dog near the kennels and the tinkering of metal was heard from inside the blacksmith's barn. Lords and ladies nodded to each other as a jester tried to entertain them by walking alongside while juggling small palm-sized bags filled with sand.

Servants rushed through the courtyard with baskets of bread, and she saw a merchant showing his wares from the back of his cart.

A strolling minstrel walked through the crowd playing a small flute, bringing a light-hearted tone to the surroundings. Everyone here seemed to be in high spirits. Everyone but her, that is.

She sought out her handmaiden, Oralie, standing near the cart that held the dowry her father had given with his acceptance of her marriage. The cart still dripped with water, and broken wooden barrels and torn dirty bolts of cloth were stacked in a pile atop it. She moved to run toward her handmaiden, but Nyle reached out, putting his hand on her shoulder, holding her steady.

"You'll go nowhere until I allow it," he told her.

"Lord Sheffield, you've finally arrived." His squire rushed up, taking the reins of his horse.

"Locke, have you managed to collect all my dowry?" His concern painted his words.

His squire's face darkened as he shook his head. "I'm afraid the coins as well as many of the weapons were lost at the bottom of the moat, my lord. The earl was kind enough to say he'd have his men try to collect the goods and bring them to you, but it doesn't look promising."

"Damn," he spat. "How about the rest?"

"The grain and spices were scattered over the courtyard,

my lord. The chickens and goats ate most of it before we could retrieve it."

Lord Sheffield just shook his head. "What about the jewels? Please tell me I haven't lost those as well."

When Ruby saw Locke just shake his head, she knew his answer was not good.

"We were attacked by bandits as we traveled on the road by night, trying to make it back quickly," his squire relayed. "The guards managed to scare them off before they took everything, but there were many of them and few of us, and the darkness of the night kept us from tracking them. I thought it best not to pursue the chase, knowing we had Lady Ruby's handmaiden with us. The guards agreed and so we brought her back to safety and returned as soon as possible."

"Aye," he said with a nod and a sigh. "You did the right thing, Locke. I only wish I had been with you. If I had been, I'd still have the jewels." He glared at Ruby, and she felt as if it were all her fault. After all, if he hadn't been chasing her through the woods, the jewels of her betrothal would still be in his possession.

"I'm almost afraid to ask, but what about the fabrics and silk?" Nyle asked. "Do I still have that at least?"

"Aye," Locke answered with a smile, pointing toward the wagon. "That you do. Although they are in poor condition as they haven't fared well from the putrid moat water, at least they are still in your possession."

The look of despair on his face was enough to make Ruby feel pity for the man. He'd gained a fortune and lost it all within a day's time. She wondered what he'd have to say about this when he got her alone.

"All is not lost, my lord, as you still have the best part of the dowry," said Locke, obviously trying to sound reassuring.

"What else is there?" Nyle grumbled.

"Why, Lady Ruby, of course. I see you've managed to find her and bring her home safely."

He released his hand from her shoulder, and Ruby heard the disgust in his voice.

"Aye," he said sarcastically. "I at least have that, don't I? Such a Ruby in the rough. And what a treasure she is."

He motioned for her handmaiden to join them. The woman ran up to him and curtseyed, waiting for him to acknowledge her.

"Get up," he told her, causing her to rise.

"Aye, my lord," she answered.

"What is your name?"

"Her name is Oralie," Ruby answered for her.

"I believe I was speaking to the handmaiden," he said in a low voice, "now let me ask again. What is your name?"

The woman looked at Ruby with confusion in her eyes as she had just told him. Still, Ruby just nodded for her to tell him again.

"I am Oralie, Lady Ruby's maidservant," she relayed. "I am at your service, my lord."

Ruby realized her handmaid was nervous and rightly so. She figured she needed to try to calm her.

"If you'll kindly instruct her where to put my trunks," said Ruby, "I would like to retreat now to my chamber."

She heard him chuckle softly, and then he turned his head to look directly at her.

"Your chamber?" he asked. "You will be my wife by the morrow so as of tonight you will be staying in the solar. . ."

"The solar is fine," she answered.

Ruby

" . . . with me," he finished.

She saw Oralie's look of surprise and she felt her own body stiffen. She hadn't expected this – not yet. She couldn't sleep in the same bed with the man. She didn't even know him! This was preposterous and she would not stand for it.

"I demand the wedding banns be posted before I share a pallet with you, my lord."

"You will demand nothing from me, and stop interrupting when I am speaking." He looked at the handmaiden and continued. "Now get her things and take her to the upstairs solar to wash the traveling dirt from her body. Have her prepared and ready to join me for the midday meal in the great hall anon, where I will introduce my new wife to the rest of the castle."

"Please stop speaking as if I am not even here," Ruby told him. "Let me also remind you, I am not your wife, as I am only your betrothed."

"That's right," he said, perusing her with his dangerous stare. "And let me remind you that you might never make it as far as becoming my wife."

Her eyes opened wide and she felt a bolt of fear crash through her. She wasn't sure if that was a threat but didn't want to wait around to find out.

"Come along, Oralie," she said to her handmaiden, heading toward the castle. "The Lord of Death has spoken."

Chapter 6

"Just set the trunks by the wall," Ruby told the pages.

They did as ordered and left the room and Oralie closed the door behind them. Ruby's handmaiden was a woman of close to forty years of age who had never married nor had a child of her own. She was a small, frail woman with ebony hair. She always acted so prim and proper but when they were alone, Oralie let her guard down, living vicariously through Ruby's wild ways, enjoying the woman she could never be.

When Ruby's mother, Mirabelle, died five and ten years ago while giving birth, Oralie had taken all the girls under her wing so to speak, trying her best to fill in as role of their mother. Ruby had taken a special liking to the woman more than her sisters and that's why she insisted Oralie come with her to Sheffield.

"Lady Ruby, let me help you change into a proper gown." Oralie hurried over and opened her trunk, which thankfully had not gotten ruined when the cart dumped.

"I don't care about being proper," she told her, crossing

her arms over her chest. "I like who I am and will not change for anyone."

"Oh, but you must," said Oralie hurrying over to help Ruby remove her soiled gown. "If not, aren't you afraid you'll anger Lord Sheffield? After all, you are about to become his wife, and there is no telling how he'll react."

"It probably would anger him," she admitted, "but I'll be prepared to defend myself with this." She proudly took her dagger from her waist and held it high in the air.

Oralie removed Ruby's belt and pouch, then took the dagger from her and laid it on the bedside table before helping her remove her gown. Ruby eagerly grabbed the dagger again and held it up in front of her. Oralie slowly folded the gown and looked down as she spoke.

"If I were you, I'd not be flaying that in his face, my lady, or he may decide to match you with the tip of his sword."

"Just let him try," she said, lowering the dagger to her side and feeling an emptiness within her. "Oh, I miss my ruby dagger. Do you remember it Oralie?"

"I remember," said Oralie, "or are you forgetting I was once your mother's lady-in-waiting as well?"

"I haven't forgotten. I just like talking about it, that's all." Ruby placed the dagger on the bed and held out her arms as Oralie pulled a green gown over her head. Ruby would have rather just worn an oversized tunic and a pair of hose, but decided not to anger her husband-to-be any more at this time.

"Ruby, I know you've grown up acting more like the earl's son than his daughter, but those times are behind you now."

"No, never," she said. "I know how to use a dagger and

a sword and won't hesitate to use them if I have to."

"Your mother would have wanted you to act like a lady. And while I see your bravado with a blade, I sincerely don't think you understand what it means to actually kill someone."

"What do you mean, Oralie? The knights do it all the time and don't even bat an eye."

"Mayhap so, but you have no idea what goes on in their heads afterwards."

"I'm sure I could do it too, if I had to. I wish I could have been a knight, as I think I would have rather liked it."

"You don't mean that, and better keep those thoughts to yourself around Lord Sheffield." Oralie buttoned her into her gown as she spoke. "You act so hardened, my lady, but don't forget I've known you since you were a child. I know that even though you show a strong demeanor, you hold things inside that truly bother you. Sometimes it would do you good to feel the emotions of a lady, and even cry once in awhile."

"Oralie, you are wrong. I don't hold anything in, and am sure being a knight would be much better than being a lady."

Her handmaiden was just finishing up fixing her hair when a knock came at the door.

Oralie went over and opened it. A young page stood there.

"Lord Sheffield requires Lady Ruby's presence in the great hall anon."

"Thank you," said Oralie, closing the door.

"I'm not going." Ruby plopped down on the bed.

"I think you should, my lady. You really should obey your new husband, as most men are not as tolerant as your father."

"You mean most men would not put up with the way I speak my mind or ride a horse or practice my joust."

"You know that your father was soft with you. Those acts are all punishable and not tolerated at all by most men. You are going to be married to Lord Sheffield and need to stop challenging him and instead act the part of his wife if you want this marriage to work. You will be Lady Sheffield now and should be proud of it. You also need to show respect for your husband, just as your mother showed respect for your father. It's what your mother as well as your father would want you to do.

She thought about it, then nodded. Mayhap Oralie was right. She was playing with fire and since the devil ruled fire, she was sure not to win anyway.

"All right, I am hungry, so I'll go," she told her. "But I am only going because of that, not because I'm frightened of him." She placed her dagger into the sheath on the belt around her waist.

"Of course, my lady. I understand."

Ruby made her way to the door, not sure she understood anything. Why did Lord Sheffield choose to marry her, and why did he seem in such a hurry that he wanted to say the vows even before they posted the banns?

* * *

Nyle stood at the dais with the chaplain at his side. The great hall was filled with not only the servants and his knights, but the knights' families as well. The buzz of conversation grew louder as they all waited, once again, to watch their lord get married.

"My Lord," said Locke, holding out a ring. "Don't forget this."

"Oh, aye," he said, taking the simple gold band in his hand and turning it over in his palm. This had been the same ring he'd used for each of his past three wives and he hoped it wasn't bad luck. It didn't matter, he told himself. He only needed a wife in order to secure that he'd receive the boy. And since the king's messenger arrived just that evening with his missive, Nyle now knew that the date of the boy's arrival was scheduled for tomorrow. He was sure he'd have a much better chance this time of having a wife to present when he met with the king in secret. Or so he hoped.

His gaze shot upward as Ruby and her handmaid entered the great hall. She wore an ugly green gown that was ill-fitting on her, and did naught to show her curves at all. It didn't matter. He just needed her to say the vows and then they'd be able to eat. Being as famished as he was at the moment, he hoped this wouldn't take long.

He walked over to Ruby and took her by the arm, guiding her to the dais.

"This is the castle's chaplain, Father Francis," he said, nodding to the man.

"Oh, you're waiting to say the prayer before the meal so we can eat," she said, noticing the book in his hand. "Go ahead, Father, as I am very hungry."

The chaplain opened his mouth to tell her why he was there, but Nyle laid a hand on his shoulder to stop him. "Go ahead and start," he said, holding on to Ruby's arm so she couldn't get away.

"Shouldn't we sit first?" she asked innocently, and Nyle knew she had no clue what was about to transpire.

"We will sit and eat afterwards," he told her.

"I see," she said looking around the hall. "I guess everyone stands for the prayer here. This is not the way we

Ruby

do it in Blackpool."

"Please start, Father, and make it short and simple," commanded Nyle.

"Of course, my lord." The short, balding man nodded and opened his book looking for the right page.

Nyle reached out and gently closed the book and handed it back to the man. "No need for the formality," he said. "Just the basics are fine."

The chaplain looked up, wiped his brow in his sleeve and continued. "Do you, Lord Nyle Dacre of Sheffield take Lady . . . I'm sorry what's her name?" he whispered.

"My name is Ruby de Burgh of Blackpool, but why does your meal prayer sound to me more like a wedding vow?" asked Ruby.

"Well . . . because . . ." the chaplain wiped his brow again.

"Just continue," ordered Nyle.

"Of course, my lord." The chaplain cleared his throat and started once again. "Do you Lord Nyle Dacre of Sheffield, take Lady Ruby de Burgh of Blackpool –"

"I do," he said, not bothering to let him finish.

"What?" asked Ruby, her mouth opening wide. "Are you truly having this man marry us right here in the great hall while our dinner awaits us on the table?"

"And it's getting cold," said Nyle. "Now go ahead Father, please continue."

"Do you Lady Ruby de Burgh of Blackpool take Lord Nyle –"

"Nay!"

"Nay? God's eyes, what are you doing?" growled Nyle.

"Lord Sheffield," said the chaplain. "Please refrain from language such as that."

"I am not going to marry you," she said, her hands going defiantly to her hips.

"You will marry me," he matched her. "I have made not only a deal but an alliance with your father. You cannot refuse, so don't even try."

"You have not even posted the wedding banns," she told him, obviously only trying to postpone the inevitable.

"God's teeth, there is no need for that."

"Please, Lord Sheffield," the chaplain broke in again, "refrain from your blasphemy."

"You are wrong. There is a need," she told him.

"Fine," he answered. "Scribe, lend me a quill and parchment please." The scribe who'd been recording the events of the wedding ceremony handed him what he asked for. He scribbled something on the parchment and held it out for her to see. "Our wedding banns," he told her.

She squinted, looking at the parchment and reading the words aloud. "Lady Ruby of Blackpool and Lord Nyle of Sheffield are to be married anon."

"Good enough," he said, handing the parchment and quill to Locke. "Have this posted on the door right away," he told his squire. Then he looked back to her. "Alright, the banns are now posted."

"That's not the proper way to do it," she complained. "It should be posted on the door to the church as well as the castle and for three Sundays in a row before we're married."

"I thought we've been over all this already. You are far from proper and so it does not matter that we're not following procedure."

"Well, we need to plan the ceremony and the celebration to follow. If I'm being forced to marry, then I want a large wedding with all my family present as well."

"Nay. That's not going to happen."

"Why not?"

The little spitfire was trying his patience and he didn't have time for this. He didn't want to do it, but he knew the only way to get her to agree to this farce of a marriage was to scare her into it. And as much as he hated what he was about to say, he really had no other choice.

"Because . . . " he told her, forcing the words from his mouth. "There is no need for the expense of a large wedding when we don't know how long you are going to live."

"My lord!" Locke gasped from beside him. And when Nyle looked at Ruby's handmaiden, her eyes quickly shot downward and she stared at the ground. The chaplain was blessing himself, not once but thrice, and Ruby's eyes were opened wide as if she couldn't believe what she'd just heard.

"Continue," he instructed the chaplain.

"Wait!" She pulled her arm away from Nyle and when he glanced her way, the fear he thought he'd see there was really an angry fire in her eyes. "I will marry you in this absurd way if you insist, but not because you are trying to scare me into it. I fear you not, my Lord of Death, and if you think I am going to be the ever-obedient wife then you are sadly mistaken."

He knew she was going to be nothing but trouble and now he was starting to regret that he hadn't chosen one of her more soft-spoken sisters instead. But one thing for certain, whoever had been killing off his wives better stay clear of her.

She continued, and he didn't even bother trying to stop her. "I will uphold the agreement of my father to honor this marriage of hell, but only because of him, naught else."

"Are you quite finished?" he asked through gritted teeth,

trying to ignore the astonished faces in the room, doing all he could to maintain his composure and not reprimand her for her words and actions. "Because if so, will you please recite your vows so we can eat?"

"Yes," she said and smoothed down her skirts and looked up at the priest and said, "I regretfully do."

"My lord?" said the chaplain shifting nervously to one foot. "That is not what she is supposed to say."

"Say it right," he warned her, watching her chin tilt upward and her hand toss her single braid back over her shoulder.

She looked back at the chaplain and said, "I . . ."

Nyle cleared his throat at that moment as a subtle reminder of her expected cooperation.

"Do," she finally answered.

The chaplain let out a deep breath, and closed his book looking more relieved than even Nyle, that this was over. "I pronounce you man and wife," he said. "You may now kiss the bride."

Nyle looked over to Ruby and she was glaring at him and he knew she would probably slap him if he tried to kiss her. He was going to forget the whole blasted idea until the crowded room started chanting, "kiss, kiss, kiss."

"I can't disappoint them," he told her softly.

"You can't disappoint me either," she said.

He didn't know what she meant by that, but without waiting any longer and in order to calm the noisy room, he reached his hand around the back of her head and pulled her toward him, fastening his lips over hers tightly, not giving her the opportunity to bite him again.

Her fists came up and she pushed against his chest, but when he deepened the kiss, her arms slowly lowered, coming to rest against him. The crowd cheered and clapped and he found himself enjoying kissing her when she wasn't trying to bite him. He felt an odd feeling in his chest and would have liked to discover what it was, but instead he pulled away quickly.

"All right," he said. "Now that it's over with, let's start the feast. I'm starved."

Ruby never meant to let him kiss her, but it all happened so fast that she barely had a chance to react. She'd meant to push him away, but when his lips caressed hers and she felt the warmth growing as she came to life under his touch, she'd closed her eyes and threw back her head. Instead of the angry, punishing kiss she'd thought he'd give her, his lips were soft and sensuous and inviting. She was shocked at her own eager response to his advance, and found herself wanting even more.

Never had she thought a kiss from a man like him would feel so passionate and alive. It was dangerous in an exciting sort of way, and had her wondering what other responses he'd be able to coax from her.

His lips had slowly pulled away, taking with him the vibrations that were flowing freely through her and leaving her mouth burning with desire. She opened her eyes only to find him already halfway up the dais, leaving her standing there as if nothing out of the ordinary had just happened. Of course, for him, this wasn't out of the ordinary as he seemed to marry someone every week or so.

"My lady, let me help you to the dais," said Oralie.

"I'm fine," she told her handmaiden, her eyes locked onto her new husband as she spoke. "I do not have a long train on this gown, so I can manage on my own, but thank you just the same."

She headed up the dais, and instead of pulling out the chair for her, he sat himself down, holding out his goblet to the cupbearer to be filled with wine. She settled herself at the table next to him, then spoke, her eyes looking out to the crowd rather than at him.

"And you say I am the one who is crude and not proper."

He nodded to the cupbearer who went on to fill the drinking vessel of the chaplain sitting next to him. She noticed that there was only one cup between them and that they would have to share. There was also only one trencher, hollowed-out crust of brown bread, between them to hold their food.

"Pardon me, Wife? What was that you said?" His eyes searched her face as he brought the goblet to his mouth. After taking a sip, he held it up for her to drink as well.

"'Twas nothing," she said, tilting the goblet from the bottom of the stem rather than to touch his hand holding the proffered cup. She drank where his lips had been just seconds ago, only making her feel his essence running through her once again as she remembered his kiss. She released the goblet and leaned back in her chair and let out a sigh.

"Oh," he said, placing the drinking vessel on the table. "I almost forgot." He patted his surcoat as if he were looking for something then pulled out an object from inside his tunic and laid in on the table in front of him and pushed it over halfway between them. "It's yours if you want it."

She fastened her gaze onto a simple gold ring. She felt disappointed that he wasn't putting it on her finger and also that he sounded so nonchalant as if it didn't matter if she took it or not.

Ruby

She picked up the ring gingerly in two fingers, the reality of being married settling against her brain. This wasn't at all how she'd envisioned her wedding day. But then again, she also thought she'd stay unmarried and with her father for the rest of her life so she really hadn't any visions in her head of how it was supposed to be.

"Shouldn't you put it on me?" she asked, still holding it up in front of her.

"I can if you want me to," he said, taking the ring from her, his fingers brushing against hers in the process, causing that damn tingle against her skin to return. "I just didn't know if you'd want to wear it, considering the circumstances and all."

He picked up her hand in his and was about to slide the ring onto her finger when an awful thought flitted through her mind.

"Wait!" she said, stopping him by pulling her hand away. "By any chance . . . is that the same ring the rest of your wives wore?"

"Aye, it is. Now give me your hand."

"Nay!" She pulled her hand to her chest. "I can't wear a cursed ring."

"Cursed?" He inspected the ring, his mouth pursed in the process. "Why would you think the ring is cursed?"

"Has not every woman who has worn it wound up dead?"

"Well . . . I suppose so."

"Then I cannot put it around my finger and please don't ask me to."

"Suit yourself, then." He put the ring into the pouch at his side, and she felt a surge of disappointment stab at her heart. Here she was – married and without her family present

- and she didn't even have a ring to seal the vows.

"Use this," she said, slipping the ruby ring that used to be her mother's off the finger on her right hand and holding it out to him.

He whistled and held it up to the light to peruse it. "This is quite nice. Much nicer than the ring I had to offer. But 'tis already yours, so it won't do." He went to give it back to her and the stab of disappointment grew stronger.

"Nay! Please use it . . . for now," she said. "To seal the vows of marriage."

"As you wish," he told her, "but I thought it would not matter to you."

She thought so as well, until she'd seen the gold ring he'd tried to give her and reality hit her hard. She was married now, like it or not. She was his wife, and this man beside her was now her husband.

"Hold out your hand," he instructed.

"Have the chaplain bless it first," she said. When she saw the scowl on his face and thought he was going to object, she added, "please."

The chaplain looked over, having heard his name mentioned, and she blurted out the request just in case Nyle decided not to go along with it.

"Father Francis, will you please bless this ring for our marriage?" she asked.

"Of course," he said, taking the ring in his hand and saying a prayer over it, then pulling a small bottle of holy water from his pouch and sprinkling it atop the ring. "Here you are," he said, handing it back to Nyle.

She held out her left hand, and this time the look in his eyes was not of aggravation, but more reserved, and if she didn't know better – caring. He slipped the ring onto the proper finger and looked into her eyes. She saw want within them, as well as need. Both of these things scared her. Then she thought of their wedding night and this scared her even more.

She remembered the stories she'd heard the men relaying years ago when she'd disguised herself as a page and went along on their hunting trip. She felt her heart beating faster and she was sure her face was reddening as well, as she felt a sudden surge of heat. She pulled her hand away and grabbed for the goblet, downing the wine in one swig in order to calm her nerves.

"You keep that up and you'll be prone on the floor before I ever take you to our wedding bed," he said.

Her hand shot out to the cupbearer to have him refill it. Then once again, she quaffed the wine, hoping that was exactly what would happen. Because if she wasn't passed out before they made it to the bedchamber, she didn't know if she could go through with the act of coupling with such a dangerous – and handsome man.

Chapter 7

Nyle sat near the fire drinking heartily with his men. The meal was finished and the minstrels in the gallery were providing the music for the feast. He knew they expected him to dance with his new bride, but dancing was the last thing on his mind right now.

Ruby stood at the far end of the hall conversing only with her handmaiden and he felt as if he should be by her side, yet he couldn't bring himself to do it. He hadn't divulged the information to her that all three of his past wives had died on their wedding day – and before he even had the chance to consummate the marriage. It bothered him to no end that they were murdered right under his nose and he'd been too blind to see it.

Shame washed over him at his own carelessness as to not have protected his wives. But each murder had been done so cleverly that there was no way he could have known and tried to stop it. After all, how was he supposed to keep an eye on them in the garderobe or know that they'd be poisoned drinking from the wedding cup or that they would die in his own bed waiting to consummate the marriage? Still, he couldn't help but feel it was all his fault.

Ruby

His eyes darted around the crowded room. He felt it in his blood that the killer was lurking somewhere in his castle's walls. He took a swig of his ale and looked around the room at so many unfamiliar faces. He'd been gone serving King Edward III for many years and really did not know all the knights or servants which were now in his own castle. He'd only inherited his father's domain less than two moons ago. He'd tried his best to get to know everyone, but his duties were many and so were the people that inhabited his domain.

"Sir Godin," he said to his captain of the guard who was one of the oldest knights there, and also one of the most loyal, or so his father had always told him.

"Aye, milord?" The man came and sat at his side. He was a rather large man, but still in good shape for his age. He also had a great sword arm that gave Nyle a fair challenge in the practice yard.

"Tell me, are there any new knights or footsoldiers or other men in my service as of the last few months?"

"Well, aye, there are, my lord," he said, running a hand over his dark, short beard in thought.

"Point them out to me," he instructed, surveying the crowded room.

"There, talking to the minstrel is a new footsoldier, Umphrey," said the knight, motioning with his head. "He came to the castle pledging his service and loyalty just after your father died but before you'd arrived, my lord. I thought it best to have the castle well protected until it once again had a lord, so I welcomed him to the garrison."

Nyle surveyed the man's scarred face and hands and also his burly build and hardened composure. "So he's naught more than a mercenary, no matter what he claims. Does he have any family here with him?"

"No one, my lord. He is more or less a loner. But he has a calm disposition for such a large man."

"That means nothing. Assign a man whom you trust the most to keep an eye on him day and night. Report back to me if anything at all seems out of the ordinary."

"Of course, my lord."

"Who else is new to the castle?" he asked.

"Well, the falconer took on a new apprentice a few weeks ago," Sir Godin told him. "There the boy is now, showing your wife one of the falcons."

Nyle shot to his feet, seeing the boy holding the bird forward and Ruby running a finger along its back. He worried for her safety, as this boy could easily be the murderer.

"Shall I assign someone to keep an eye on him as well, milord?"

"Nay, I have a better idea. Locke," he called to his squire standing not far from him.

Locke hurried over, holding a tankard of ale in his hand.

"Yes, Lord Sheffield?" he asked.

"I want you to keep an eye on the new falconer's apprentice," he said. "Befriend the boy and get to know him."

"Oh, you mean Darby," he said with a nod of acceptance. "He is very good at his skill. He's shown me how he's trained the falcons to swoop in and kill on his command."

"That's what I was afraid of."

"My lord?" he asked, obviously confused.

"I want you to watch him like a . . ."

"Hawk?" asked Locke with a large smile.

Ruby

"Just keep a close eye on him, will you? And keep him away from my wife."

"You think he'd try to woo her from you?" Locke looked up, confused, and shook his head.

"Nay, you simpkin, I think he may try to murder her. There is someone within these walls killing off my wives and I need to discover who before they decide to strike again."

"Oh, yes, the unfortunate deaths of your wives. I understand. I will keep my ears and eyes open, my lord. But I don't think he is a murderer. Mayhap you should keep an eye on that new cook, Forwin, instead. He seems to like sharpening those butcher knives constantly, and has a menacing look about him."

"That I will." He motioned for his steward, Lewis, to join them.

"What is it, my lord?" Lewis was in charge of the household and the books, and also in charge of the servants. The man was short and plump and looked like he spent a lot of time near the food in the kitchen.

"I feel there may be a murderer within the castle walls," he told him.

"You mean – because of the deaths of your wives?" he asked.

"Aye. And since I've yet another new wife, I'd like to see her last more than a day. Now keep a close eye on the new cook, Forwin."

"Right away, my lord." After a nod of dismissal from Nyle, the man turned and headed toward the kitchen.

Just then the straight trumpet blared and the herald called out that they had guests.

"Someone is arriving this late and uninvited?" Nyle

looked over to Locke and Godin. They just shrugged and shook their heads.

"Oh, didn't I mention it to you?" asked his steward turning and coming back to join them. "Lord Sheffield, your sister sent a missive while you were gone that she was arriving here this evening."

"Linette is here?" He looked up to the solar door and saw a small entourage of servants, a few soldiers and a bent-over woman who looked like an old handmaid walking through the hall following his younger sister.

Linette was only eight and ten years of age, and nine years younger than him. She was tall in stature, and her hair was just as dark as his. But her eyes were bright blue instead of his eyes of weathered silver. His twin, Nigel, had had bright blue eyes as well, and Nyle found himself missing his brother, as he had died in the same battle that had brought Nyle fame in the king's eyes.

As the sole heir to the estates with Nigel's death, Nyle should have returned then to make amends with his father, but instead he stayed away and held a grudge that would haunt him for the rest of his life.

"Nyle," she called, rushing to him with her arms outstretched.

"Linette." He rushed over to greet her with a quick kiss and an embrace. Over her shoulder he saw Ruby just staring at him. "I didn't think you'd come," he told her.

Linette had married a Scotsman from the Highlands close to two years ago. She'd moved to her husband's homeland with him not long after their marriage, and following the death of their mother when she passed-on from a weak heart. Linette thought their mother's death was her fault since she had been opposed to her marrying a

Ruby

Scotsman.

"I got your missive that father died," she said. "I am sorry it has taken me so long to get here. What happened to him?"

Nyle saw the regret in her eyes and knew that she had wished she were here to be with her father before he'd left this world.

"He died from his battle wounds, Linette. "Though he'd fought it for a long time, it finally consumed him."

"First Nigel, then mother, and now father. I am so saddened, brother." She threw herself against his chest and wept bitterly.

"I am sorry, Linette, but at least we still have each other." He put his arm around her shoulder as she wiped the tears from her eyes. "Do not fret, dear sister, as they are all together now."

His eyes darted over to Ruby, and the falconer's apprentice seemed to be getting closer to her. He didn't like this in the least. "Come, I want you to meet my new wife," he said, taking his sister's arm and guiding her across the hall toward Ruby. Her handmaiden followed.

"Lady Ruby," he said, reaching out and taking her by the arm, "I'd like you to meet my sister, Lady Linette."

"How nice to meet you," said Ruby, so respectful he barely thought it was the same untamed girl he'd married.

"Yes, I heard you were married, brother," Linette said, nodding an acknowledgement to Ruby.

"And which of his marriages were you referring to?" asked Ruby. "This or one of the other three?"

"Other three?" asked Linette in question, looking at her brother.

"I'll tell you later, sister."

Nyle squeezed Ruby's hand, trying to warn her to keep her mouth shut, but she just continued.

"He tried to give me their cursed wedding ring, but I wouldn't accept it, because I don't plan on ending up dead like his other wives."

Yes, the shrew was back. Why had he expected anything less? He felt like crawling behind the ornate tapestry lining the wall for warmth. He didn't want his sister hearing this as the first thing when she'd just arrived and was in mourning.

"I have heard some kind of rumor in my travels, but I assure you my brother didn't murder anyone," Linette replied.

His eyes shot up to his sister and he spoke to her in a low tone. "How did you hear?"

"My handmaiden, Ascilia told me," she said splaying her hand toward the silent woman right behind them.

Nyle turned around quickly and confronted her. "How did you know?" he asked. The woman had black hair tied up under a wimple that not only covered her head, but wrapped around under her chin in folds, covering most her wrinkled face that looked to be deformed from some sort of burns. She looked to the ground quickly, stopping him from viewing her face.

"I . . . heard it while occupying the household of the king in Windsor," the woman said, not looking at him.

"Windsor?" He looked up at his sister. "I thought this was your handmaiden from the Highlands."

"No," his sister relayed. "Actually, my handmaiden was injured on the journey here. I was lucky to find Ascilia when I stopped at an inn for the night. The innkeeper recommended her. She tells me she was a handmaiden for one of the ladies at King Edward's court. Since you spent time there, mayhap you know the lady whom she served."

The handmaiden's name sounded familiar, but Nyle truly did not remember her from his time at Windsor. "Which of the ladies there did you assist?" he asked. The handmaiden answered without looking at him.

"Lady Jocelyn," she said, catching him by surprise. "Perhaps you know her?" she asked. "After all, I do remember you, Lord Nyle, and unless I'm mistaken, you seemed to have spent much time with the Lady Jocelyn." The woman's voice was soft and held a crackly odd tone to it.

Nyle's heart stood still. He clenched his jaw tightly, still affected by the name of the woman he'd loved and who'd betrayed him by coupling with the king, as well as others. He was not about to admit he knew her now. Not after the king banished her from his dwellings and took her baby. And now the king was bringing Jocelyn's child here on the morrow. Egads, this was bad timing. He only hoped the handmaiden wouldn't remember the child, but that was probably too much to ask.

"I remember Lady Jocelyn," he admitted. "But only vaguely." He noticed the handmaiden's body stiffen and she glanced up quickly, then dropped her gaze again. He saw a flash of blue eyes in the process.

"Excuse me, my lord and lady," said Oralie, coming to Ruby's side. "But if it is by your order I will go to the solar and see to the preparations for your wedding night."

"Of course," Nyle interrupted, before Ruby could object to coupling with him. "Please make the necessary preparations as we will be coming to the solar soon."

"I beg your leave as well," said Linette's handmaiden from behind him. "As I need to see to my lady's belongings and prepare her chamber too."

"You will find my steward in the kitchen," he told the woman. "He will direct you to a chamber that my sister can use while she is here."

The handmaidens both left and Nyle took his sister on one arm and his wife on the other and guided them across the hall toward the fire.

"Are you hungry?" he asked his sister. "I can have the cook prepare some food, as we have already eaten."

"Nay," she answered, settling herself on a bench at the trestle table. "What I would like, is to get to know your new wife. Please, sit next to me," she said smiling at Ruby and tapping the seat with her hand. Ruby did as instructed and Nyle called a servant boy over with more wine, as he knew he probably would need it before this conversation was over. He had no idea what words would be flying from his new bride's mouth.

"Tell me about yourself," said Linette. "How and when did you and my brother meet?"

Ruby found herself liking Nyle's sister. It felt good to have another woman to talk to, and the tall, dark-haired woman reminded her of her own sisters that she already missed dearly. She felt comfortable around her, and it helped to ease her jitters from her nervousness of having to couple with her new husband soon.

"Well, I met the Lord of Death first yesterday," she admitted.

"Lord of Death?" His sister's eyes held amusement as she laughed behind her hand and looked up toward her brother. "Oh, Nyle, I've heard you called many things through the years but never the Lord of Death. And never from a woman!"

Nyle took two goblets of wine from the servant boy and handed them to the women. Then he took one for himself, taking a swig before he answered.

"Well, you'll hear many shocking things falling from my wife's lips, but I warn you not to believe a single word."

"Oh brother," scolded Linette. "Let your wife speak. Please, continue," she said nodding to Ruby.

"Really, there's not much to tell. He came to my father's castle in Blackpool to choose a wife, as I have three sisters. I was on a horse practicing my joust at my homemade quintain when he chose me."

"Quintain? You?" she asked in bewilderment.

"Yes, I know how to wield a sword and use a dagger to hunt as well."

"Are your sisters like this too?" she asked.

"Nay, they are proper ladies who are obedient and know the skills of sewing and weaving, which I refuse to do."

"Really?" She raised a questioning brow and looked over to her brother. "Yet my brother chose you. Curious."

Just then a scream was heard and the sound of something tumbling down the steps. Commotion flowed through the room and Ruby saw Nyle jump to his feet and place his hand on the hilt of his sword.

"Lady Ruby," someone called out from across the hall. "Your handmaiden has just fallen down the steps and she is not moving."

"What?" Ruby sprang from the bench, alarmed. Picking up her skirt she ran through the hall with Nyle passing her up and making it to the foot of the steps first.

"Clear the way," he said, pushing his way through the crowd. He hunkered down next to the woman and placed his fingers on her neck.

Ruby stopped next to him, a knot in her stomach twisting as she surveyed Oralie lying face down at the bottom of the steep stone staircase.

"Is she . . . dead?" She didn't want to even hear the answer, but had to ask. Nyle rolled her over and the woman moaned.

"Nay, she lives," he announced, "but is lucky she didn't break her damned neck. Her leg looks awkward and hopefully it is not broken. The healer needs to look at her immediately."

"I am here," called out the healer from the crowd.

"What happened?" asked Linette running up to join them.

"She stumbled and fell down the steps," said Linette's handmaid, Ascilia descending the steps with linens in her hands as she spoke. A moment later the chambermaid appeared at the top of the steps with a hand clasped to her mouth when she surveyed the scene.

"Did you see it happen?" Nyle asked the handmaid.

"Nay," she answered, "as I was in the upstairs chamber getting linens from the chambermaid. But I heard it."

"Did anyone see what happened?" Nyle asked, his eyes searching everyone in the crowd.

No one responded, and Nyle knew this looked like the murderer was on the loose again. Still, he couldn't prove it.

He instructed several of his men to take the hurt woman to the great hall where the healer was already opening his bag of herbs and ointments.

"Oralie," he said as they carried her away. "What happened?"

"Oh, my lord, I am sorry, but there were no linens on the bed and Ascilia told me she'd seen a chambermaid and to contact her. I was heading downstairs to tell Lady Ruby about the delay when I fell."

"Yes, I took her to the chambermaid myself," said Ascilia. "I was still there or I may have seen exactly what happened."

"Did you just stumble or were you pushed?" he asked, following behind as they moved toward the great hall.

"I felt something on my shoulder but before I could turn to look, I fell forward down the stairs, Oralie told him. "I am not certain, my lord, but it could be possible that I was pushed."

"I see." He walked back to the crowd at the foot of the steps, all the while in deep thought. "Sir Godin," he spoke lowly so only his loyal knight could hear him. "Did you have a man watching Umphrey?"

"I did," he said, "but Umphrey managed to slip away."

"Locke?" he asked, pulling his squire over to him. "What about the falconer's assistant? Did you have an eye on him?"

"I'm sorry, my lord. I stopped for a moment to speak with the stablemaster about your horse, and when I looked up he was gone. But I am sure he went back to the mews."

Nyle looked up to see his steward arriving from the kitchen and the new cook was right behind him.

"Brother," said Linette, her hand on his shoulder. "This is your wedding night. Why don't you and your bride retire to the solar for the night and you can concern yourself with this on the morrow?"

He thought about what she said, and realized the safest place for Ruby to be right now would be with him.

"Perhaps you are right," he told her.

"But now that Oralie is injured, I don't even have a handmaiden to help me prepare," said Ruby, and Nyle knew she was only stalling for time.

"That's true," he said. "Your handmaiden will be of no help to you for now. Possibly not even for a while by the looks of her leg. I will have to find you another."

"I'd be happy to help out," offered Ascilia.

"Yes, I agree. She can have my handmaiden for the night," said Linette. "Then we can look for another in the morning." She walked forward and placed one hand on Ruby's back and the other on her handmaiden, Ascilia. "Now go already, as your husband waits."

As she pushed them gently toward the stairs, Ruby wanted to object, but with everyone watching, she knew she shouldn't. She felt so nervous to begin with, and now without Oralie at her side to comfort her, she knew she would feel even worse.

She walked up the stairs toward the solar, with Linette's handmaiden at her side, wondering if this woman could give her any words of wisdom on this special night.

"Ascilia," she said. "I heard you say earlier that you once served in King Edward's household and that Nyle resided there as well. Can you tell me at all what it might be like to bed my new husband? I am very nervous."

The woman led her across the second floor corridor and opened the door to the solar. She held out her hand for Ruby to enter first, and when Ruby stepped inside the first thing she laid eyes on was a very large bed. All of a sudden terror ripped through her at the thought of what was she was expected to do next. But for some reason that didn't bother

her as much as the next words that came out of the old handmaiden's mouth.

"I can tell you much," the old woman said in a garbled voice. "For you see, I was handmaiden to the woman your new husband once loved. That is, the woman who bore him a child."

Chapter 8

"What are you saying?" Ruby felt a wave of shock flash through her by the handmaiden's words as the woman reached out slowly, closing the door behind them. "That Lord Nyle has a child? I know he was married three times and just recently, but was he married to this Lady Jocelyn as well?"

"Nay," she said, pulling off Ruby's belt, running a hand over her dagger. "He was very in love with the woman but wouldn't marry her. Even when he knew they'd had a child together."

"Well, that's awful," she said, watching the woman remove her dagger from the sheath and test the sharpness against her thumb. "He is more of an ogre than I'd imagined."

"Aye." The woman put the dagger down on the table but not back in the sheath. She then reached over and helped pull Ruby's gown over her head. "Sit down." She pushed Ruby into a chair a little harder than she'd expected. The handmaid then used her fingers to quickly unbraid her hair. After that, she started digging through the trunks that were Ruby's.

Ruby

"So if he's in love with someone else, then why has he been trying so desperately to get married?" she asked.

"Why don't you ask him?" The handmaiden found Ruby's hairbrush and brought it over. She ran it over Ruby's head quickly and her hair tangled. The woman just kept on pulling, causing Ruby to cry out.

"Ow! Be careful," she instructed. "Oralie would never treat me so roughly. You are a lady-in-waiting and should know the treatment that is expected of you."

"My many pardons, my lady, as I meant no harm. I am just not used to tangled hair, as Lady Jocelyn's hair was always smooth as silk."

Ruby didn't like being compared to Nyle's lover, Lady Jocelyn, and it made her feel uncomfortable since this was her wedding night and she was nervous enough to begin with.

"Now stand up and let's remove those undergarments as your husband will be here at any moment," ordered Ascilia.

"Nay," she said, clutching her hand to her shift as the handmaiden reached forward. "I don't think I want to bed him. I'm afraid. Does it hurt?"

"Worse than you'll ever know," said the woman. "Especially if you think tangled hair hurts. I thought I heard he chose you because you were strong and could take care of yourself."

"Who told you that?"

"I heard it from the chambermaid who heard it from the steward who heard it from Lord Sheffield's squire himself."

"Oh. Word travels fast, I see. Aye, I can take care of myself."

"You don't act like it. Now let's see what you have to offer him on his wedding night, and I can only hope you

107

won't disappoint him."

"Disappoint him?" Ruby hadn't even considered that Nyle might be disappointed. She didn't like to think that she would not please him between the sheets. This only made her anxiety even worse.

Before Ruby could stop her, the woman had pulled off her shift and she stood there in only her braies and hose.

"Not as large as Lady Jocelyn's breasts," she said, reaching out and weighing Ruby's breasts in her hands as if she were doing naught but checking the firmness of a melon at the market. "Lord Nyle likes his women with a much bigger buxom, this will never do."

"What do you mean?" she asked, looking down at her breasts, never having considered herself small, though she knew her sister, Sapphire, was much more endowed than she. "I can't help how I look," she said in her own defense.

Ruby used her arms to cover her breasts before the woman touched her again. Oralie had never done anything like this to her before. But then again, Ruby had never been in the position of being prepared for a wedding bed, so she knew not if this was truly the process.

"Let's see what lies below the waist." She pulled down Ruby's braies so fast that it almost knocked her over. She untied the hose that were secured to it and pulled them from her legs as well.

"Hmm. Lord Sheffield likes his women tight," she told her. Before Ruby knew what was happening, the woman reached out for her womanhood, her finger pointing forward.

"Stop it!" Ruby had had enough, and no longer cared if this was custom or not, she didn't like it. She pushed the woman backward, causing her to stumble and land against the bed. Her long sleeves rode up a little and she noticed a strawberry birthmark on the inside of her right arm, and for an old woman, she had very firm and beautiful arms. Still, her face looked old and hideous, so much so that Ruby didn't like to look at it.

"How did you get those burn marks on your face?" she boldly asked. "And why are you not with this Lady Jocelyn, wherever she may be?"

The woman looked at her curiously, then pushed herself up from the bed and wandered over to the bed stand. She spoke to Ruby without turning around.

"Lady Jocelyn dismissed me the night I fell into the fire having fallen asleep at the hearth. No one wants a woman who is disfigured by burn and scars. Please don't dismiss me, Lady Ruby, as I feel as if I am not wanted anywhere."

Ruby's heart went out to her and though she really didn't like the way she'd been treated, she didn't want to turn her away in her time of need. She couldn't even imagine how it felt to be disfigured by scars and burns.

"Of course not," she told Ascilia from across the room. "I wouldn't think of dismissing you, so wipe the thought from your mind."

"Thank you so much, my lady," she said lowering her head as if mayhap she were crying. Her back was still toward Ruby. "I only mean to help you."

"Of course you do," she answered.

"That is why I must tell you that you shouldn't couple with Lord Sheffield."

"Why not?" Ruby asked curiously wondering what the woman knew about the man she'd just married.

Ascilia turned her head slightly and spoke in a soft voice over her shoulder. "He doesn't love you."

"I know he doesn't love me, nor do I love him. It doesn't

matter. Love has naught to do with a marriage."

"He only wants you for one reason."

"I know. For me to bear him children. Just like any man."

"Nay. To take care of the child he already has."

"You make no sense. He has mentioned no such child, nor have I yet to see one." She wanted to find out more from this mysterious woman, but just then the latch on the door moved and she knew someone was about to enter. "It's him!" Ruby dove to the bed and slipped under the covers quickly to hide her nudity. Ascilia just stood with her back toward her, still facing the bedside table.

As the door opened, the sound of raucous laughter was heard, and to Ruby's horror Nyle walked into the room followed by several of his knights as well as the chaplain.

"My lord!" she called out. "Do not let those men into our wedding chamber."

"'Tis custom, my dear," said Ascilia, straightening her gown and fussing with her sleeves as she turned around. "It is customary for the wedding penetration to be witnessed by many, in order to prove you are a virgin."

"I am a virgin!" she cried out. "Lord Nyle, please. There is no need for anyone to watch. Please remove the men from the chamber at once."

Nyle stopped in the doorway, a tankard of ale in his hand as he spoke. "Are you telling me that you no longer want to do this the proper way?" he asked. "After all, I know how upset you were when I didn't post the wedding banns as was proper."

"I don't care about being proper. I will not couple with you with others watching."

"Go on, men," he said shoving the tankard of ale into

one of his knight's hands, then turning and closing the door. There were many groans and protests from behind it.

"I will stay and witness the penetration," offered Ascilia, her head down, the wimple covering her face as she spoke.

Ruby's body stiffened beneath the covers. She was sure if Ascilia was allowed to stay she would probably be reaching between them and joining in on the coupling. She was only too relieved to hear Lord Nyle's answer.

"Nay, you will leave as well. This is our wedding night and I don't want anyone else present, so go."

"Of course, my lord," she said and hurried out the door.

Once she'd gone, Nyle walked slowly toward the bed. Ruby felt her heart beating wildly and she couldn't stop thinking about everything the handmaiden had told her.

He reached down to his belt and undid it slowly, all the while his eyes being fastened on her. Next he slipped it from his waist and reached over to place it as well as his sword on the chair next to the bed.

"So, are you ready to consummate our marriage my little spitfire?" His hooded eyes held lust, she was sure of it. And she was sitting naked with only a thin coverlet between them.

"Is that what you said to all your wives before you bedded each of them?" She knew she shouldn't be baiting him at a time like this and when she was so vulnerable, but yet it bothered her at how many women this man had had, and she felt like naught more than just another notch on his sword.

He looked at her intensely but didn't answer. Instead, he just pulled his tunic off over his head. He threw it atop her things on the bedside table. Her eyes scanned his strong chest and muscled arms and she licked her dry lips wondering how he would feel beneath her fingers. "For your information, I didn't say the same thing to my past wives, because they all died before I had the chance to ever consummate the marriage."

"Seriously?" she asked in disbelief. "So you mean to say – you were married, but not really married since you never bedded a one of them?"

"I guess you could say that." He reached down and removed his shoes and hose as he spoke. "They were each murdered before we could couple. Actually, I was rather surprised to see you still alive when I entered the room. I purposely came quickly before you had a chance to die."

"Well, wasn't that nice of you," she said, hearing her own sarcasm dripping from her lips. "After all, I wouldn't want to disappoint you by ending up –" She stopped her words in midsentence as she watched him pull off his braies and stand before her straight as an arrow. She'd seen animals in her father's courtyard aroused and mating before, but never had she seen a fully aroused man. 'Twas truly an amazing sight.

"Can't take your eyes off me, can you, my little gem?"

"I . . . I . . .." She didn't know how to answer.

He pulled back the corner of the coverlet with one hand and kneeled one leg on the bed. He leaned forward, his long hair unbound and hanging around him, tickling her skin as he positioned himself above her and touched her cheek gently with his hand. Then he lowered his mouth to hers in a sensuous kiss. She felt a shiver of delight fill her entire body as his satiny lips released hers and his mouth pulled at her bottom lip in the process. It was an erotic move and she liked it, though she never thought she would.

He set free a burst of emotions inside her from just one

kiss. Then he let his mouth skim down her neck, kissing a trail to the hollow of her collarbone as he came very near to her hidden breasts.

"I don't love you," she blurted out, trying to stall for time as she didn't know what to do and was afraid she might displease him. "And I know you don't love me."

"Is there a problem with that?" His fingers gently pulled her tight fist apart and she released the coverlet she was clutching to her chest. Then he rubbed his hands over her shoulders and slowly trailed the tips of his fingers down her chest, cupping her breasts in the process.

Her breathing deepened and her chest rose. His hands were strong, yet gentle, and his exploration sent a delicious shiver through her as he grazed his thumbs past her nipples causing them to go taut in his hands. He lowered his mouth to one nipple, sucking gently and nipping playfully as it turned into a rigid peak. She involuntarily arched her back, gripping at his long hair, pushing herself further into his mouth. She didn't know what was happening to her. She felt warmth between her thighs and a wetness there as well. Her body was responding to his touch and she never in her wildest dreams thought the act of coupling would make her feel this way.

"So are my breasts too small for your liking?" She had to know, after what the handmaid told her.

"Nay, they are perfect," he replied. Slowly, his hands slipped downward past her waist, his fingers caressing the outside of her thighs. Then one hand settled atop her womanhood, causing her to squirm beneath him. She gasped when she felt him fondle her there, and when his finger slipped gently inside she found herself parting her legs further for him, liking the way it felt to have him inside her body. She became alive under his touch and found herself accepting his advances toward her as she responded to the seduction of his passion.

"So am I tight enough for you?" she asked, thinking of what Ascilia had said once again.

"Very much so," he said with a slight chuckle, placing his leg over her, settling himself atop. She felt his hardened form stretching against her body. Then he tested her readiness first with his hand and then rubbed his manhood against her. He was satin over steel and excitement coursed through her as she could think of naught else but coupling with this handsome and very experienced man.

"I don't want to hurt you," he whispered into her ear, his tongue flicking out playfully, causing a wave of anticipation to overtake her. He knew how to excite her in ways that she'd never imagined. She found herself liking her new husband in bed more than she thought she ever would. She also found herself liking the idea of being married.

"You won't hurt me," she said. "I feel my body calling for you and a burning desire between my thighs that is causing me to go mad. I have never known this feeling before."

"Never?" he asked, with a raised brow.

She smiled, as he was wise to the ways of a young woman who had to please herself if she didn't have a man. "Never with any man, and to this extreme," she said, finding herself lifting her legs around his waist, urging him to enter.

"I know we are married, Ruby, but I also know how much you despise me. If you don't want me to continue, I will stop right now."

"But then our marriage won't be consummated," she told him.

Ruby

"Nay. But I rushed you into marriage and I won't rush you again into coupling if you don't want to do it."

"Now's a fine time to tell me," she said with a smile. "I don't think you'd be able to pull away if I said to stop."

The muscles in his arms stiffened and turned rock hard. She was just teasing him, but still she wanted to know how he would respond.

"Is that really what you want?" he asked, all the while in position to couple. All he had to do was thrust forward and the marriage would be consummated.

"Perhaps," she said playfully and watched a cloud of disappointment cover his face. She heard him let out a deep sigh, and he rolled off of her to the side.

"What are you doing?" she cried out, not thinking he would really pull away right now.

"I told you, Ruby, I want you to agree to this coupling or I will not do it. You are my wife now and though I have every right to claim you, I cannot bring myself to do it if you don't agree. Not after what I put you through lately by taking you from your home against your will and denying you a proper marriage, or to have your family present."

"You fool!" she cried out. "Take me now before I die from want and you have another death of a wife on your conscious."

"Do you mean that?" He pushed up on one elbow and she could see the hope, the want, and the need within his inquiring eyes.

"I do," she said loud and clear, as a reminder of their wedding vows.

He didn't ask again. He entered her then and she felt her body stretch to take him in completely. There was a slight tinge of pain and then it was followed by glorious vibrating of her nether regions as he thrust into her over and over again and claimed her as his wife. She reached a peak of elation that she'd never felt before, and knew that the fear she'd held of the stories she'd heard about making love were all in vain, as this felt wonderful and she couldn't get enough. He let loose with his emotions and spilled his seed within her. Then he rolled over, calming his breathing and they both just lie there staring at the ceiling.

"You are amazing," she said, meaning it in every sense of the word. She had never known that a man could make her feel this way.

"You are now my wife in every way," he told her, and she liked the way it sounded as well as the way it felt. Mayhap she could accept being married to him and learn to like it after all. Because this was a side to Nyle that she'd not seen before now, nor did she expect. He actually seemed as if he cared about what she wanted for the first time since she'd met him. She could only hope it would last, as she rather liked it. "Do you still believe I am trying to kill you?" he asked.

"Well," she said with a smile. "I almost died when you were going to pull away, so mayhap you are after all."

That made him laugh, and she liked the way the corners of his mouth turned up and way his straight white teeth looked against his sun-kissed skin. His silver eyes seemed to sparkle like gemstones, being several shades lighter when he was happy. That pleased her. Ascilia seemed to think Ruby could not please her lord, yet she knew she'd made him very happy. She was happy too.

This man was her husband. This beautiful man with his muscles and tanned skin, and long, dark hair, and sparkling eyes. Why hadn't she noticed before, not only his beauty but the genuine caring side of him? There were parts of him that he seemed to keep hidden away. He would have stopped and not made love if she had so desired. He'd actually cared what she thought and had given her the choice. No man capable of murdering a woman could act so gentle and caring as he'd just done. She could see now she was wrong about him all along. She wasn't sure what happened to his wives, but he couldn't be the assassin she'd thought him to be.

"Can I ask you something?" She ran her finger in lazy circles through the hair on his chest.

"Only if I can do the same to you," he said, pulling her closer so she could nuzzle her head into the crook of his neck.

"Aye," she answered. "Do you want to start?"

"Nay, go ahead," he said to her.

"I'm sorry to bring this up now, but can you please tell me how your wives died?"

"Of course. I owe that to you, Ruby," he said. "I should have told you before now." He rubbed his face against the top of her hair as he spoke. "My first wife, Henrietta, died in the garderobe. I was told she slipped and hit her head on the stone and died instantly."

"Oh, that's horrible."

"My second wife, Prudence, was lying in bed waiting for me to consummate the marriage, and when I entered I found her dead."

"From what?" she asked.

"No one knows but 'tis my suspicion she was smothered with a pillow."

"So you think someone truly killed her?"

"It could be so."

"What about your third wife?" she asked curiously.

"Millicent never made it past the wedding feast. She choked on the wine and died right there at dinner."

"Couldn't you save her from choking?"

"Nay. Because I believe the wine was somehow poisoned. She spilled her goblet and I noticed an odd odor from the cup, but I cannot prove it."

"But wouldn't you have drank from the cup as well and been poisoned too? After all, we shared a goblet of wine today."

"Millicent had her own goblet she liked to use. No one but her drank from it as it was a gift from her father."

"So I'll bet all these girls' fathers are upset about this."

"Of course they are. And in order to prove my innocence, I had to return each of their dowries."

"I see. Well, at least you won't have to do that with me. I survived the cursed wedding night. I do believe my ring is luckier than the one you wanted to give me." She held up her hand and looked at the ruby on the ring flickering in the firelight from the bedside candle.

"The night isn't over yet," he said. "That's why I am not leaving you even for a second. You will stay by my side and I will protect you every minute of the night."

"I'm sure I'll be fine," she said. "After all, I have my dagger should anyone come after me." She reached over to the bedside table and under the tunic he'd thrown on top, looking for her dagger. When her hand came up empty, she sat up quickly, throwing his tunic to the floor and looking for her weapon.

"What's the matter?" he asked, his eyes half closed. He yawned and flipped onto his back.

"My dagger is gone."

"Where did you leave it?"

"On this table, but now it's not here."

"It probably fell under the rushes when I threw my tunic atop it." He pulled her back to him and wrapped an arm around her. "Now it's my turn to ask a question."

"Oh, that's right." She looked over to the table again and then down to the floor. Perhaps he was right. It must have just fallen under the rushes and herbs of lavender and rosemary that were covering the floor creating a sweet scent.

He reached over and turned her face toward him. "Why did you ask me if your breasts were too small?" he wondered. "What would ever make you think I even cared?"

"Because Ascilia told me that you liked big busted women."

"What the hell?" He scrunched up his face and narrowed his eyes. "What would give her that idea?"

"She said that Jocelyn had big breasts and that you were in love with her."

That took him by surprise. He pulled back his arm and sat up on the bed. "Why would she say that?"

"Mayhap because it's what this Jocelyn told her?"

"It's not true," he said. "Don't believe it."

"You seem to be getting very upset about something that is not true."

"I don't want you to say that name again, do you understand me?"

"Whose name? Jocelyn?"

"Stop it! I mean it." His smile faded and his sparkling eyes turned dark once again.

"All right," she said, turning on her side so as not to have to face him.

"Goodnight," he said, turning on his side with their

backs now together.

"Goodnight, husband," she said, thinking how foreign the word husband sounded on her tongue. She wanted to ask him about the child and also about the fact that Ascilia said he only married her to take care of it. None of it made any sense, since there was no child of his in Sheffield that she knew about. Mayhap the handmaiden was just addled and making this all up. She closed her eyes and fell asleep, hoping it was all just a lie.

Chapter 9

Ruby was having a bad dream that Nyle was holding a pillow over her face trying to suffocate her. She tossed and turned and then stopped suddenly, as she thought she heard the sound of the latch moving on the door. She opened her eyes, realizing it was still night and the candle in the metal holder next to the bed had yet to burn out. Then she heard it again. The sound of someone trying to enter the room.

She looked over to Nyle who was snoring on the bed next to her, then back over to the door. It was probably nothing, she realized. She thought about waking her husband, but after that nightmare she'd just had, she was glad just to awaken alive.

Instead, she slipped from the bed, finding her shift and throwing it over her head quickly. She looked once again on the table for her dagger, and when she didn't see it, she got down on the ground on her knees and dug around in the rushes, hoping it had just fallen.

The door squeaked open then, and she looked up to see a big man – one of the soldiers she'd seen in the great hall last night, sneaking into the room. He had a knife in his hand, as she could see the blade glimmering in the candlelight above her. Since she was low, he didn't see her at first, but then he caught sight of her and she gasped. Too frightened to call out to Nyle for help, she was frozen to the spot as he lifted his blade and rushed toward her.

Nyle shot out of the bed and in one motion reached over her and grabbed his sword and knocked the man to the ground. He kicked the attacker's blade away with his foot and held the tip of his sword to the man's throat.

"Don't even breathe or this blade goes through your neck," he ground out. Then he talked to her without turning his head. "Move, Ruby. I want you far away from this murderer."

She quickly stood and crawled across the bed, straining her eyes in the dark to see what was going on.

"Who are you and why have you been killing off my wives?" Nyle asked.

Before the man had a chance to answer, the door opened and in rushed the old handmaiden with Nyle's sister, Linette, following with a lit candle in her hand. One of his knights was right behind them. Nyle's back was to the door.

"Nyle, what are you doing?" When Linette saw her brother standing there naked, she hid her face with her hand and looked away.

"Stay back," Nyle warned her, glancing quickly from the corner of his eye, then bringing his attention back to the attacker.

The knight rushed past Ascilia with his sword raised. Then he tripped, putting out his arm to stop himself, and stumbling right into Nyle. The impact jerked Nyle forward, sending the tip of Nyle's blade right through the attacker's neck.

Ruby

"Nay!" she heard Nyle shout out. The soldier's eyes bugged open wide and blood covered him instantly. Nyle turned around with eyes of fire. "Sir Elwood what in the name of devil is wrong with you? I almost had that man spilling his guts and now because of you he spills his life blood on my floor instead."

"I apologize, my lord, but I seem to have tripped on something, but I don't know what, as it is very dark."

"Damn it," Nyle ground out. "I was so close to finding out who hired him."

"Brother, are you clothed yet?" asked his sister, still not turning around.

Nyle removed his blade from the man's throat and threw his sword to the floor in disgust. He grabbed his braies and pulled them on. "You can turn around now," he told her.

Ruby noticed the way the handmaid was still eyeing Nyle's chest and she didn't like it. She crawled over the bed and grabbed his tunic and handed it to him. "Please put this on," she said. Then she looked over to Sir Elwood. "What did you trip on that made you fall forward with such force?"

"I don't know," he said, looking to the ground. "'Twas almost like something just shot out and tripped me."

Then Ascilia bent down and picked up something and held it up for them to see. "It must have been this." She had Ruby's dagger in her hand.

"My dagger!" Ruby rushed forward and grabbed it from the woman.

"See, I told you 'twas here somewhere," Nyle said, donning his tunic.

"Yes, I guess you were right." Ruby eyed the distance from the table where she'd left it over to the other side of the room where it had just been found. Nothing made sense.

And tripping on a dagger seemed ridiculous to her.

"Who is he?" Linette held her candle over the dead man's face.

"He's a hired mercenary sent to kill my wives, that's who he is," answered Nyle. "However, now that he is dead I'll never find out who he was working for or why someone wants my wives dead to begin with." He reached out an arm and put it around Ruby. "Are you all right, sweetheart?"

Reality finally hit her. This man had truly meant to kill her. And if it wasn't for Nyle jumping over the bed and coming to her rescue, she would be dead right now. Her body shook with fear and she pulled herself closer to him in a protective hug. She had never been in this position before and didn't like it.

"I'm fine," she said. She looked to the dagger in her hand and grasped it tightly. "But I'll tell you now that this is never leaving my side again."

"You don't have to worry about that anymore," said Ascilia. "Now the murderer is dead and you can all relax."

"I'm not so sure this is the end of it," said Nyle. "After all, the man had to be taking orders from someone. Now I need to figure out who that is. If only he was still alive." He looked at his sister and her handmaiden and an odd expression crossed his face. "What are you two even doing here anyway?"

"Ascilia woke me and told me she'd heard a noise and looked out the door to see a strange man entering your chamber," Linette explained. "She was afraid for Lady Ruby's life and we came to see what was happening."

"I followed him here, my lord," said Sir Elwood from behind them. "I'd been watching for him in the great hall and am sorry to say I dozed off. When I awoke I saw him leaving and came after him."

"And no one thought to wake me in the process?" He looked down to Ruby when he said it.

"I didn't want to disturb you," she said, knowing how ridiculous that sounded, but not wanting to tell him about her bad dream.

"Get this dead man out of here," he ordered Sir Elwood, picking up his blade and wiping it against the dead man's tunic. "And make sure the room is cleaned from his blood, as I want my wedding chamber in order. Everyone else - out, as I'd like to speak to my wife in private."

Sir Godin arrived at the door just then and together he and Sir Elwood removed the dead man from the chamber. The women left as well, and Ruby felt a little apprehensive to be left alone with her husband when he seemed so angry. She wanted to trust him, and did in a way, as he had saved her life. Still, she couldn't really trust him completely. He wasn't being honest with her and telling her everything she needed to know.

"So what did you want to speak to me about?" She walked over to one of her trunks and pulled out an oversized tunic and donned it. Today she would be comfortable while working with her weapons in the practice yard, and she wasn't going to wear a restrictive gown. Besides, she needed to be prepared and able to move quickly should another murderer come after her.

He looked at her and shook his head at her choice of apparel. Then he walked over to her trunk and pulled out a gown for her to wear. "Put this on instead."

"That's not proper attire for practicing with my weapons."

"You won't be practicing with weapons today, because

we have to meet someone at the crossroads at daybreak."

"Whom are we meeting?" she asked.

"It doesn't matter, now just get ready." He opened a trunk of his and pulled out fresh clothes and dressed quickly.

"I think there are things you are keeping from me that I need to know."

"Such as what?" He sat on the edge of the bed and donned his hose and shoes.

"Such as the fact you have a child." She blurted it out, not knowing if it were true, but wanted to see his reaction.

"What would give you an idea like that?" He stopped what he was doing and his eyes fastened to her.

"I . . . heard it," she said, not wanting to mention the handmaiden right now. She wanted to get more information out of the woman and if Nyle thought Ascilia was spilling his secrets he might just remove her from Ruby's service.

"Has Ascilia been filling your ears with lies about me again?"

Too late. He knew.

"Again?" She ran a hand over her tunic as she spoke. "Are you saying there are other things she's lied about?" She didn't want to bring up Jocelyn after he'd been so adamant that she didn't mention the woman's name ever again. Still, she wanted to know more.

He stood and grabbed his belt and weapons, fastening them on as he spoke.

"I don't want that woman near you again. There is something about her I just don't trust. I will find a replacement for you today."

"Ascilia will do fine," she said.

"Nay. She is my sister's handmaid anyway. Now ready yourself quickly, or do you perhaps need my help?"

Ruby

She thought about them making love last night. She'd hoped they would have had the chance to do it once again this morning. But instead, he seemed in a hurry to be on with his plans for the day, as if the intimacy they'd shared last night no longer meant anything.

"Nay, I need no help. But I would like to know about your lover, Jocelyn."

His head snapped up and his eyes grew darker than a moonless night. She saw him biting the inside of his cheek and he looked as if he were going to explode with anger. Mayhap she shouldn't have mentioned the girl's name after all.

"I told you to never mention that name again. Now ready yourself and meet me in the stable as we are departing anon."

Before she had a chance to answer, he was out the door and slamming it behind him. She would get the answers she needed, and no one - not even her husband - was going to stop her. She donned her gown quickly, wondering where to find Ascilia.

Chapter 10

Nyle paced back and forth just outside the stable, wondering what was taking Ruby so long. It was almost daybreak and he was to meet the king at the crossroads with his new wife in tow, and he mustn't be late.

He'd felt bad for not answering Ruby's questions about Jocelyn, but he didn't have time for it this morning. He'd tell her everything in due time, but right now he had other obligations to fulfill. The king would not be forgiving if he were not there to meet him as planned.

"Locke," he called to his squire who had just readied a second horse for Ruby. "Go to the solar anon and see what is keeping my wife."

"Aye, my lord." The boy took two steps and then stopped in his tracks. "I think I see her coming now," he said. "However, I don't think you'll be happy."

"Why the hell not?" He looked in the distance and saw Ruby escorted by that damned busybody old handmaiden and his sister. To his horror, Ruby had not donned a gown as he'd instructed, but was wearing exactly what he'd ordered her not to - a man's oversized tunic instead. She had it belted at the waist with hose and short boots instead of a lady's pair of soft shoes. Her hair was long and loose instead of braided, and while it looked beautiful and very alluring as it lifted gently in the breeze, it was not proper of a married woman to wear her hair unbound. And as if that wasn't bad enough, she had weapons sheathed in her belt. Her dagger, a small dirk, and a man's sword were all lined up as if they were her soldiers and she were headed to war.

"What the hell are you doing?" he ground out, meeting her halfway across the courtyard.

"Why, I'm doing exactly what you instructed, husband. I'm joining you at the stables so we can meet your secret liaison at the crossroads."

Damn, why'd she say that in front of everyone? He wanted to leave in secret, with just her and his squire, but now she'd leaked the information to the odd handmaiden and his sister as well. And with the wagging tongue of not one woman but three, the rest of the castle would be privy to this fact before he even returned. Not to mention, Locke was not the best at keeping a secret. He was only too glad now that he'd not told his wife whom they were meeting.

"I thought I told you to wear the gown," he said in aggravation.

"I was going to, but Ascilia convinced me that I needed to be comfortable if we were going to be riding."

"She did, did she?" He found himself hating the handmaiden more and more every day. He'd have to talk to his sister about dismissing her as soon as he returned with the boy.

"Ascilia will be accompanying me on our journey today," Ruby informed him.

"I'd like to come as well," said his sister.

"Nay, neither of you will be coming with, so forget the absurd idea," he said adamantly, ready to do whatever it took to stop them. There was no way in hell he'd let all these people traipse along with him to join in a secret liaison with the king. He dismissed them, and when they left, he turned to his wife. "You, my wife, need to get back to the solar and change at once."

"My lord," interrupted Locke. "'Tis already daybreak. As it is, we'll never make it there by the time the sun rises."

"God's eyes, I don't need this," he said. He reached out and grabbed Ruby by the arm and dragged her over to the horse. "There's no damned time for you to change, now get on the horse and be prepared to ride hard as we are late."

She pulled out of his grip and looked at the horse. "But this is a saddle for a lady. I don't need that, dressed as I am. Besides, I can ride faster on a saddle made for a man."

"You'll ride this horse and not complain. Do you hear me?"

"I would prefer a different horse with another saddle."

"We have no time for that, now are you getting on the horse or do I need to put you there myself?"

"Lord Sheffield," interrupted Locke. "She can take my horse and I'll follow you with another, but the sun rises quickly and you really need to be going."

"Fine," he said, not wanting to waste any more time arguing over a damn saddle. He mounted his own horse quickly. "But I warn you, wife, you'd better be able to keep up."

"Nay, husband. I think you are the one who will be left in the dust." She mounted Locke's horse so quickly that he hadn't even seen her do it. She kicked her heels into the sides of the horse and headed out the castle gate before he even had a chance to move.

"Follow us to the crossroads quickly," he told his squire. "I have a feeling I'm going to need you, as now I'll have not only one child to watch over, but a wife acting like a child as well." With that, he headed out the gate after her, thinking he'd gotten more than he'd bargained for by marrying such an untamed woman.

Ruby rode like the wind with Nyle right behind her. Every time he got close, she'd urge her horse faster and once again leave him in her dust. She prided herself for being able to outride any man. She also prided herself in her ability to handle a weapon and only hoped someday she'd get to show her husband her skills, though she knew he'd never condone it.

She'd made it almost all the way to the crossroads, but what she saw ahead of her made her slow her horse, allowing Nyle to catch up. An entourage sat waiting on the road just ahead of them. Not one person as she'd assumed by what he'd said, but a good dozen soldiers as well as a cart attached to a horse.

This took her by surprise, but not half as much as the fact that she recognized the banner of the coat of arms flying from the pole held by the squire. 'Twas the royal quartered shield of red and blue with the golden lions of England mixed with the fleur-de-lys of France. It was none other than the man who'd claimed both thrones as his own, King Edward III himself.

Nyle shot by her on his horse and she urged her steed forward to catch up with him.

"Why didn't you tell me we were meeting the king?" she asked, feeling ever so nervous.

"I didn't think I needed to announce my every plan to you." He slowed his horse and so did she as they approached the gathering in the road ahead of them.

"If I had known," she said softer and from the side of her mouth, "I would have worn the gown."

"Well a little late for that, isn't it?" he replied. "Mayhap next time you'll just trust me."

"Mayhap next time you'll confide in me since I am your wife."

"Please refrain yourself from embarrassing me in front of the king." He looked at her attire and shook his head in disgust. "Too late for that," he muttered, riding forward to greet his sovereign.

"Sheffield, I thought you weren't going to show." The fair-haired king sat tall atop his steed looking so regal that Ruby wanted to crawl under a rock for the way she was dressed. Though her father fought for this man many times, she had never seen the king so close-up before. He was tall in stature, and had a long nose. His beard and hair were a fair color and his eyes a pale blue. He was adorned with the fine clothes of nobles, with an ermine lined cape and a golden jeweled crown as well. On almost every finger he wore a ring, and around his waist he had an array of very ornate and expensive looking blades.

Ruby looked back to her husband who didn't seem to like a showy composure. He wore a simple black tunic and beige hose with short boots upon his feet. Besides his sword strapped onto his waist, the only other adornment he had was his signet ring made of gold with an etched griffon atop it which was his coat of arms.

She hadn't meant to embarrass Nyle – or had she, she wondered. Either way, if he had told her they were meeting with the king she would have dressed presentable.

"Sire," said Nyle jumping off his horse and bowing in front of the mounted man. "I can never apologize enough for being late."

"Aye, why were you late, Sheffield?" he asked, not even acknowledging Ruby.

Ruby half expected Nyle to blame it on her and rightly so, but instead he put the blame on himself, surprising her immensely.

"I apologize once again, my liege. 'Tis my fault, as I'd made merry late into the night yesterday at my wedding and was moving slowly this morning."

"Good, good," the king chuckled. "Then you have taken a wife as I've instructed?"

"I have," he assured him.

Ruby found it interesting that the king had ordered him to marry and wondered why. She would have to ask Nyle later.

"Well, where is she?" The king looked up and down the road, never once looking at her. "You know I need to meet and approve of your wife before I hand over the child."

So there was a child, Ruby realized. But what was this whole connection, and with the king?

"This is my wife," he said, reaching up his hand to help her from the horse. "Please dismount and greet the king properly, darling."

"Sheffield, you've got to be jesting," growled the king. "This is your wife? I thought she was naught more than a servant."

"I'm pleased to have the opportunity to meet you, Sire," Ruby said, curtseying in front of him though she wore the clothes of a man.

"King Edward, I can explain," said Nyle, his words sounding more stressed than ever.

"Nay, let me explain," said Ruby which only earned her a frown and eyes of fire from her husband. "Please," she added, trying to sound soft and sweet like a good wife should.

"Nay," said Nyle, but the king interrupted.

"Aye," he said looking down at them both, never dismounting his horse as he spoke. "I'd like to hear this explanation. Lady . . .?" he asked.

"Ruby," she answered and reached to adjust her sword which was disheveled from her journey. The sound of a dozen scraping swords being unsheathed and the sudden enclosure of twelve knights on horseback closing in around her made her stop in mid-motion.

"What the hell are you thinking?" whispered Nyle.

"Sorry," she said. "I was just adjusting my sword."

"Well, do us both a favor and keep your hands off your weapons unless you want to die after all," warned her husband.

"Your Majesty," she said, raising her hands above her head as she spoke. The tips of the swords around her lowered but only slightly. "I am the daughter of Earl Talbot, of Blackpool. I am the first born of his four daughters."

"Earl Blackpool?" he asked and then nodded. "Aye, he is a fine warrior and has served me well through the years. Continue."

"Had I known I was meeting with you today, Sire, I would have dressed in my finest gown and worn my jewels as well as coiled my hair atop my head and tucked it beneath a proper headpiece."

"Umph," grunted the king.

"But I was married just yesterday and my husband, Lord Sheffield, has not yet learned to communicate with me fully. You see, I planned on practicing in the weapon yard this morning and that is why I am dressed as such and also carry so many weapons."

"You, a female, know how to use a sword?" he asked.

"Aye," she said proudly. "Would you like to see the sword my father gave me?" She lightly tapped the hilt of her sword and once again the tips of twelve others greeted her from the knights atop their horses.

Nyle grabbed her arm and held it down at her side. He squeezed hard, and spoke in a low and very irritated voice. "You do that again and you'll be meeting with the tip of my sword next time." Then he looked up toward the king, still holding her arm tightly as he spoke. "I apologize, Your Majesty. We've just been married and she has not yet learned what is expected of her. I haven't had the time to train her, and she is a bit . . . shall I say . . . untamed."

"Train me?" She yanked her arm away from him. "Untamed? You speak as if I am naught more than one of your hounds," she said, not caring anymore that she was in the presence of their king. Then she looked up to King Edward and spoke directly to him. "I beg your forgiveness for my appearance, Your Majesty, but I cannot apologize for who I am and for what is truly in my heart."

"I see," he answered, then spoke to Nyle. "You will have your hands full with this one, Sheffield. I am surprised you chose her in the first place."

"I assure you, I will handle her," Nyle told him. "As well as the boy," he added. "Please, allow me the chance to prove it."

Ruby still didn't what boy he spoke of, as she'd yet to

see a child. King Edward didn't say anything, but seemed to be thinking. His hand raised and he smoothed his fingers over his beard. He looked first at Nyle and next at her, and then gave a slight nod of the head.

"I like her, Sheffield," he said and grinned. "Aye, I think she'll keep both you and the boy in line."

"Your Majesty?" By Nyle's clipped words, Ruby knew he did not like the king's prediction.

"Calm down, Sheffield. All I meant was that while your wife is untamed and quite rough around the edges, she'll do fine."

"Thank you, Sire," said Nyle with a slight nod.

"Get the boy," the king called to one of his men. The guard made his way to the wagon and reached down and took a small child from within as a handmaiden handed it up to him. He put the child atop his horse and rode forward. The boy looked to be no more than one year of age at most, and had a head of dark brown hair, almost black. Just the opposite of the king's fair hair. The guard approached them, and the boy shouted out, "Nyle," surprising her completely. He reached out his little arms, and she watched her husband collect the boy and hold him to his chest protectively.

"Now take good care of my bastard," said the king. "I am leaving today for London, but when I return I am going to decide if I will acknowledge him as mine or not."

"He's your son?" she blurted out, as this took her by surprise.

"Aye, I believe so," said the king, looking at her oddly. "Do you know differently? If so, you need to tell me, as I would slay the man by my own hand who I found had sired a child with my mistress Jocelyn."

"Lady Jocelyn was your mistress?" she asked, once

again never expecting to hear him say this. She saw Nyle's expression and she wished now she hadn't said anything, but 'twas already too late.

"Lady Ruby," the king said, perusing her curiously. "I get the feeling you want to tell me something. If you have information about this child or the Lady Jocelyn, you need to tell me. Because withholding information would be betraying your king."

She looked at Nyle whose eyes begged her to still her tongue. Then she looked at the boy clinging to Nyle seeming to feel safe in his arms. She didn't want to say anything that could jeopardize this, nor did she want to have the king slaying her husband as she stood by and watched.

"Nay," she answered, knowing she needed to say something more in order for the king not to be suspicious. "I just . . . heard Ascilia mention Lady Jocelyn's name, that's all."

"Ascilia the old handmaiden?" asked the king. "I thought she'd died right after I banished Lady Jocelyn from Windsor, but mayhap I'm mistaken."

"Oh yes," Ruby told him. "She is alive and in the walls of Sheffield right now, I assure you."

"Well, I will take your word on that," said King Edward. He turned a half circle on his horse and looked over to Nyle. "Sheffield, I need to retreat now, but I am counting on you to keep the boy safe until my return. The queen is getting suspicious and I need to get the boy out of her sight for awhile. Actually, the boy has been weaned so I won't have to leave the wetnurse with you. Since you now have a wife, she will raise the child as if it were her own, with you looking out for its safety."

"You can count on me to watch after little Tibbar," said

Nyle ruffling the boy's hair with a quick flick of his hand.

"Good, good." The king nodded. "Until I return, then."

"Until you return, Your Majesty," echoed Nyle with a bow.

The king raised his hand and gave the order, and the whole entourage turned around and headed down the road.

Ruby waited til they'd left and then turned back to Nyle.

"Why didn't you tell me we were meeting the king and you needed a wife to help you look after his bastard?"

"Well, now you know," he said, climbing atop the horse with the boy in his arms. She wanted to talk to him more, but saw Locke racing up the road on his horse with a puff of dust behind him, and knew this conversation would have to wait. She mounted her horse and turned and followed her husband who was holding proudly onto the little boy.

She should feel relieved the boy was the king's bastard and not Nyle's as Ascilia had said. But for some reason, it just didn't feel right. Nyle looked so natural with little Tibbar in his arms as they rode down the road. He looked so happy as well. In her heart, she knew he was hiding something, and wondered if this boy was indeed his own son.

A sudden sadness blanketed her thoughts that he may not be able to keep his child. Then a sheer bolt of panic ripped through her thinking what the king would do to him when he found out. Then she felt that stab of jealousy through her heart, thinking about the woman named Lady Jocelyn whom Ascilia had told her Nyle had loved. She wanted to feel that love from her husband and also as if they had a child together and were riding down the road as a family.

This young boy reminded her of the loss of her own

baby brother, as well as the loss of her mother. She wondered how her life would have been different had her mother lived to tell her the ways of married life, as well as if she'd had a brother to look after and nurture while she'd been growing up.

An emptiness engulfed her as she looked over to the little boy who was laughing and trying to grab Nyle's fingers on the reins. Nyle played with the child and teased him by moving the reins to the side every time he tried to touch them. This was a side of her husband she truly admired. A gentle, caring, loving side - and she liked it immensely. She wanted to know more about this side of her husband, because she felt as if she were starting to have feelings for him though she never thought it possible. Now if only he could act this caring with her. But then again, she realized she hadn't given him many reasons to show her this kind of attention and admiration. Mayhap Oralie was right in saying she needed to act the part of his wife and stop challenging him. And that she should be proud to be Lady Sheffield, and also show her husband respect.

She wanted to go home and see her father and talk to her sisters about all this. She'd never felt so alone or so confused in her life. She knew she needed to get far away from Nyle right now or he'd see the tears welling in her eyes. She kicked her heels into the sides of the horse and passed up both Locke and Nyle, ignoring their calls for her to slow down and ride with them. She needed to get away from them and just think, because she would do whatever it took in order to escape the feelings that were threatening to consume her.

Chapter 11

Nyle watched Ruby ride away, and though she'd tried to hide it, he'd seen the tears in her eyes. He needed to talk to her. He needed to discuss the plan that the king wanted them to pretend it was their baby and they'd just brought it here from her home in Blackpool. No one was to know it was the king's bastard, and Nyle had to do everything to convince her to keep it a secret.

Only Locke knew the truth about the boy, but Nyle had not told him his suspicions that Tibbar may be his son, not the king's. He rode up next to Locke and placed the baby on the saddle in front of him.

"Can you ride with the boy on your lap and the reins in your hand?" he asked.

"This horse would go back to the castle without me guiding it," said Locke, fastening his arm around the young boy. "And I would ride with the reins in my teeth if I had to," he assured him. "The boy is safe with me."

"Good. Ride up to the gate then, but don't enter until I return with Ruby. I see her heading off toward the woods and I need to tell her about the plan."

"Of course. I'll be waiting," Locke told him.

Nyle took off at full speed, able to overtake Ruby as she no longer seemed to be challenging him. He rode up to her side, trying to gain her attention.

"Stop, Ruby, I need to talk to you."

She kept riding.

"I said, stop." He reached over and grabbed her reins, causing her horse to rear up. She held on expertly without falling off, and Nyle found himself impressed by her unnatural skill. He guided her horse over to a tree, then dismounted and tied up both mounts. "Come down from there anon, wife. I need to speak with you."

Instead of fighting like he thought she would, she slipped from the saddle and stood next to him, her arms crossed over her chest.

"So speak," she said. "But please don't ask me to do anything before you explain to me what is going on."

"Take a walk with me," he said, reaching out to put his arm around her shoulder. She pulled back and walked a good distance from him as they made their way down to the creek.

"Why didn't you tell me we were going to meet with the king?"

"I couldn't. He swore me to secrecy."

"Locke didn't seem surprised, so I doubt that's the truth."

"Please, Ruby, sit down, and let me explain." He pointed to a large boulder and she leaned against it with her arms still crossed.

"We are married now, Nyle, and I would hope you could start trusting me and not lie to me anymore."

"All right," he said. "I owe you that." He leaned against

the boulder next to her. He reached out and took her hand in his but she still refused to look directly at him.

"I'm listening," she said.

Nyle wet his lips thinking how dry his throat was right now. He wished for a drink to help him get through this, as he couldn't tell her everything, but he needed to tell her enough so she'd agree to help him.

"The king wants me to watch his son, Tibbar, for awhile," he said.

"You mean his bastard, don't you?"

"I don't like calling the boy that," he said, feeling irritated at her words.

"Well, that's what he is, isn't he? After all, King Edward wouldn't be asking you to hide one of his heirs away in a castle that is not fortified enough to be able to have stopped three murders in a row. Why is he even allowing the baby to stay here after the murders?"

Nyle knew she was going to ask that, and he didn't fancy telling her the answer. Still, he had no choice.

"I . . . don't think he knows about the deaths of my other wives," he said.

"You mean, you didn't tell him, don't you?"

"The opportunity never arose, so I didn't think it necessary."

Ruby just shook her head. "Unbelievable. And tell me, what was that comment the king made that he ordered you to take a wife? Why?"

"He wouldn't leave the child with me unless I was married."

"So that's why you were in a hurry to marry so many times in a row?"

"Aye. Without a wife, the king would not have put

Tibbar into my care."

"Why do you want to watch this child so badly that you'd go through all this?" she asked. "Can't the king just have a nursemaid watch the child in his own castle?"

"You heard what he said, Ruby. The queen is becoming suspicious, and he doesn't want her to know about his bastard child. After all, she has birthed him a dozen children, their youngest only a half year old. She has also lost several to the plague. She has been through tough situations and he doesn't want her concerned that he might not be loyal to her."

"But he's not loyal to her," she said.

"That is not for us to judge."

"He sounds as if he spends most of his time in bed – and not always his own. Tell me about his mistress, Lady Jocelyn."

He didn't answer at first, and his hesitation caused her to become suspicious.

"Is his mistress the same Jocelyn that Ascilia spoke of, the one she said you loved?" She obviously already knew the answer but wanted him to tell her.

"Ruby, I can't speak about the king's affairs. All I can say is that King Edward has ordered you to help me with this child."

"I didn't hear him tell me directly to do anything." She pulled her hand away and walked toward the creek. He waited a moment and then followed.

"Please. I am asking you, will you help me – as my wife?"

"I – I'm confused," she said. "You seem to be so attached to the boy and want him at Sheffield so desperately that you not only kept the murders a secret from the king, but also married and buried three wives without a bit of remorse."

"That's not true," he told her. "I mourned every one of my wives, though I barely knew them."

"The fact remains they are dead, and someone tried to kill me as well," Ruby told him. "This all has something to do with this baby, doesn't it?"

"I'm afraid so," he admitted. "I think someone was trying to keep me from being married so the king wouldn't leave Tibbar with me. And before you ask, yes I knew there was a good possibility there'd be an attempt on your life as well, but I also knew you could protect yourself. That is the reason I chose to marry you over your sisters. But after you almost died at the hands of that mercenary, I realized how wrong I was wrong to have put you in danger. My heart aches to think I almost lost you. I am truly sorry, Ruby, I really am."

He waited for her to explode now that she knew the truth why he'd chosen to marry her. But instead of the outburst of anger he expected, she was silent for a moment, and then just looked up to him with wide eyes.

"So you were impressed with my skills and knew I could protect myself?" she asked.

"That's right. I've never seen a woman do the things you can do, Ruby. I must admit, though it might repel most men – I rather like it, though you'll never hear me say this aloud in front of my men."

She smiled and they both laughed, and it seemed to him they were slowly breaking down the walls between them.

"So what do I have to do?" she asked.

He felt a sense of relief wash over him, and reached out and gave her a hug. "The king wants us to pretend this is our baby for now."

"Nyle, we were married only a day ago, so I'm sure no one will believe it," she said with a laugh.

"Nay, but they would believe that this is your baby from . . . from another time."

Her eyes opened wide and she stopped laughing.

"So you're asking me to pretend I wasn't a virgin on our wedding night after all? And that I was some sort of harlot who birthed a bastard and then left him behind and went off to marry you? You have got to be jesting."

He could see those walls rising between them once again. "Well," he said, running a weary hand over his face, "everyone in the castle already knows me and 'tis no secret I haven't a child. But they don't know you. And if you don't like the idea, then tell me, do you have a better one?"

"So you're saying you wanted to marry me just to take care of a child that you will never see again as soon as the king returns?"

"I . . . I . . . yes," he answered instead of telling her if things worked out the way he planned, Tibbar would be staying with them at Sheffield forever and be their son.

"Before I agree to anything, I need you to tell me the truth."

"I have," he said.

"Not about everything, you haven't. The handmaid said that you, not the king, had a child with this Jocelyn. So tell me, whose child is this boy – yours or the king's?"

Nyle thought about that for a moment, and he knew that no one really knew the answer. But if he told her he wanted her to help him because he thought it might be his child, he knew she'd never agree. But if it were a request from the king to watch his bastard, which it was, then she would have no choice.

He couldn't risk her telling everyone this could be his child and it getting back to the king. After all, he chopped off the head of the last man found in Jocelyn's bed. He really didn't fancy being the king's next victim. He put his fingers around his throat rubbing his neck, already feeling the blade of the axe or perhaps the burn of the noose tightening. He didn't want to be dishonest with his new wife, but he also couldn't risk losing his own life or losing a boy who may be his son – forever.

"'Tis by the order of the king that you play out the part and watch over his child," he said instead of answering her question.

"I see." Her words were cold and clipped and her arms were crossed over her chest again. "So by doing this, I'd show respect for you as my husband?"

"Not just respect for me, but also the king."

"Would any of your other wives have done this?" she asked.

"All of them," he answered. "Without complaining or questioning it at all," he added, hoping she was starting to understand the role of being a wife.

She thought for a moment as if she were mulling things over in her head, and then she finally answered. "Fine," she said, heading toward the horse and mounting it quickly.

"Really?" he asked, surprised she'd agree so easily.

"I will play the part in your little, deceptive game, but if you just once tell me I can't use a blade in the practice yard or wear a tunic and hose instead of a gown, then I will tell everyone your little secret."

Well, he didn't expect blackmail, but at least she'd agreed to work with him. And though she should be reprimanded heartily for her tone as well as her threats, he could do naught about it. If so, his secret would be out. She was winning this round, but that would change soon.

He lifted himself into the saddle, turning his horse a full circle and looking back to her as he spoke. "The king's secret, not mine," he corrected her. "And you would do well to remember that, Wife."

He rode off before she could answer, hoping to hell he'd be able to tame her before she made a mess out of the whole blasted situation.

Chapter 12

Ruby rode into the castle gates following Nyle with the boy in his arms. Locke was right behind her. A crowd of people rushed up to him, the stableboy grabbing the reins of Nyle's horse.

"Lord Sheffield," called out his steward, Lewis. "Who is the young boy?"

Nyle looked over to her, and she ignored him as she dismounted.

"This is Lady Ruby's child," he told them. "She has had the child brought here from Blackpool."

Ruby dismounted and handed the reins of her horse to a groom. Nyle's sister, Linette, ran up to join them, and her handmaid followed behind. For some reason, the old woman didn't seem to be bent over as much as the other day, and was moving much quicker.

"You have a child?" asked Linette, putting her arm around Ruby's shoulder. "I want a child badly but have not yet had one." Then she turned and looked at her brother still sitting atop his horse. "Nyle, why didn't you tell me this yesterday when I arrived?"

"I wanted to let Ruby tell you," he said, dismounting with the one-year-old in his arms. "Come, darling," he said with a nod of his head toward Ruby, "take the baby."

"Take the baby?" Ruby froze, not knowing a thing about rearing children. Her sisters had always tended to the young ones of the castle, and helped the nursemaids with the children of the lords and ladies of her father's castle. In the meantime, she'd been out watching the knights practice instead. She knew naught about children and neither did she think she could fake it.

"Oh no, he needs to know his new father," she said.

"He needs his swaddling changed . . . Mother," Nyle said with a smile, holding out the baby who she could see had wet himself.

She walked up cautiously, and no more than raised her hands to take him before Nyle was pushing the baby into her embrace. The child started crying immediately, and she felt like crying as well.

"There, there now, little Tucker, calm down for your mama."

"Don't you mean Tibbar, darling?" Nyle corrected her in a low, hoarse whisper.

"Oh, yes. Tibbar, my boy," she said trying to bounce the baby in her arms. He only cried more and she could feel the wetness of his swaddling leaking onto the front of her tunic. She held the crying baby at arm's length in front of her, wondering just what to do.

"I'll take him," said Ascilia," moving forward to grab him.

"Nay!" Nyle stopped her with an outstretched arm and Ruby just pursed her mouth in response.

"Ascilia can help me," she told him, but he just shook

his head, meaning for her to do it by herself.

"Haven't you got the stomach yet for changing a dirty swaddling?" asked Linette. "Here, I'll take him and you come with me and we'll do it together." Ignoring the protests of her brother, Linette pulled the boy out of her arms and he calmed right away. "After all, in the Highlands I get plenty of practice with all the babies and children within my husband's large clan."

She walked away talking gibberish to the baby and Ascilia followed right behind.

"Don't let that handmaid touch my baby," Nyle told her. "I don't trust her."

"*Your* baby?" Ruby looked at him and raised a brow.

"I meant our baby. You know I am only playing out the part," he said softly.

"Yes, I see. And you play it so convincingly that I would have sworn you really were the boy's father."

With that, she hurried off after Linette hoping she would only be a bystander in the swaddling changing ceremony, as she wasn't looking forward to playing mother.

* * *

Nyle watched Ruby walking away with his sister and the handmaid, and just shook his head.

"She seems to be trying," said Locke, coming to his side.

"She isn't trying hard enough," he said. "If so, mayhap she would have remembered the boy's name."

"Do you think this is going to work, my lord? I mean the ruse of her being a mother and all?"

"It doesn't look promising. She doesn't seem skilled with children at all. Now besides having to teach her how to

Ruby

act like a lady, I will have to teach her how to tend to a child as well." Nyle ran a weary hand through his hair.

"You have a real challenge on your hands, my lord."

"You don't need to remind me," he said. "I only wish I knew what to do to make her more receptive."

"To you, or the baby?" Locke asked with a smile.

"Both," Nyle answered. "Keep an eye on her, will you? I am worried about what may transpire."

"But I need to keep an eye on the falconer's apprentice," he told him. "I've only got two eyes, my lord."

"Then an eye on each of them will be beneficial, now go."

"Aye, my lord."

Locke took off at a run after them, and Nyle headed toward the barracks of the garrison. He needed to tend to the knights and their training and also the many other duties required of him in trying to run and maintain such a large household. He was really hoping Ruby would be able to help out with the baby, but now he was having his doubts. He was only glad his sister had showed up, but he knew she wouldn't be staying here long. If only he could trust a nursemaid with the baby, but it was too risky. They needed to watch over this child personally.

He also needed to take Linette to his father's gravesite soon. His father was buried at the back of his mother's favorite church in Lancaster, near the coast. While it was far from Sheffield, 'twas where his mother wanted to be buried, as it was the same graveyard as her relatives. Nyle needed to spend time with his sister and take her there, as he knew she needed to mourn and he hadn't even allowed her that since she'd been here. Aye, he decided. He would tend to the needs of his family very soon indeed.

Elizabeth Rose

* * *

Ruby spent most the day with Linette and the baby, and had to keep reminding herself the child's name was Tibbar. What kind of silly name was that and what did it even mean? She was sure Nyle had a hand in naming the boy, because, to her recollection, King Edward's sons had normal names like Edward, Edmund, John and Thomas.

Who, she wondered, would ever burden their child with such an oddity?

"So, Ruby," said Linette carrying the baby, walking next to her as they made their way across the courtyard. Ruby had managed to get rid of Ascilia by sending her out to get supplies for the baby, but it wasn't easy as the woman seemed to be shadowing her lately and it was starting to make her feel uncomfortable. "Where did you get such an odd name like Ruby, anyway?" Linette asked.

All of a sudden Ruby realized she'd been fast to judge Tibbar's name when she and her sisters were saddled with odd names also. She smiled and almost laughed.

"Well, we were all named after daggers with gemstones in the hilts that my mother bought from a blind hag in desperation as she was trying to conceive."

"What?" she asked with a giggle, bouncing the boy up and down as she walked. "The old hag was trying to conceive?"

"No, no," said Ruby with a giggle of her own. "My mother was barren and trying to give my father an heir. 'Twas an old superstition that anyone who bought a blade from this woman would conceive. One child for every blade bought."

"I don't believe in those things," she said. "Don't tell me you do?"

"Well, it worked. My mother bought four daggers with gems in the hilts and I have three sisters."

Ruby explained her story of the past to Linette.

"So since you don't have your dagger, you don't think Nyle is your true love?" asked Linette.

"Nay. We don't love each other. I think he despises me."

"That's not true. I've seen the look in his eyes when he watches you when you don't know he's looking."

"That's not love, that's lust," she pointed out. "And I don't think your brother knows the meaning of the word love. At least not for me. But if what Ascilia said is true, he's known love with a woman named Jocelyn."

"Really?" she asked. "I've never heard him mention anyone by that name. But tell me, did you not love the man who gave you this beautiful baby?"

"I have no baby," she said, realizing only too late what she'd just said.

"So, if Tibbar isn't your son, than whose is he?"

"Oh, Linette, please don't let Nyle know what I just told you, or he will kill me."

"I don't understand," she said. "What is going on?"

"I can't tell you, but I promise if I wasn't sworn to secrecy, I would. Because I would love to have a woman to talk to right now."

They walked up to the practice yard and no one was there. But the pell, or tall wooden pole used for sword practice, was at the near side of the field.

"Do you really know how to use that sword?" asked Linette, pointing to the weapon at Ruby's waist.

"Would you like to see me use it?" she asked, feeling the

life begin to flow through her again for the first time since she'd arrived in Sheffield.

"I would. Let me hold Tibbar out of the way, and you show me what you can do with that blade."

Ruby pulled the sword from her side, the scraping sound of metal exciting her already. She'd missed her daily practices since being married to Nyle, and she was only glad he was nowhere in sight right now, as she really felt as if she had a lot of stored up emotions she needed to let out.

* * *

Nyle was conducting his men in a meeting atop the battlements with Locke at his side when something down in the practice yard caught his eye. Someone was fighting furiously with the pell, and he knew no practice was scheduled until after his meeting was finished.

"Who's that?" asked Sir Godin, looking over the wall and squinting in the sun.

"They are pretty good with the sword," said Sir Elwood. "Did you bring in a new man, my lord?" They all ran to the wall and peered over, pointing and talking amongst themselves.

"Nay," he answered, pushing his way through his men to see over the wall as well. "I've brought in no one new." Then his eyes settled on the small person fighting the wooden pell with a sharpened sword and not a wooden one as was proper. In the person's other hand they held one of his own shields with his crest of a gold griffon painted upon a field of crimson. There was only one person who would do something that was not proper and think naught of it. And also only one person he knew that had hair that was almost white and halfway down to their waist. Ruby. And nearby he saw his sister standing and watching with the baby in her arms.

"Damn," he spat. "She is supposed to be watching the baby."

He hurried down the battlements with all the men right behind him.

"She?" asked one of his men. "Are you telling me that's a girl fighting like a man down there? Impossible."

"Is that your wife?" asked Sir Godin, rushing down the stairs and across the courtyard to catch up with him.

"She may not be my wife when I'm finished with her," he said, heading straight for the practice yard. He rounded the corner and stopped abruptly, ducking as a sword came slicing through the air right toward his head. Ruby stopped suddenly from twirling in a full circle, the wooden shield having blocked him from view. Her sword was high above her head.

"Oh, no! I'm sorry," she said, lowering her sword and dropping her shield when she saw what she'd almost done. His men joined him from behind.

"Ruby, you are supposed to be watching the baby," he growled.

"I am." She pointed with her sword in the direction of Linette and Tibbar. Linette smiled and waved.

"Put that thing down before you take out someone's eye." He grabbed her arm and lowered it to her side. "And you are not watching Tibbar, you are playing knight again."

"I am doing no such thing," she said. "I am working off some of my frustration."

"Well put the blade away and get back to you motherly duties."

"If I remember correctly, we had a deal," she told him right in front of his men. "You agreed I could use my weapons whenever I want, and dress however I please as well."

"You did?" The shocked voice of Locke and the mumbles of surprise from his men had him cringing inside.

"Can't you just do it later when no one's around?" he whispered.

"Nay," she answered. "This is the time of day I normally practice."

"Well, me too," he said. "So this looks like it's going to be a problem."

"Why don't you two spar?" asked Locke. "I would like to see that."

"I'd like to see that too," came a voice from a man behind him, and before he knew it they were all urging him to spar in a sword practice against a girl. His wife. He shot Locke an angry glance, wishing for once his squire would just remain quiet.

"Nay, I don't fight girls," he said. Then he smiled and looked over to his men. "I wouldn't want to hurt her."

"What's the matter, brother?" called out his sister. "Afraid she might beat you?"

"Enough of this nonsense," he said, walking away. Then he stopped as he heard his wife's voice.

"Please?" she begged from behind him. He turned to see a little pout on her face. He didn't know if she was doing it just to control him, but it didn't matter. She'd said please, and he wanted to start making amends with her. He also knew that they were going to have to sleep together again tonight and it wouldn't be pleasant for either of them if they were at odds with each other.

"All right," he said pulling his sword from his scabbard and stepping back a few paces. "I promise I'll try not to hurt you."

The crowd moved back giving them plenty of room and he heard little Tibbar squeal as if he were excited to watch as well.

"Now, the rules are – whoa!" He raised his sword just in time to block her blow.

"I don't do anything properly," she reminded him. "No such thing as rules for me."

He matched her more than once, not liking the way she was coming after him with a vengeance. The little chit was trying to hurt him, he was sure of it. But he would never do anything to hurt her, and was trying to hold back and be careful. Still, he rather enjoyed her spirit, as well as the challenge. She was definitely not a normal wife, and he liked that.

Though she had a strong sword arm and blocked him well too, she seemed to be faltering when he lunged forward little by little, and he finally hit her sword, sending it flipping up into the air. He reached out and caught it by the hilt, handing it to her over one arm.

"Your sword, my lady," he said with a smile and noticed the stains of scarlet appearing on her cheeks. She was obviously surprised at what he'd just done as well as embarrassed. His men laughed and cheered from behind him, and he even heard a giggle from the baby.

"You cheat," she said.

"How so?" He toyed with her, raising his chin and looking down his nose.

"You use your left hand to fight. That threw me off."

"Exactly what I count on when I fight."

"That gives you an advantage," she complained.

"All right, then how's this?" He removed the sword from his left hand and put it in his right. "Let's try it again."

"But that isn't your fighting arm."

"It doesn't matter. Now are you going to fight me or not?" His men cheered from behind him, encouraging another dual. He playfully used the tip of his sword to lift the hem of her tunic up slightly, raising a brow in the process, but making sure no one could see underneath but him. She pushed it back down with her hand, and shot him a scolding eye.

"You will be begging me to stop this time," she said, lashing out with her sword. He met her with his and the sound of clashing metal echoed through the practice yard once again.

"I will be begging for nothing, but I think you will be begging me for something instead."

"And what might that be?" she asked, their swords still meeting in the air as they danced around the courtyard in competition. Nyle was able to fight with either hand, but preferred his left, as that was more accurate as well as more confusing for those he fought in battle.

"You will be begging me for kisses to make all your pain go away."

"I will never beg you for kisses and neither will I have pain, but you will."

The men were roiled up now, and he was rather enjoying this little foreplay. He hoped it might even lead to a nice tumble in bed later. His blood pumped through his body with excitement from this little skirmish and he could only imagine she was feeling the same way. Yes, he decided, this was a good idea after all.

Ruby

Once again he managed to unarm her, her sword flipping up into the air and he handing it back to her. Everyone laughed from behind him and he spun around to acknowledge them. When he turned back to give her the sword, he saw her picking up a broomstick and heading for a horse.

"Ruby, come back here," he called, noticing the way she stomped over the ground. She mounted a horse and he knew he had to go after her. He put down the swords and ran across the practice yard, stopping just next to the quintain as he heard his squire, Locke call out.

"Lord Sheffield," he called, and Nyle stopped in his tracks and turned to see what he wanted. He heard the rumbling of the horse's hooves against the earth behind him as Ruby rode across the field.

"What is it Locke?" The men were all shouting and he couldn't hear him, so he just turned around intending to try to talk with Ruby. That's when he saw her with the broomstick in her hand, her eyes set with determination to hit the shield on the quintain.

"Ruby, stop," he said waving his arms in the air, until he realized she had no intention of doing that. The horse came closer and her pole moved forward, and once again Locke called out.

"Damn it, what do you want?" he asked turning around quickly. Then the realization hit him that she really wasn't going to stop and he was standing directly in the way. He turned abruptly trying to get out of the way as his wife hit the quintain with the broomstick and something hit him as well. The sandbag on the other end of the swivel arm turned as she rode by, and though he tried to avoid it, he still managed to get clipped in the eye.

"Ooomph." The air was knocked from him as he hit the ground hard. The sound of running feet had him looking up to see all his men as well as his sister with the baby standing there looking down at him.

"Like I said – watch out," Locke told him.

Nyle just moaned and held his eye. He was so embarrassed and also so enraged that he couldn't even speak. Then Ruby rode up on the horse, all smiles until she realized just what she had done. She jumped off the horse and ran to his side, kneeling on the hard ground next to him.

"I am so sorry. I didn't mean to hurt you," she said. Through the eye that wasn't starting to swell, he noticed the sincerity on her face. "I just wanted to show you I know how to use the quintain," she explained.

"Well, that fact has been established."

He got to his feet, trying to maintain his composure, and she reached out and brushed the dirt from his tunic as she spoke.

"I will never do it again, I promise. I am so sorry I –"

He stopped her apology as he pulled her to him and kissed her hard on the mouth in front of everyone. That gave the crowd something to cheer about and it shut her up as well. He pulled back and she just looked at him with wide eyes, and before he knew it, she'd reached up and pressed her mouth over his in another kiss.

His eye didn't hurt so badly all of a sudden. If she was this passionate in the middle of the practice yard with a dozen men watching, he couldn't wait to see how she'd be acting come tonight when he took her to his bed.

Chapter 13

"Let me see your eye," said Ruby, leaning over Nyle as he sat at the trestle table of the great hall.

"I'm fine," he mumbled, gently pushing her hand away and looking up to the crowd gathered around him. "Now men, get to the practice yard and servants get back to work. His eye throbbed like the devil from being hit by the sandbag, and he held a cool, wet rag against it to help ease the pain. Now he'd have a black eye for the next sennight and he had his unruly wife to thank for that.

Linette sat across from him, letting little Tibbar crawl around the top of the table as she broke up pieces of bread and soaked them in milk and gave them to the little boy to eat.

"Nyle, that was the funniest thing I've seen in a long time. Actually, it reminds me of the story Nigel used to tell of when you two were first learning to hunt."

"Linette, please," he said, already feeling the embarrassment of the story he knew she intended to tell.

"Nyle, I'm sure Ruby wants to hear about your past."

"Nay," he ground out.

"Aye," Ruby answered excitedly. "Please do tell the story, Linette." She hurriedly sat herself next to him and leaned in eagerly to listen to his sister.

"Well," Linette said with a big smile, "I only know it as my brother Nigel used to relay, as I was not yet born when it happened. But Nigel never could stop laughing as he told the story of how Nyle got tangled in the hounds' leads. The kennelgroom tried to hold them back when Nyle held up his pet rabbit, wanting to show it to the dogs." She burst out laughing, and Ruby giggled as well.

"You brought a live rabbit in front of the hounds and didn't think they'd go after it?" asked his wife.

"I was eight," Nyle said in his defense.

"Yes, he was eight," relayed Linette, "I remember this story clearly. He had caught his first rabbit with a snare and wanted to keep it as a pet instead of having it for dinner."

"Linette, please," he said, putting down the rag and reaching out to feed some bread to Tibbar. "Haven't I been embarrassed enough already today?"

"Well, what happened?" asked Ruby, anxiously. "Did you end up keeping the rabbit?"

"It never made it past the hounds," said Linette. "And Nyle was lucky to make it out of the tangled mess alive. I laugh every time I think of this story. Nigel used to make Nyle so angry every time he mentioned it."

"Enough," he told her, tired of being laughed at by everyone today. He didn't need it from his own sister nor from his wife.

"To this day he won't eat rabbit," Linette broke in, not able to resist telling more.

"That is funny," said Ruby, laughing with her, and Nyle

had about all he was going to take.

He noticed the handmaid at the back of room, having just come in with a bag in her hand. Tibbar started fussing, and Linette reached out for him.

"Oh, I see Ascilia is back," said his sister. "I'll just have her take Tibbar to my solar for a nap."

"Nay," said Nyle, stopping her. "I'm sure my wife would like to do that. And the baby will be staying in our solar now where I can keep an eye on him."

"Well, let me call a nursemaid over then," said Linette.

"Nay. I want only Ruby, myself, or you, to care for the baby. No one else. Is that understood?"

"Why not?" asked Linette.

"Let's just say, I don't trust anyone else with the baby right now, and please don't ask questions."

"But I was planning on finding the armory as I have not yet seen the rest of the castle nor your demesne," Ruby told him. "Locke offered to show me the barracks and the mews as well."

"You will not be going anywhere near my garrison dressed like that," he told her.

"Then I shall change first, and then go," she said, getting up from the bench. "Besides, I have no idea how to make a fussy child take a nap."

"Then let me show you," he said. "It's not hard. If you can make a quintain from scraps and figure out how to give your husband a black eye on the first day of being married, then I think you can figure this out as well."

He stood and grabbed Tibbar from the table and held the boy to his chest and rubbed a gentle hand over his back. In a matter of minutes the boy settled down and closed his eyes, his thumb in his mouth as he drifted off to sleep.

Elizabeth Rose

"You are amazing!" She looked at him in wonderment and it helped him to forget about the way they'd all laughed at him earlier.

"Aye, I've heard that on more than one occasion from you now," he said with a wink that wasn't missed by his sister.

"Mayhap I should take the baby for his nap," Linette said. "I am guessing you two may want a nap of your own." She held out her hands for the baby but he just shook his head.

"Actually, dear sister, I think I will take Tibbar as I am feeling drained from that rambunctious sparring with my wife in the practice yard earlier."

"Did you want to spar again?" He almost laughed when he saw the hope in Ruby's eyes. He wondered how her father had put up with her antics all these years. He knew if he did nothing soon to help her, she would never learn to be a lady. But in order to do that, he needed his sister's help.

"I'd love to spar with you, darling, but not until later tonight in the privacy of our bedchamber. Right now, I'd like you to go change into a gown. And Linette, if you'd please take her to the ladies' solar and teach her to sew I'd be ever so grateful."

"Teach her?" Linette looked at Ruby as she got to her feet. "Sewing is the first thing a lady learns when she is just a girl."

"Well, if you haven't noticed, my wife is a little different than your normal lady. But with your help mayhap she can learn to do what is expected of her now that she is Lady Sheffield."

"I don't sew," Ruby reminded him.

"I believe if you go up to the ladies' solar you'll find my

164

cloak there," he told her. "You do remember the one you stepped on and tore and threw in the mud puddle the day we met?"

"Oh," she said, with a guilty grin. "So you know about that?"

"I know that since you were the one to rip it, you would want to fix it for me too, wouldn't you?"

"Well, yes, I suppose so," she said.

"And when you are done, Linette can take you to the kitchen and teach you how to instruct the kitchen servants in preparing the meal. Linette can tell you what I like to eat."

"That's right," his sister said, then smiled devilishly. "Just as long as it's not rabbit."

"Go!" he instructed, and both the women walked away laughing and talking. He saw the handmaid follow them as they went down the corridor.

He was happy to see Ruby getting along so well with Linette. It did both of them good, as it was helping to get Linette's mind off of the loss of their father. He would have to convince his sister to stay a few extra days in order to teach his wife the duties of the lady of a castle. Besides, he liked having Linette around again, even if she did tease him.

He kissed the top of little Tibbar's head, feeling like he never wanted to let the boy go back to King Edward. But if Ruby didn't start acting her part as a mother to this child soon, he knew the guise would never work. She didn't seem eager to take care of the baby and this concerned him. She would rather be out on the practice field like one of the men.

Even if she wasn't fond of watching this child, he could only hope when they had children of their own her heart would warm toward them.

He knew Tibbar's mother had basically abandoned him,

only interested in bedding men and luring them into giving her everything she wanted, from jewels to fine clothing to coin. But he wanted the mother of his children to be nurturing, loving and caring. He was fond of Ruby but didn't know if she would ever be the wife and mother he wanted her to be.

* * *

Ruby sat in the ladies' solar with Nyle's cloak on her lap. After she'd changed into a gown, she'd spent most the afternoon sewing and chatting with the other women. She hadn't thought she'd enjoy it, but being around some of the other women in the castle was actually just what she needed. She missed her sisters immensely and this seemed to help fill the void.

While the work was tedious and her fingers had fumbled with the needle more than once and she'd stuck herself until she bled, she'd managed to learn from Linette how to mend Nyle's cape. All the ladies in the solar were very skilled at stitching and even weaving and it made Ruby feel like a very incompetent wife. She knew Nyle was right in saying that she needed to learn the skills of a lady, and she wanted to work her hardest at pleasing him.

The needle came unthreaded, and she couldn't seem to get it threaded again. She knew Linette was busy on the other side of the room and felt bad bothering her. Then she saw the handmaid just sitting there staring at her and she motioned for her to come over.

"Ascilia," she called. "Please help me with this." She held it out to the woman, but she seemed hesitant to take it. Then she finally did, but was no better at threading the needle than she. Odd, she thought since a handmaiden needed to know everything about taking care of a lady, including sewing.

"I . . . can't do it," she said, throwing it down onto Ruby's lap.

"Why not?" asked Ruby. "I've never known a handmaid who couldn't sew."

"I just . . . don't see well anymore," she said, straightening her wimple and pushing some strands of hair back underneath that had come loose. The wrinkles on her face looked lighter than the other day, but Ruby figured her eyes were just playing tricks on her from all this tedious sewing.

"Oh," said Ruby. "That's fine, then." She finished on her own and folded up the cloak and went to talk to Linette.

"I will meet you in the kitchen," she told her. "I just want to drop off this cloak in the bedchamber first."

"Of course," said Linette with a smile. "You did a fine job sewing, Ruby. I am sure Nyle will think so too."

"Do you really?" she asked. "Because I have the feeling he is upset with me, and I want to learn some skills so he can see that I can do more than just fight."

She headed down the corridor with the cloak in her hands, inspecting her needlework as she walked. Not bad, she thought. That is, for her first time. Had her mother still been alive when she was growing up, she was sure she would have taught her these skills. But since she'd been raised by her father and tried to please him by acting like a son, she had really missed out on a lot, she realized. Well, she planned on making up for all that now that she was married.

She pushed open the door to their solar and entered,

stopping in her tracks as she looked up and saw the most precious sight. There on the bed was Nyle, lying on his back without his tunic, his black eye covered with a wet rag. Little Tibbar was curled up in his arms with his head lying against Nyle's chest. They were both sleeping.

Ruby felt a warmth in her heart, and a tear came to her eye. Nyle was such a good father, even if the baby wasn't his. She didn't know for sure, but neither did it matter. She just saw another soft, loving, caring side that she hadn't thought her hardened warrior husband could possess.

Her opinion of him since the first day she met him at her father's castle was changing drastically. She liked being around him when he was like this, and was starting to enjoy the idea of being married as well. Even sewing, and the chores of being the lady of the castle weren't really as horrible as she'd thought they'd be. Her life was changing quickly, and though she'd thought she hated Nyle, lately she realized she was very fond of him after all.

They both looked so adorable, and she realized that they really did look like father and son. The same dark hair, the same cheekbones and slope of the nose. She knew in her heart now Tibbar truly was his son. She felt jealous in a way that this wasn't her son too. She also felt angry that any mother would just abandon her baby and not try to get it back, no matter what the circumstances.

She heard a noise behind her, and turned to see Ascilia standing in the doorway, her eyes fastened on Tibbar and Nyle upon the bed. Ruby put the cloak down quickly and escorted the handmaid out of the room, not wanting to wake Nyle and the baby from their peaceful slumber.

Once out in the corridor, she closed the door and whispered to the handmaid. "Isn't that adorable?" she asked.

Ruby

"Nyle really loves that baby. He is a good father, isn't he?"

"Let's go to the kitchen," Ascilia said with no reaction to Ruby's comment. "There is a new cook there who has something special planned for dinner. He has things he wants to teach you."

"Oh, good, as I really want to learn to cook so I can impress my husband. I think I will enjoy being Lady Sheffield after all. I am so excited to learn from the cook that I can barely wait."

"Neither can I," said the woman with an odd bitterness to her tone. "Neither can I."

* * *

Ruby was a fast learner in the kitchen, and this surprised her more than anyone. After spending time with Linette, she realized that in time Nyle would be impressed with her domestic skills as well. Ruby always liked a challenge, and she was determined to be the best lady her husband had ever seen, no matter what it took.

"So tell me," said Linette. "Why is it you never learned to cook?"

Ruby plucked the feathers off a chicken as she spoke. "I guess 'tis just because with three sisters I never had to do it. Or sew, or even manage a household. They were all proficient at these skills and I let them do the work while I spent the time with my father."

"Doing what?" she asked.

"Mostly riding and hunting. Actually, he even let me play cards and dice with the garrison up on the battlements on the nights I couldn't sleep. The men were bored on night watch, but with me there it made their time go quickly."

Linette took a pestle and mortar from a kitchen maid and started to grind herbs. "Well, don't let Nyle catch you playing dice with the garrison because I don't think he'd like it."

"Probably not," she said. "Linette, I saw him sleeping with the baby on his chest up in the solar. It made me realize that I want to become a lady and bear Nyle heirs some day."

"Then you'd better start taking care of Tibbar, because I can tell Nyle is frustrated with you where that is concerned."

"But . . . I can't," she said.

"I can teach you what to do if that's what is worrying you."

"I know," she said. "But it's more than that."

"Then what?" She stopped grinding the herbs and looked to her with a questioning brow. "Do you not like Tibbar? Because I can't see how anyone couldn't like such a cute baby."

"That's not it," she said. "It's just that – I'm not really the child's mother and I can't stop thinking about who she might be."

"Why don't you tell me what all the secrecy is about?" she asked.

"I really can't belie my husband's trust," she said.

"Well, I think the baby looks just like Nyle. I wouldn't be surprised if it was his."

"Do you really think so?" asked Ruby.

"Well, even if it was, would it matter to you? You are his wife now, no matter who may have birthed him that baby. So if I were you I'd start acting like a mother to little Tibbar. You could use it as practice for when you two start having babies."

"There is something else," she told her.

Ruby

"What is it? Linette grabbed the chicken and plucked a few last feathers and handed it to the big man with the sharp knife. He slammed the knife into the wooden table, lopping off the head of the chicken and looked at Ruby and smiled. It sent a chill up her spine.

"You see, Tibbar reminds me of the baby brother I lost," said Ruby. "I was very young at the time, but I do remember his dark head of hair."

"You said he was stillborn?" asked Linette.

"Yes. And my father thought he was a demon and the cause of my mother's death."

"Do you really think your brother was a demon? That is the most ridiculous thing I've ever heard."

"You are right," she said. "And I think I would like to get to know Tibbar. Mayhap he could take the place of the baby brother I lost."

"Now, that is a good idea." She picked up the mortar and pestle. "I need to bring this to the cook making the stew. I will be right back."

As soon as she left, Ascilia came over to Ruby.

"Cook needs you to help him in the larder," she said, nodding toward the man with the big knife.

"Me?" Ruby looked over to the big man who had chopped off the chicken's head and shivered slightly. There was something about him she just didn't like. "Can't you help him?" she asked.

"Linette needs my assistance, but we will be there soon. You said you wanted to learn to cook to please Nyle, so this is your chance."

"Oh, of course. You're right," she said, already regretting that she agreed. The cook smiled and motioned to her and headed into the larder.

"Follow me," he said. Ruby looked up, wanting Linette there with her, but Ascilia was talking with her and she couldn't get her attention. She ran her hand over her dagger at her side and followed the man into the room used to store fish and salted meat.

As soon as they entered he lit a candle, and the door swung closed behind him. Salted carcasses of pigs and goats and even pheasants and rabbits hung from the rafters, swinging lightly as he passed by and disappeared into the darkness with only the slight light of the candle sitting atop the barrel in front of her lighting the room.

"Are you coming?" he called from the darkness, and she hesitated and looked back to the closed door. She had a feeling she should not follow him deeper into the larder, but then she thought about truly wanting to please Nyle and wanting to learn all she could of being a lady. She had never been in this larder before and curiously ended up following him, picking up the candle to guide her way.

Something didn't feel right, but she walked forward anyway, thinking she was letting her nerves cloud her judgment. She stopped just under the partial carcass of a cow, straining her ears to listen for the cook. She heard a creaking from the rope that held the meat above her, and looked upward just in time to see the rope snap and the beef come tumbling down. She jumped out of the way, but was still knocked to the ground. The candle fell on its side, sputtering, threatening to extinguish itself. The heavy carcass fell atop her leg and she was trapped, now unable to move. She reached for her dagger at her side and saw the cook's shadowed form as he made his way toward her.

"I need help," she called out, thinking he meant to assist her. Then she saw the glittering of his knife as he held it up high. She thought at first he'd meant to cut the meat off of her to help release her, but when she saw the mad look in his eyes and the turned down line of his mouth, she knew she was mistaken. His hand came down with his knife in it, right toward her chest. It was obvious he wasn't trying to free her, but kill her instead. She fumbled for her dagger and screamed at the top of her lungs.

Chapter 14

Nyle made his way to the kitchen with little Tibbar latched onto his hip, and his sword swinging at his waist on the other side. The boy kept reaching out for it, mumbling gibberish, and Nyle pulled his hand away so he wouldn't touch it. The baby then grabbed at Nyle's ring.

"Why is it the only word you know how to say is Nyle?" he asked. "Everything else is total nonsense."

"Nyle," the boy said in a high voice, then reached out and took a fistful of Nyle's hair in his hand and tried to eat it.

"Slow down, you hungry monster," he said, entering the kitchen. "We'll find something for you to eat. I think that nap we had made us both hungry. Plus, it put me far behind in my work, but it was well worth it."

"There's the baby," said Linette, walking up with outstretched arms. "How was your nap?"

Nyle pried the boy's hand from his hair, letting his sister take him.

"Well, if you're asking him, it was fine," he said. "If you are asking me – painful." He put his fingers up to his aching eye. "Tibbar is restless in his sleep and managed to kick me right in my injured eye."

"Oh, you sweet little thing," said Linette, kissing the boy atop the head.

"What about me?" he asked with a grin.

"Both of you are sweet." She reached over and kissed him lightly on the eye.

"Where's Ruby?" He looked around the busy kitchen. "I thought I sent her to help you."

"She was here a minute ago." Linette looked over to her handmaid who had her back to them and was across the room. "Ascilia, have you seen Ruby?"

"Well, I think I saw her go to the larder with the cook," she said softly, still not turning around.

"Cook?" he asked, suddenly realizing Ruby was alone with a cook and in the larder. "What cook?" His eyes scanned the room frantically.

"I think mayhap it was that large man who was enjoying lopping off the heads of chickens," said Linette, "but I'm not sure."

"Dammit, no," he said, racing toward the larder, just as he heard a woman scream from within. He ripped open the door and pulled his sword from his side. He stepped forward into the darkness, but there was no candlelight and he could not see far. "Ruby? Where are you?" he called.

He heard what sounded like two people struggling, and a moan as well as another scream that sounded a lot like his wife. He rushed forward, stumbling against barrels of salted herring while trying to make his way in the darkness to where he'd heard the voices.

The door opened behind him and he heard more voices and a candle lit up the room. To his horror, in the firelight he saw Ruby lying on the ground partially covered by some salted beef that looked to have fallen from the ceiling. And lying atop her was the crazed cook with a sharp knife in his hand. Blood leaked down into a large puddle beneath them, and upon seeing this, he let out a scream.

"Nay!" he screamed, rushing over and grabbing hold of the cook, turning him over to stab his sword through him, but stopping when he saw the hilt of a dagger already sticking out from the man's chest. The cooks eyes were frozen wide in surprise and there was no doubt he was dead. Nyle pushed him to the side and grabbed for his wife next.

"Ruby, are you all right?" He threw down his sword and reached for her, but her eyes were closed and there was blood covering the front of her gown. She almost looked as if she, too, were dead.

"Lord Sheffield? Are you in here?" Locke ran in with his sword raised and the steward was right behind him holding a candle.

"Over here," he cried, ripping the large hunk of salted beef from atop her, that had her pinned down. "Ruby," he said, pulling her to his chest and holding her tightly in his arms. "Ruby, sweetheart, please don't leave me. Please don't die, my beautiful wife."

While he'd felt remorse at the loss of his other wives, thinking of losing Ruby had him terrified. He'd been attracted to her wit and wild ways, even though she always managed to anger him. But now that they were married and had spent intimate time together, he felt as if his life was better and more complete because of her. He was still guarded with his emotions, but Ruby had a way of chipping through that wall to reach his heart. Seeing her lying here like this only sent a wave of panic through him. He couldn't lose her, and didn't know what he'd do if she was really gone from his life forever.

Locke and Lewis rushed up, stopping to survey the bloody scene.

"What's happening?" he heard Linette call from the door.

"Stay out, and keep the baby away," Nyle shouted. "And don't let anyone else enter."

"Is she dead?" asked Locke, looking over his shoulder toward Ruby and then over to the bloodied body of the cook.

"Dammit, Lewis, you were supposed to be keeping an eye on the cook," he cried out.

"I am sorry, my lord. I was watching him, but there was much commotion in the kitchen and I became distracted."

"Ruby," he said, shaking her limp body. "Ruby, wake up," he cried, kissing her face and also the top of her head. Then, when he thought for sure she'd been murdered, she stirred slightly and moaned. He let out a breath of relief as she slowly opened her eyes.

"Did you mean it . . . that I'm beautiful?" she asked softly, and smiled.

"Dammit, Ruby you scared me," he said, picking her up in his arms and standing. "Aye, you are the most beautiful sight I've even set eyes on at this moment. Tell me, are you hurt? You are covered with blood."

"Nay, I'm fine," she said, shaking her head. "That is the cook's blood you see." Then her eyes filled with fear. "Nyle, where is he? He tried to kill me."

"Shhhh," he said, trying to calm her. "Everything is fine. He can't hurt you anymore, he is dead, sweetheart." He put her back on her feet.

"Dead?" she asked, turning to look in the direction of the

cook lying on the floor with the dagger sticking out of him. She screamed and hid her face against Nyle's chest.

"That's my dagger in his chest, isn't it?" she asked.

"Aye," he admitted. "I came to help you, but as we all can see you didn't need help. You really were able to take care of yourself, just as I'd hoped when I chose you to marry."

She looked up to him, the fear in her eyes turning to tears. "Nyle, I . . . I killed a man."

"You did it in self defense," he said, noticing her body shaking slightly.

"I am a murderer," she said, crying against his chest.

"No, you are not," he told her, "and I don't want to ever hear you say that again." He looked over to his steward. "Get a bath prepared in my solar anon."

"Aye, milord," he said, rushing from the room.

Sir Godin entered just then, rushing up with his sword drawn and stopping when he realized what had transpired.

"You're a little late aren't you?" growled Nyle. "Where were you when this was happening?"

"I was on the battlements, my lord," said Sir Godin. He reached down and picked up Nyle's sword and handed it back to him.

Nyle placed it back in his scabbard. "Get this mess cleaned up," he ordered, guiding Ruby toward the door.

"This is starting to become tiresome cleaning up dead men," mumbled the knight behind him.

"Then do something about it," he answered. "Tell the garrison to meet me in the great hall, and Locke, tell my sister I want to see her with the baby in the solar right away."

Nyle left the larder, ignoring everyone who was standing

there with wide, questioning eyes. He made a dash to the solar holding onto Ruby's hand, angrier than he'd ever felt in his life. He'd almost lost another wife, and this could not continue. He was not going to lose Ruby – ever. He would find the culprit behind all this and put an end to it before anything else happened.

Chapter 15

Ruby slid down into the hot water of the tub, trying to stop her body from shaking. She had almost been killed tonight, for the second time since she'd become Lady Sheffield. And as a result, she had become naught more than a cold-blooded murderer herself.

Oralie had warned her that there would be repercussions if she'd ever had to kill a man, and that her mind might not be able to handle it. She'd dismissed the absurd idea, thinking it was no different than hunting an animal for a meal. Now she knew Oralie was right, because she just couldn't shake the image of the dead cook from her mind, and she was the one who had taken the man's life.

The door opened and she looked over to see Nyle enter the room, and noticed the backs of two guards outside the door. He shut the door and walked into the room, not taking off his sword, but instead pacing in front of the tub and running a hand through his hair.

"Where is the baby?" she asked.

Ruby

"Linette has Tibbar in the great hall, and I have half the garrison standing over her to guard him."

"Don't you think you are overreacting?"

He stopped and looked at her and his eyes narrowed. "Someone tried to kill you tonight, Ruby and almost succeeded. This is a serious matter. And if I must remind you, this is the second attempt on your life since I've married you. This is all my fault. It's also my fault three other innocent girls went to their deaths that should still be alive today."

"It wasn't your fault," she told him. "Please don't blame yourself."

"Then whose fault is it?" he asked. He continued to pace. "I should have known there'd be another attempt on your life. I should have stayed by your side constantly."

"We all thought the attempts would end after you killed that mercenary. How were we to know?"

"I should have known better. The only thing I don't understand is why. Why is someone doing this and who the hell is behind it all?"

"Come into the tub, Nyle, the water feels wonderful. It'll help you relax."

"Tell me again, what happened in the larder?"

"Nyle, I really don't want to talk about it just yet. Don't you understand that I am just as upset as you or mayhap even more? After all, I killed someone today." She sat up higher in the tub, feeling the tears welling in her eyes. "I never meant to kill anyone. For all I know, that man could have a wife and several children that will never see him again. It is such an awful feeling, that I don't want to ever experience it again."

"You get numb to it after awhile," he told her

nonchalantly. "What's the matter with you, Ruby? I thought you knew how to handle a weapon and all that went with it. You're acting like a . . ."

"A lady?" she asked, and she heard him sigh and just nod his head slightly. "I like practicing with weapons, but now that I know how it feels to kill, I don't want anything to do with weapons again. I just want to be your wife. I want to learn to sew and cook and take care of babies and be a lady. And most of all, I want you to be proud of me."

"I am proud of you, sweetheart. Proud that you defended yourself today when I wasn't around to do it. It's just your fear talking, and you'll get over it. I don't want that part of you to ever change, do you understand?"

She didn't understand. She felt more confused than she'd ever felt in her life. First he wanted her to be a lady, and now he sounded as if he wanted her to be a warrior instead. She didn't know what to think any more.

She couldn't help herself. She didn't mean to break down, but she just started crying and couldn't stop. She thought she was stronger than this, but she never realized killing someone would feel so horrible or affect her so much, even if it was in self-defense. The knights and soldiers killed people all the time, yet it never seemed to affect them. She didn't know how they could go to one battle after another, killing man after man, and live with themselves the next day. She knew now that all the glory of weapons and fighting she'd admired while growing up was not glorious at all, but rather horrifying.

"Don't cry, Ruby." He let out a deep breath and removed his weapon belt and sword. His clothes followed. He slipped into the water beside her, and reached out and pulled her into his arms.

"I want to go home," she told him, burying her head in his chest.

"You are home," he said, kissing her atop the head.

"No, I mean to Blackpool. I miss my sisters and I want to see my father."

"You're right," he told her, pulling her closer. "Mayhap that is a good idea right now. I feel you would be safer there anyway."

"I won't leave without you," she told him. "Please don't send me away from you in the process."

"I won't," he said, rubbing her shoulder wondering what the hell he should do. All he knew was that Ruby was homesick and he was tired of not feeling like he was capable of protecting his own wife. "We'll go to Blackpool soon," he told her. "We'll go together. I promise."

"Nyle, don't you miss your family? You never talk about them."

"I do miss them," he admitted. "Although I didn't get along with my father, and my brother Nigel and I were always in competition."

"Tell me why you didn't get along with your father."

"I don't want to talk about it, Ruby."

"I am your wife, Nyle. Please start opening up to me, as you have been so secretive."

"You're right," he said. "I will tell you. My father favored my brother, and though I was the first born twin, he'd planned to make my brother his heir."

"Oh, I'm sorry."

"But now none of that matters. Nigel died in the same battle that put me in favor in the king's eyes for saving his life. Just another reason for my father to be upset that I couldn't have saved Nigel as well." Nyle held up his hand with his father's ring on it. "This is all I have left to remember him by. And I know now that life is too short to hold grudges. I only wish I could go back in time and do it over."

"What happened to your mother?"

"My sister is nearly ten years younger than me. My mother treasured her, but her heart was broken when Linette married a Scotsman that my parents did not approve of and moved to the Highlands. She died from a weak heart and Linette believes she is responsible."

"My, your family's story is sad. I am so sorry."

"You have told me very little of your family, Ruby."

"Well, then I'll tell you as well, since you have shared your story with me. You already know my father, as well as have met my sisters," she said. "But you don't know that my mother died birthing my brother who also died the same night."

"I am sorry, but I know these things happen."

"Aye, they do, but this is different. My mother bought jeweled daggers that we were named after, hence assuring we would find our true loves. But my mother had done wrong trying to steal a fifth dagger years ago from the blind old hag who sold them to her. My father believes she was cursed by the hag and that is why she and my brother died. He got rid of the daggers, and to this day I miss them, as it was the only true remembrance I had of my mother."

"I understand," he said, holding up his ring and looking at it. "So your dagger had a ruby in the hilt?"

"It did. And I can only hope to find another some day that will at least remind me of what I've lost."

"We will visit Blackpool again soon," he told her. "I know how important it is for you to be around your family."

Ruby

He pulled her closer to him, wishing he knew just what the hell he was going to do about all this. He really shouldn't leave Sheffield with the baby because he had no idea when the king was going to summon him to return the child. But if he had to leave Sheffield in order to protect Ruby and little Tibbar, then so be it. Because he knew in his heart that the three of them were somehow a family.

* * *

Ruby woke the next morning with Nyle on one side of her and little Tibbar right in the middle of the bed between them. Actually, she was the one who insisted they put the baby in the bed with them in order to watch over his safety. After yesterday, Ruby had had a change of heart when she'd almost lost her life in the larder.

She'd been so upset after what had happened that she couldn't even make love with her new husband though they had both sat naked in the same tub. Of course he tried to make advances as any man in his right mind would, but when she'd refused him, he'd respected her wishes. She knew that he, too, was very upset by the danger that seemed to lurk around every corner in their own home.

The baby opened his eyes and looked directly at Ruby and smiled. Her heart went out to the boy, and she couldn't help but think of the baby brother she'd lost. She'd been avoiding this child, not only because she had no experience with children, but also because it pained her to look at the boy as it always brought back memories of that horrible day.

Tibbar sat up and reached out and started splaying his arms, hitting Nyle in the chest. Nyle mumbled something with his eyes still closed and rolled to his side, one arm going over the baby in a form of protection though he was asleep. She knew this boy meant so much to him, and she also knew in her heart that somehow Nyle was his father. They looked so natural together. They both had the same dark hair and though the boy's eyes were blue, she saw a part of Nyle within Tibbar's eyes as well.

The boy started sucking on Nyle's finger and her husband giggled in his sleep and rolled back the other way. She knew he must be exhausted from everything he'd been through lately. She wanted to give him time to sleep and she also wanted time to get to know little Tibbar for herself. So she slipped out of bed quietly, quickly donning her gown, hose and shoes. Then she reached out her arms for the boy, meaning to pick him up, her heart already about beating from her chest.

What if the boy didn't accept her? What if he started crying and woke up Nyle? She felt like a fish out of water and only wished now that she had taken the time to practice the ways of a lady at Blackpool and that her father had not been so lenient with her wild antics and instead forced her to change her ways.

To her surprise, Tibbar held out his arms, wanting her to pick him up. When she did, she realized his swaddling was very heavy. She looked around the room but did not see extras with which to change him, nor had she done it yet on her own and wasn't really sure she knew how. She decided to go to Linette's room and ask her to help. She picked up the boy, once more looking over to the bed and Nyle.

"Where are you going?" he mumbled, as if he knew what she did though his eyes were still closed.

"I'm just going to take care of the baby so you can sleep," she said.

"Fine," he answered. "Just don't leave the room without me." She heard his breathing change and knew he'd fallen back asleep quickly. The baby cuddled to her and she liked that. She took a step toward the door and something made her turn back and look at her dagger lying on the bedside table. She'd never gone anywhere without it, but for some reason she couldn't bring herself to take it with her. She saw a small amount of dried blood on the blade yet, and realized Nyle had cleaned it for her in a hurry yesterday and missed a spot.

She felt her stomach tighten and flashes of her sticking it into the cook's chest with his eyes bugging out and blood gushing everywhere was lodged in her mind. She didn't want to put it on her belt, and would just go without it today. She knew Nyle had guards around every corner watching her now, and so she would be safe even without it.

"Come on, Tibbar," she said with a smile. "Let's go get you a dry swaddling and something to eat."

She pulled open the door to find not one, but two guards standing watch.

"My lady," said one with a nod of his head.

"Good morning," she said, leaving the room and heading down the corridor. They followed on her heels, right behind her. She looked over her shoulder and walked a bit faster, but they continued to follow. She stopped in her tracks and turned around.

"Thank you," she said, "but you don't need to follow me."

"'Tis Lord Sheffield's command that we stay with you at all times, my lady."

"Of course," she said, and continued on to Linette's chamber. She stopped just outside the door, her fingers on

187

the handle. She pushed it open and started to enter, and realized the guards were going to enter as well.

"Nay!" she said, holding up a hand. Tibbar squealed and grabbed at her fingers. "You cannot follow me into Lady Linette's chamber. It would not be proper." She surprised herself with her own words, wondering when she had started to think of doing anything the proper way. Still, she did not want the men following her into the room.

"Lord Sheffield ordered us to stay with you at all times," one of the men said.

"Well, I am sure he didn't mean following me into the chamber of a woman who is probably not even clothed. Now stay here and stop following me, please."

They looked at each other and shrugged. "We will stay outside the door then," one of them said.

"Fine." She entered the room and closed the door behind her. She turned around, surprised not to find Linette, but her lady-in-waiting instead. She was just getting out of a tub of water and Ruby was taken aback that she would be bathing in a lady's tub and in her solar nonetheless.

Ascilia looked up quickly and turned away fast, but Ruby couldn't help but notice her breasts and buttocks were full and tight and not at all what one would expect of an older woman.

"My lady," cried the handmaid, grabbing a towel and wrapping it around her. She ran to the other side of the room and with her back facing Ruby quickly dressed.

"Where is Lady Linette?" Ruby asked, looking around the room.

"She has already gone down to the stable to have her horse prepared, as she plans on riding today, my lady," she answered.

"Really? And did she tell you that you could use her bathwater?"

"Aye. Lady Linette allowed me to use the water since she was finished," said the woman, covering her head quickly with a wimple that wrapped around her neck and shoulders as well.

"I was hoping she would help me change the baby's swaddling," Ruby told her. "But since she is not here, you can do it for me instead."

"Me, my lady?" The woman seemed surprised.

"Of course. You are a handmaid and know about these things."

"You are the baby's mother," she reminded Ruby. "I believe you should do it instead."

Tibbar started crying and she knew she needed to get him into something dry. A foul stench was starting to permeate the air and she had no doubt that her first experience with a baby's swaddling was going to be quite a challenge.

"We'll do it together," said Ruby, lying the baby on the bed. "Now bring me a clean swaddling please."

Ruby unwrapped the baby's covering, the smell making her already sour stomach feel worse. But it was more than she wanted to handle when she saw the mess that covered the little boy.

"You do it," she said, putting her hands up in the air and taking a step backward.

"Nay, you are the boy's mother, I believe you should do it," said Ascilia, placing the clean swaddling on the bed.

"But this is a mess," Ruby said. "I don't even know how to approach it."

"I am sure you will be capable," said Ascilia, taking one

look at the baby and crossing over to the other side of the room. Ruby found it odd that a servant should be acting in this manner. Still, she had no idea how Lady Linette thought to discipline those in her service and knew that her father had let her act in inappropriate manners, so mayhap this was more common than she thought.

"Well," she said, eyeing the baby and then the tub of water. "Mayhap 'tis time for the baby to have a bath as well." She removed the child's swaddling, carefully picking up the crying boy and rushing over to the tub of water, hoping this would work.

* * *

Nyle woke from a sound sleep, hearing the slight sound of a crying baby from somewhere in the distance. He opened his eyes, listening, remembering the baby had been sleeping between them during the night and now it sounded to be farther away.

He sat up quickly, his eyes scanning the room but not seeing Ruby nor the boy anywhere.

"Damn!" He jumped from the bed, donning his clothes in a hurry, cursing himself for being such a sound sleeper. Not at all an admirable trait for a knight. He needed to be aware of his surroundings even in his sleep. But lately, the events had taken a toll on him and he found himself disturbed and anxious most the night, and then too exhausted to move when he finally did fall asleep.

"Guards!" he called out, but no one answered. "Where the hell are they?" he spoke to himself as he pulled on his shoes. "Ruby!" he called, but no answer from her either. He grabbed his weapon belt and donned his sword, realizing

Ruby

Ruby had taken off somewhere with the baby. Then he spotted her dagger still lying on the table, and he felt a streak of panic run through him.

"What the hell is the matter with her?" he asked, picking up the dagger and sticking it into his belt. "Doesn't she know she can't be out and about without a means to protect herself?"

He ripped open the door and headed down the hall, following the muffled sound of a crying baby. He turned the corner and saw his two guards standing outside of Linette's chamber.

"What are you doing here?" he asked, but the guards just turned to him and pointed to their ears, unable to hear him over the sound of the crying baby that was getting louder. He headed toward them to find out what was going on.

Ruby did her best to wrap the dry swaddling around the clean baby and secure it into place. She picked up the boy, liking the way it felt when he suddenly stopped crying. She knew now that she one day wanted to become a mother. Ascilia watched with wide blue eyes and sauntered closer. The baby giggled as Ruby bounced him, and she giggled as well.

"He's happy now," she said, seeing a longing in the handmaiden's eyes. "Do you have children of your own, Ascilia?"

The woman's eyes darted to the ground. "Nay," she said, fussing with her wimple.

"Well, here, hold little Tibbar, as you must feel a loneliness not having your own child." She shoved the boy into her hands before she could object. She'd been watching Ascilia lately and she knew the woman had some sort of sadness behind her eyes. If she was anything at all like herself, then the woman just needed a little coaxing.

"Nay, take the baby," said Ascilia as if she were frightened by the child.

"He doesn't bite." Ruby walked over to the basin to clean her hands. "You really should try to find someone like Nyle to marry," she told her.

She heard the woman's gasp from behind her. "What do you mean by that?"

"Well, I mean that I thought he was an ogre at first, but now I see I was mistaken." She dried her hands and turned to see the woman just staring at her. The baby was fussing and trying to get away.

"How so?" she asked.

"Well, I thought Nyle was a man who had no caring feelings within him, but I saw the way he loves this baby and also how upset he was when I almost got killed in the larder. I know now that he would do anything at all for me, and tho he didn't say it, I truly think he loves me." She smiled as she sat down in a chair next to the bed. "He is a wonderful father and I am not sure what he would do if he ever lost little Tibbar."

"Really?" The woman looked at the baby and finally smiled at the boy. "Do you love Lord Sheffield as well?"

"Aye, I do believe so," she said with a sigh. "I didn't think I could ever love anyone since the death of my mother and baby brother has affected me horribly throughout my life. But now I realize I had closed off my heart to a wonderful man in fear. This little boy has taken the place of the brother I lost so many years ago. I don't know what either of us will do if the king decides to take him back."

"This is the king's child?" she asked, smiling slightly at

the baby as if that thought pleased her. Ruby realized she had just spilled the secret and clamped her hand over her mouth and just shook her head.

"Oh, please, don't say anything, as I wasn't supposed to tell you," she begged her. "Whatever you do, don't tell Nyle I told you Tibbar is the king's bastard or he would never forgive me."

Just then, the door burst open and Nyle stood there with his hands on his hips. "These walls may be thick," he said, "but I have keen ears that can pick up the crying of a baby as well as the tone of your wagging tongue, Wife."

"Oh, Nyle, I am sorry," she said, running over to him. "It was an accident. But don't worry, Ascilia will keep our secret."

He looked across the room and saw the handmaiden with the crying baby, and stormed over and tore the boy from her arms. Tibbar stopped crying instantly. "Who said you could hold the baby?" he snapped. The handmaiden lowered her head quickly and turned away.

"I told her she could hold him," said Ruby from across the room.

"I don't want anyone touching this baby except the two of us and my sister," he reminded Ruby.

"I didn't see the harm," she protested, having seen the smile on the woman's face when she'd held the baby.

"There is a killer on the loose and we can't take a chance," he growled.

"Oh Nyle," she said with a small laugh. "Ascilia is a handmaiden, not an assassin. You are overreacting again."

He looked once more at the handmaiden and then headed out the door. "Come, wife," he said. "And after the meal you and I are going to have a little chat."

Chapter 16

Ruby slipped away from Nyle after the meal when he was busy instructing his men as to the new security of the castle. He'd decided to post more guards at the gate and have them check every person who came to sell their wares and even the villeins who served him as they tended to their chores.

Ruby couldn't go two steps without having a guard following her. While she appreciated Nyle's concern for her safety, she was getting tired of being shadowed. She made her way across the hall to see her handmaiden, Oralie, whose leg had been wrapped by the healer, as she wanted to know how she was faring.

"Oralie, how are you?" She sat down next to the woman on the bench and put her hand on her shoulder.

"I am feeling much better," she told her. "However, I fear 'twill be some time before I am healed and I can resume my duties of your lady-in-waiting. My leg was not broken, but badly hurt."

"I understand," she said, feeling sorry for the woman as she truly seemed unhappy. "But I am fine for now, as Linette has been sharing her handmaid with me. Personally, I would rather not have one at all until you return to my service."

"How are you faring, Ruby? I heard you killed the cook in self-defense."

"I'm not sure, Oralie. You were right. I don't like the way I feel from what I did."

"I see you're not wearing your dagger."

"I can't. Not yet."

"Well, just give it some time and I'm sure you'll be back to your old ways in no time."

"I'm not sure. I kind of like being a lady, so I might just try living a different way for a while."

"Never give up the things you love because of fear, Ruby. You are who you are, and I'm sure Nyle understands and accepts that."

"Enough about me," said Ruby, not being sure how to answer. "Tell me what you've been doing lately."

"Nothing at all, because I can't. I tire of sitting around all day and only wish I could be of use to you, my lady."

"Well, you can!" She waved Linette over who was playing with Tibbar. "Linette," she said, "I would like to let Oralie, my handmaid, watch over the baby as well."

"Of course," she said, putting the child in Oralie's lap.

"Oh, that would be wonderful," she said, "however I cannot move around and it may be difficult."

"Why should it?" asked Ruby. "Tibbar doesn't walk yet and is really no trouble at all. "We could all take turns, and I will assign a servant to help you if you should need it."

"Lady Ruby, you have made me so happy," she said.

Ruby next called over a young servant girl that came with her from Blackpool whom she knew she could trust. "Blodwen," she said. "Please stay with Oralie and help her take care of the baby at all times."

"Of course, Lady Ruby," the girl said with a curtsy.

Ruby got to her feet and noticed that Nyle was still engaged in conversation with his steward and the bailiff as well. She knew he'd be busy for some time and wanted to go explore the castle as she'd yet to really get to see her new home.

"Linette, will you go with me to explore the castle and its surroundings?" she asked.

"Of course," she said. "That sounds wonderful."

Nyle watched from the opposite side of the room as Ruby not only left the baby in Oralie's care, but left with his sister, when she knew he had told her he needed to talk to her, as well as not to leave the baby with anyone besides the three of them. When would she ever learn?

"So, did you want to go over the tallies now, my lord?" His steward pulled a scroll from his side and unrolled it. Nyle could see it was very long and knew this was going to take much longer than he'd hoped.

"And the villeins need you to settle a dispute, as well as one of the serfs is requesting your permission to marry, said the reeve. "They are waiting for you outside the church as we speak."

Nyle turned to Locke who was standing next to him, and gave him an order in a low voice. "Follow my wife," he told him. "I have a feeling she's going to try to lose the guards and I want someone following her to protect her until I can finish up. Tell Sir Godin to assign two guards to watch over the baby as well."

"Of course, my lord," he said, and took off to carry out his orders.

Ruby

* * *

Ruby and Linette had climbed the battlements and seen the armory. They'd also convinced one of the guards following them to let them see the barracks as well. They walked along the elevated walkway now, two guards right behind them as they stopped and looked out over the wall.

"I always loved climbing the battlements at my father's castle at Blackpool," said Ruby. "I feel so free when I am up so high."

"You should visit me in the Highlands some day then," Linette told her. "The hills and moors and fields of heather are breathtaking. You would really like it."

"I just might do that some day," she said, facing out toward the open air and raising her face to the sun. She reached back and unbraided her hair and let it blow in the breeze.

"Are you happy here?" Linette asked her. "And are you happy being married to my brother?"

"I am," she said with a smile. "I never thought I would like being married but I do. However, I miss my father and my sisters."

"Then why don't you go back to visit them?" she asked.

"I would like to, but I'm not sure Nyle would take kindly to that idea right now, although he has promised to take me. As you can see, he has me so well guarded that I cannot take two steps without being shadowed by a guard. I feel like I am no longer free, but more like a prisoner here."

"He only does it for your own safety," she told her. "I can see he cares about you immensely."

"I understand," said Ruby. "But I am used to being reckless and doing whatever I want. I love being the lady of the castle but I still feel the need for excitement in my life as well. Oralie said I should never give up the things I love, and she is right."

"Well, I have had more excitement since I've come here than I've had since the day I got married," she told her.

"Do you love your husband?" asked Ruby.

"I do," she said. "I married a Scotsman and moved to the Highlands, however Adair is often gone for long periods of time. I, too, long for excitement."

"Then let's do something about that," said Ruby, looking back toward the guards. "And the first thing we have to do is to lose these guards."

"Nyle won't like that," said Linette with a smile.

"Did you never do anything your brother disapproved of when you were growing up?"

"My brothers were already away being fostered by the time I was old enough to remember them. Being almost ten years younger, I was like an only child."

"Well, we need to make up for lost time then," said Ruby. "Be ready to pick up your skirt and run. I think it's time we had a little fun."

"But a lady never picks up her skirt, but rather glides," Linette told her.

"There'll be no gliding today," said Ruby. "Now follow me and try to keep up."

* * *

Ruby ducked into the mews with Linette right on her heels. She ran around the dark corner and dove into the hay, startling several of the hooded falcons in the process. She fell to the ground laughing, and Linette joined her.

Ruby

"We did it," said Linette. "We managed to lose the guards."

"Shhhh." Ruby held her finger to her lips and peeked out the crack in the side wall to see the guards running by.

"I think they went this way," said one of the guards, and they took off in the opposite direction.

The girls fell to their backs laughing.

"I haven't laughed like this in a long time," said Ruby.

"I have never acted so reckless or carefree," added Linette.

"Who goes there?" came a voice from the mews.

Ruby sat up quickly peering into the darkness. She hadn't known anyone was inside. "'Tis only Lady Ruby and Lady Linette," she answered, trying to see who it was who had spoken to them.

A boy walked forward who was perhaps several years younger than herself. His arm was outstretched and a hoodless falcon sat perched upon it, turning its head to look at her with one eye.

"Who are you?" asked Linette, sitting up next to her.

"I am Darby, the falconer's apprentice," he said. "I am new here."

"Aye," said Ruby, getting up and brushing off her skirt. "I met you the other night. So, tell me, how is the training going with the birds?"

"I enjoy it immensely," he told them. "However, Bertram, the falconer does not seem to train me as much as I'd like. He tends to be gone a lot lately, as he sometimes leaves for town and does not return until the next day."

"Well, that's not right," said Ruby. "Where does he go?"

"I'm not sure," said the boy. "My lady, would you like to hold the falcon?" he asked. "'Tis a young bird that I have been training."

"I would," said Ruby taking the extra glove from him and putting it on. "I had a falcon in Blackpool that was mine, but one day on the hunt it was killed by one of the hounds who mistook it for a pheasant I guess."

"You are the lady of the castle and should have a falcon. This one's name is Jibbs, and I think it should be yours." The boy placed the falcon on Ruby's arm.

"You look like a true lady now," said Linette, eyeing Ruby with the bird.

"Will you work with me in training this falcon to truly be mine?" asked Ruby.

"I will," he said. "It is still a young bird but I think it will serve you well by the time we are done."

"Lady Ruby?" Locke walked into the mews, moving his head back and forth trying to see in the darkness. "Are you in here?"

Ruby looked at Linette and they both burst out laughing.

"I think our fun is over for the day," said Ruby. "And I do believe my husband is not going to be happy tonight."

"I'd have to agree to that," said Linette. "And I can only say that it was worth any of his ranting and raving."

Ruby gave the bird back to Darby, thinking of how mad Nyle would be with her and that mayhap she shouldn't have done anything to anger him after all.

Chapter 17

Nyle sat next to his wife and little Tibbar the next morning on the bench, as mass had just finished in St. Agnes's Church in the village. He listened to the church bells ring and it did naught to calm his thoughts. It pained him that he hadn't had a proper marriage ceremony with Ruby and neither had her family been present as was her wish.

God's eyes, he hadn't even given her a ring. He looked down to his own finger with his gold signet ring and thought to himself that he should give it to Ruby until he could buy her a proper wedding band. But he realized he couldn't, as it was the last remembrance of his father, and besides, it wouldn't fit her. He'd just have to find another ring at a later date.

She seemed so natural with the baby on her lap and he was impressed by the way she'd changed and was making a true connection with Tibbar. His feelings for her had been growing lately, even if she did continue to anger him by disobeying almost ever order.

He'd felt bad about reprimanding her yesterday for

hiding from the guards, but he had to do it, to let her know he feared for her safety. Yet, he knew it was in her nature to act in that manner and he rather liked the spunky, playful side of her and really didn't want to change that. Still, he felt uncomfortable that she'd refused to wear her dagger since the day she'd used it in self-defense and killed the cook.

She'd proven to him that she could defend herself in times of danger, but without a weapon, she'd have no chance. There'd been no more attempts on her life since he'd strengthened the security around the castle and also had her followed every minute of the day. But he knew she was irritated by it, and truthfully, so was he.

They'd only made love once since they'd been married. And now that he had guards following her everywhere and Tibbar slept between them in their bed every night for his own protection, he'd had no time alone with her. It was torture to look at her and not be able to touch her. She was his wife and he was a man with needs, and he would do something about this little problem today.

The mass ended and they all got up to leave. He put his hand on Ruby's back and guided her through the church with the baby in her arms. They made their way down the steps and headed for their horses. Locke was waiting for her with the reins of her horse in his hand. Nyle took the baby from her as she mounted. She held out her arms for Tibbar, but instead he gave the baby to Locke.

"What are you doing?" she asked in surprise.

"Ruby, I thought you and I should spend some time alone today. I wanted to know if you would like to go for a ride with me instead of heading back to the castle."

"I would love to," she said with a smile. Then she looked over to the guards nearby and frowned. "Will they be

Ruby

coming with?" she asked.

"Nay," he said. "There is no need. I will be there to protect you."

She smiled. "Then aye, I would like to go."

"Have my sister or Oralie watch the baby," he told Locke. "No one else." He had decided to agree to let Oralie watch the baby as well, as it meant so much to Ruby. Besides, he realized it was too much to ask that a lady of the castle raise her own child. That is what they had servants for, and he would not overwhelm Ruby or his sister with the care of a baby every hour of the day.

"Aye, my lord," Locke said with a nod. The baby stuck his little finger into Locke's eye and he grunted, but still tried to maintain his composure. Both Ruby and Nyle laughed at the sight of Locke standing at attention with one eye closed.

"If you're not careful you may end up with a black eye the same as me," he said looking over and winking at Ruby.

Then in one motion he mounted his horse, and took off over the countryside with Ruby right behind him.

* * *

Ruby loved the ride through the countryside and the part she liked best was that she was able to spend time with her new husband and not have guards right at her elbow watching. They raced each other and then they rode slowly next to each other, making their way over the grounds and along a bubbling creek.

Nyle reached over and held out his hand and they rode forward with hands clasped together.

"This is wonderful," she told him, starting to feel very

relaxed. "I had wondered if we'd ever have time alone together again."

"I must say having a baby in our bed does naught for building a man's pride of his sexual prowess."

"Well," she said, "we have no baby now to stop us."

"My thoughts exactly."

"What do you mean?"

"I want to show you something, Ruby. 'Tis a special place I'd often go to by myself when I wanted to think."

They dismounted off the beaten path and near a creek. Ruby could hear the water falling from somewhere up ahead.

"This way," he told her walking a small distance. She followed right behind, leading her horse.

Then she broke through the clearing and gasped at the most beautiful sight. A waterfall rose up majestically before them, and emptied into a secluded little pond just below.

Nyle tied up their horses and put an arm around her as they gazed upon the beauty of nature.

"This is a special place," she said.

"Indeed it is." He reached over, obviously no desire for talking, and kissed her. The sun warmed the top of her head and she found herself melding her body to his as she reached up and put her arms around his neck.

His tongue entered her mouth and she met his with her own, in a sparring that only lovers used. His hands slid down her back, settling on her waist. Then he cupped the cheeks of her backside and squeezed playfully.

"Two can play that game," she told him, sliding her hands down his waist and to his backside for a squeeze as well. She felt the hilt of his sword jab into her and reached out to move it – but it wasn't his sword.

"Keep that up, wife, and we won't get as far as taking

off our clothes."

She looked down and realized just what she'd grabbed and started to laugh. He stepped away and released his belt and sword and tossed them to the ground. Then he reached over his back, pulling off his tunic in one smooth movement.

The sun glistening off his chest tempted her, and she reached out and ran her hands down it, feeling his muscles contract under her fingers.

"I think I like this game," he told her.

She knew just by his words that she had started a lover's game of which there was no turning back. Neither did she want there to be.

His lithe fingers reached forward, unlacing her bodice and slipping her gown off her shoulders, leaving them bare. She felt the slight breeze against her skin and realized he meant to undress her right there.

Part of her knew she shouldn't be doing this where roaming eyes may spot them. But another part of her found it exciting and she felt her body awakening with every move he made. He exposed her breasts to the summer air and his hands slid over her mounds, causing a flit of excitement to course through her. She pulled herself closer and once again their kisses turned to heated passion.

He reached down and removed the rest of his clothing and she didn't wait for him to help, as she undressed herself. Then they both stood there naked in front of a magical waterfall, and it all seemed so romantic.

He scooped her off her feet causing her to giggle. Then he kicked their clothes together to make a bed and lay her gently atop them.

"I have waited so long for this," he said, his eyes closing slightly as if he was anticipating what was to come.

"It hasn't been that long," she reminded him.

"Well to a newly married man whose desire is bigger than his sword, I'd say it feels like a lifetime.

"Bigger than your sword? Now that is your manly pride boasting."

"All right then, bigger than a dagger anyway."

"Don't speak to me of daggers right now as I don't want to ruin the moment."

She reached up to him and pulled him to her and they kissed and rolled around atop their clothes on the grass. Her hand reached out to fondle him and his hands both reached out and did the same to her. It wasn't long before they were both ready to consummate their marriage yet again.

He mounted himself atop and entered her, causing her emotions of passion to open like a blossoming flower in the warm sun. Then he thrust into her and she raised her hips to meet him. She reached up her legs and wrapped them around his waist and clung to him as he took one hand and lifted her off the ground. Together they made love as man and wife, and she felt all her concerns and tension leave her as they both found their release and dropped to the ground in each other's arms.

"I love you," she blurted out in the midst of passion, and she waited for him to return the endearment, but instead he just calmed his breathing and reached over and kissed her again. His long hair hung to his shoulders and brushed against her. She wanted more than anything to ask if he loved her too, but didn't. If not, she didn't want to ruin the moment. She knew he was guarded with his emotions, and also a very private man. In time he'd return her proclamation of love, she was sure. She just needed to let it unfold naturally. He obviously had something holding him back from loving her as well.

Still, the question persisted in her head, and when he rolled to his side and looked up at the sky, she found herself staring at the clouds but talking to him at the same time.

"You are still in love with Jocelyn," she said, "I know that and accept it. But I hope someday you will be able to love me as well."

"What are you saying?" He sat up and looked at her, brushing his hair from his face. "I don't love Jocelyn."

"But you once did," she countered back.

"You don't know anything about this, sweetheart, so don't think you do."

"Well if you told me, then I would know."

"I don't want to talk about it."

"You never want to talk. I am your wife and you need to start opening up to me. I told you I've already accepted the fact you were in love with this girl so why can't you tell me what happened? Or do you want me to guess?"

"You couldn't even begin to guess," he grumbled.

"Oh, but I think I can." She sat up next to him, pulling her knees up to her chest and hugging them as she spoke. "You fell in love with one of the ladies while you were at court."

His silver eyes shot over to her and then the other way. But not before she saw his secrets revealed.

"You did love her," she said, feeling like she understood everything now. "But you didn't want someone to know, did you?"

"Ruby, mayhap we should go." He motioned to leave, but her hand shot out and stilled him.

"I'm not done yet," she said, causing his eyebrows to arch in surprise.

"Is my untamed gem back again?" he asked.

"She never left and never will, she's just been on good behavior."

"Aye," he said. "I guess so."

"My guess is that you bedded the girl and the king did too."

"Ruby, I didn't know she was the king's mistress. She didn't tell me, or I never would have done such a thing."

"Ah ha, so I am right!"

"I can't hide anything from you, my little busybody. He reached out and kissed her on the head.

"You think Tibbar is your child, don't you? That's why you've taken such an interest in him."

"I don't know," he said, and she felt the sincerity in his words.

"The king doesn't know either, does he?"

"Obviously not. If so, I would be executed right now like the last man he found in his lover's bed."

"But you have a strong alliance with the king," she said. "He entrusted you with his bastard, so you don't have to worry."

"That's what worries me the most. I really don't want to disappoint him."

"You can tell him what you told me. That you didn't know."

"Oh, Ruby, I don't want to talk about this anymore. Please."

"I understand," she said. "But just tell me one thing. Can't you find out from this Jocelyn if you are truly the father of the baby?"

"I don't know where she is since the king banished her," he told her. "And even if I did, she proved to be naught more than a trollop so I doubt that she would even know the answer to that."

"Nyle, do you think Ascilia would know where to find her?"

"I don't care, Ruby. Now like I told you before, I don't want to hear another word about it. This is our time together as husband and wife and I want us to enjoy it."

"You are right. Me too." She got up and looked over to the waterfall. "Last one there changes Tibbar's swaddling for a sennight." She pushed him back down as he tried to rise, and ran laughing to the water's edge and dived in. She swam as hard as she could, hearing Nyle right behind her.

"You cheat," he said, diving under the water, and when she looked back he was gone. Then when she felt his fingers slip between her thighs she knew exactly where he was.

She stopped swimming and dove beneath the water, reaching out to do the same to him, but he just smiled and backed away quickly and disappeared.

She popped up from the water and her eyes scanned the area, and then she saw him standing naked like a sea god in the midst of the waterfall as it crashed down around him.

"Who cheats?" she said, swimming to join him.

"Have fun with the dirty swaddlings," he said, jumping into the water to join her. He wrapped his arms around her and the water rained down over them as they once more made love right there in nature. Ruby enjoyed their time together so much that she almost dreaded going back to the castle where as soon as she stepped foot inside the walls she would once again be shadowed by guards and have to also fear for her life.

Chapter 18

It had been nearly a week since their little trip to the waterfall, and Ruby had almost forgotten about the guards posted outside her door or following her everywhere she went.

She'd spent much time with Linette and Oralie in the ladies solar. And since Tibbar had yet to walk, they were able to keep an eye on him as they sewed and wove tapestries while he crawled around the floor. She'd even asked Ascilia where to find Lady Jocelyn, but the handmaiden seemed upset by the question and told her that she didn't know. Ascilia had seemed distant and sad since the day Ruby plopped the baby in her arms. The woman had something deeply troubling her, but Ruby was yet to discover what.

Linette shared her handmaid with Ruby, but truth was that neither of them really needed her. If Ruby had been as helpless at taking care of herself as most ladies, she would have gotten a replacement for her own handmaiden, Oralie. But things were working out fine. Still, she knew Oralie was far from being healed and Linette had announced that she would be leaving and going back to Scotland soon.

Ascilia excused herself, and with head down she left the ladies solar.

"Ruby," said Linette, "I do think whoever is after you is gone now, as no attempts have been made on your life in a while. But I still don't understand why someone is trying to kill you. How could anyone not like you?"

"Well, Nyle could probably give you a few reasons, although we have been getting along beautifully lately. I think I will have to talk to Nyle about removing all the guards. Actually, I already dismissed the ones from the solar door. I figured as long as I was in here with the rest of the women I was safe and there was no need for them to stand there. I told them to come back this afternoon when we are finished."

"And my brother agreed to that?" she asked curiously.

"Well, he actually doesn't know about it," Ruby admitted, pulling her needle with a long thread through the cloth. She admired her handiwork and nodded, realizing she was improving at stitching.

"I'm surprised the guards left," said Linette. "After all, they know how adamant Nyle is about security."

"Well, actually, I had to tell a little lie. They think the order came from Nyle."

"You shouldn't have done that," warned Linette.

"I felt so sorry for them standing there all day without even having anything to eat or drink, so I sent them to the kitchen. What does it matter?" she asked. "They won't be gone long."

She looked out the window, hearing the cry of the falcon, and realized she had forgotten about her special appointment for a lesson in falconry with Darby today. The falconer, Bertram, had approached her just this morning telling her that her lesson would be early this morning instead of in the late afternoon.

"Oh, I almost forgot, I have to go to the mews," she said, getting up and putting her stitching in a basket by her feet. Tibbar crawled over to inspect it and she pulled it away and handed it to Linette.

"I thought your lesson was later," said Linette.

"It usually is, but for some reason I guess Darby needed to reschedule for this morning. You should see the progress I'm making with Jibbs."

"Jibbs?" she asked, reaching out for the baby.

"My falcon," she reminded her. "You really should come watch some day."

"Did you want me to go with you?" Linette asked.

She opened the door and looked out, realizing no one would be shadowing her, and she liked the idea. She'd welcome having Linette along, but she knew the ladies were just finishing up the tapestry and she didn't want to take her away at this time. Besides, Tibbar was starting to get restless and while Oralie loved the child she just didn't have the same touch as Linette.

"No, I will be fine. After all, it's just Darby I'll be with, and we both know he is harmless. I rather like the boy."

"Aye, so do I."

She bid Linette goodbye and kissed Tibbar atop the head. Then she headed out of the keep and over the courtyard. She was late so she hurried, not stopping to talk to anyone along the way. She poked her head inside the mews and looked around in the darkness, but did not see him. She took a step inside and called out his name. "Darby? Are you in here? 'Tis Lady Ruby," she said, "I am here for my lesson."

She heard a slight noise from the back of the mews, and went back to investigate. She saw a cloaked person standing there with something in his hand and at first thought it was Darby. That is, until she realized it was the falconer coming toward her with the look of a madman in his eyes, and a club in his hand that he was raising above her head.

"Lady Ruby? Are you in here?"

She heard Darby's voice from behind her and shouted out. "Help me," she said, just as the club from the falconer came down to hit her. She tried to dive out of the way, but he still managed to graze her across the back of her shoulders. She fell to the ground and hit her head against a wooden brace. Feeling dazed and lightheaded, she looked up to see the falconer coming after her, and she found herself instinctively reaching for her dagger. When her hand came up empty, she realized she no longer carried her dagger and because of this she just might lose her life.

Locke shot forward through the darkness just then with his sword drawn, and she noticed Darby right behind him.

That's all she remembered before her world went black around her and her eyes closed, removing everything from sight.

* * *

Nyle rode over the drawbridge of the castle and in to the courtyard, having had accompanied the reeve and the bailiff on his demesne as he settled the villeins dispute over a pig and a patch of land. He'd also seen to collecting unpaid taxes and giving his approval for a serf to marry. 'Twas time consuming, and after checking the status of the crops and paying a visit to inspect the granary as well, it took up his entire morning. He had hated to leave Ruby once again, but he had his manor to run and had no choice. At least he knew she was in the ladies solar sewing this morning and that his guards were posted outside the door so she'd be safe.

"Lord Sheffield, Lord Sheffield, come quickly."

His eyes shot over to the mews where the falconer's apprentice was running toward him and waving his arms wildly. He couldn't imagine what the boy wanted.

"Lord Sheffield, your wife is in danger, she needs your help!"

"What the hell!" He jumped from his horse and pulled his sword as he ran toward the mews with his heart beating rapidly. He had no idea what the boy was talking about, but had a sinking feeling in his gut that Ruby was not in the solar with the ladies where he had left her this morning.

"Out of my way," he shouted, rushing past the boy and into the mews. He heard noises from the back of the building and ran up to see Locke with his sword drawn and under the chin of the falconer, Bertram. The falconer was a big man, but was prone on the ground and had his hands raised above his head.

"God's eyes, Locke, what is going on?" asked Nyle.

"Well, he thought he could take me down since I only had one good arm," said Locke. "But I showed him that I had two good feet as well, and here he is!"

"Where's Ruby?" he asked, his eyes scanning the grounds. Then he saw her lying in a heap a short distance away on the ground. He ran to her and dropped to his knees.

"Ruby, sweetheart, are you all right?" he asked. She moaned and opened her eyes slowly and Nyle could feel the swelling at the back of her neck.

"We walked in to find ol' Bertram here trying to club her down," relayed Darby from behind him.

"Good thing I saw her coming this way when we got back from town," said Locke. "I followed her and kept an eye on her just like you told me to, Lord Sheffield."

"Why aren't you in the ladies solar sewing?" asked Nyle, helping Ruby to a sitting position.

She sat up and rubbed her head. "The falconer told me Darby wanted to have a lesson this morning," she relayed.

"That's not true," said the boy. "Lord Sheffield, I had naught to do with this, I assure you. I would never do anything to harm your wife."

"That's true," said Locke. "Besides, he was with me all morning."

Nyle got up and stormed over to the falconer, pulling him up by the neck of the tunic. He slammed him into the wall, grabbing his dagger from his waist and holding it to the man's neck. "You worked for my father for years," said Nyle. "Why would you try to kill my wife?"

"I needed the money," he said. "I didn't really want to do it, but my family is poor and I have many children to feed, my lord. I honestly didn't want to harm her. I had no choice."

"Of course you had a choice. Why didn't you just tell me you needed money, and I could have helped you out?"

"I don't know, my lord, I am sorry."

"Sorry isn't going to get you out of this mess. You will be executed for this, but not before you tell me who paid you money to kill my wife."

He just shook his head and clamped his mouth shut. "I can't. If I do, my family will be harmed. I am sorry, but I just can't tell you."

"Then I'll just kill you right now you bloody bastard!"

"Nyle, no," came Ruby's soft voice from behind him. "He has a family and children. He needs your help, please don't kill him."

"He tried to kill you, Ruby. You don't know what you're saying."

He turned to see a crowd of people rushing into the mews. In came several of his men, and right behind them was his sister and her handmaid.

"Oh my goodness!" shouted Linette, rushing over to Ruby. "Are you all right?" she asked, collecting her into her arms.

The crowd gathered around, waiting for Nyle to do something. As much as he wanted to kill the man, he needed him alive in order to find out who was behind this.

"Tell me now, who hired you?" he asked the falconer. The man looked out to the crowd of people and his eyes widened in fear. He just shook his head.

"Nay. I will never tell you."

"Take him to the dungeon," said Nyle lowering his dagger and pushing the man forward. Several of his guards grabbed hold of him and dragged him through the mews as he struggled against him. The birds were all frightened and squawked and fluttered their wings from atop the posts.

"Everyone out of here!" Nyle shouted, making his way to help his wife to her feet. "Why the hell did the guards let you leave the solar in the first place?" he ground out.

"Oh, Nyle, I am sorry," said Ruby with tears in her eyes. "I told them to go. They thought that you gave the order. I didn't think I was in danger any longer or I wouldn't have done it."

"Well, obviously you were. Now don't do something so

stupid again." He looked to her waist belt where her dagger should have been, but knew that she had refused to wear it since she'd killed a man. "From now on you will always wear a dagger at your waist, like it or not."

"I won't touch that murderous dagger again," she told him. "Please, I can't."

"Then I'll get you another and you will wear it. And you will never go anywhere without someone with you as well as several guards at your side until I find the person behind all this, do you understand?"

"I do," she said, holding her head.

"Linette, take her to the great hall and have the healer look at her," he said. "Make sure you stay with her and don't let her out of your sight until I get there."

"Aye, brother," she answered, helping Ruby to walk through the darkened mews.

"Guards, go with," he ordered his men who were standing there as well.

"Aye," they answered and headed away with Ruby.

"I will stay with her as well," said Ascilia, walking behind them.

For some reason, that did not make Nyle feel safe. He didn't like the woman and couldn't wait until she left.

"Look at this," said Darby, pulling something from beneath the hay. He handed it to Nyle.

"This is a pouch with the king's crest on it," he said. He opened it and reached inside and brought forth a whole handful of gold coins.

"What is that?" asked Locke, looking over his shoulder.

"It's the motivation to kill a woman to help feed one's family," replied Nyle.

"Who do you think would pay that much to have

someone killed off?" asked Darby, surveying the fistful of gold.

"Someone who has a lot to lose by letting one of my wives live," he said under his breath.

"Like who?" asked Locke.

"I have an idea," he said, "but first I want to see if I can get more information out of the falconer."

"Let's go," said Locke, putting his sword back in his belt.

"There is something else I am going to need to do as well and very soon," said Nyle.

"What would that be, my lord?"

"I want my wife to be able to protect herself and for that, I need to buy her a dagger."

"We have many daggers in the armory," said Locke. "You don't need to buy one."

"She won't wear a dagger that may have killed someone," he said. "She is having some odd guilt feelings after what happened, and I'm not sure how long it'll last. Besides, she is my wife and I have never even given her a wedding ring. Nay, Locke, I need to find her a suitable dagger that is meant for a very special lady."

Chapter 19

Ruby's head and the back of her neck hurt like hell, and instead of going to the great hall, she had Linette take her to her solar so she could lie down. Ascilia said she would find the healer and send him up, and Ruby wanted nothing more than to just go to sleep for the rest of the day. She was sorry now she had gone against Nyle's wishes and sent the guards away. She realized it was a stupid move that had almost cost her her life. She also knew she should have had a dagger at her side to protect herself, yet she couldn't bring herself to carry one yet since that awful day.

"Linette, I have done Nyle wrong one too many times," she said, climbing atop the bed with her gown still on, and not caring.

"Ruby, you could have been killed today, what were you thinking?"

"I'm not sure," she said, laying her head back on the pillow and closing her eyes. "But all I know is that I can't live like this anymore."

"I agree, but I don't know what the answer is, do you?"

"Nay. But all I know is that Nyle is going to be so angry now, that that poor falconer doesn't have a chance of not being executed."

"Well, he should be. Ruby, he tried to kill you."

"Aye," she said. "I understand. Still, I can't help feeling sorry for him. He said he was only protecting his family, and is still doing that now by keeping quiet. Nyle will never get the answer out of him that he needs. I need to go try talking to him." She started to push up from the bed, but she dizzied and lay back down. The healer came into the room and stepped forward, opening his bag.

"Linette, go to the dungeon for me and try to get the falconer to talk."

"But that's not my place to do that," she said.

"Do it for me," she begged her. "Please, you need to get there before Nyle, or there is no telling what will happen."

"I can't leave you alone," she said. "My brother will have my head."

"I'm not alone, the healer is with me," she said motioning to the man. "Besides, Ascilia will be back soon, so I'll be fine."

"All right," she said. "I'll try, but I can't promise anything."

"Thank you," she said with a smile, moving her hair to the side so the healer could see her wound.

* * *

By the time Nyle had made it to the dungeon, he had been stopped and interrupted five times. He knew everyone wanted to know if they were safe, and there were things that needed to be taken care of, but he didn't have time for this right now.

He pushed open the door to the dungeon, nodding at the guards as he passed. Locke followed right behind him.

"Where is the falconer?" he asked, already heading down the passageway with cells on both sides.

"In the last cell, my lord," called out one of the guards.

The dungeon was dark and damp, and the air hung heavy with the smell of death. The sound of dripping water from overhead seemed loud as it echoed off the stone walls. A rat ran past him, and turned back to look at him, its beady eyes glowing in the firelight flickering from a torch stuck into the wall. He knew that this was not a place that even he ever wanted to visit.

He made his way to the last cell, and could see the shape of the man huddled in the corner. He looked to be slouched over a tray of food and a cup was in his hand.

"All right, I'll ask you again. Who paid you to kill my wife?" Nyle said to the falconer.

The man's head raised slightly and his hollowed eyes looked toward Nyle. Something about him just didn't seem quite right.

"Speak," he said, but the falconer just looked into his cup and let it slip from his hand. It fell to the ground, with the liquid spilling out in a puddle around his feet.

"Go get the guard with the keys," Nyle instructed Locke. "Something is wrong."

"Right away, my lord." The sound of Locke's shoes against the stone echoed through the chamber as he hurried away to do as ordered

"Bertram," said Nyle, already getting a twisting feeling

in his gut. "Talk to me!"

The man's eyes rolled back in his head and his face became very pale. Then he slouched forward, and fell to the ground, his hand settling right next to the fallen cup.

Nyle had seen this look before, and it was on the face of his deceased wife who had been poisoned. "Nay!" He took hold of the bars of the door and shook them violently. "Don't you dare die, dammit, do you hear me?"

Locke and the guard made their way back to him, and Nyle shouted. "Hurry up and open this damn door!"

The guard twisted the key in the lock, the iron door creaking on its hinges as he pulled it open. Nyle lunged forward, dropping to his knees and flipping the man over, trying one more time to desperately get the information he needed before the secret identity of the assassin was gone forever.

"Who was it?" he shouted, shaking the man until his teeth chattered together in his head. "Who was it, I ask you that wants my wife dead? Tell me, dammit I have to know."

He'd get no answers from this man now, as he was already departed from this world.

Locke rushed in after him and started to pick up the cup but Nyle stopped him.

"Leave it," he ordered. "The man was poisoned." He let go of the dead man and let him drop to the ground.

"Poisoned?" Linette stood behind him with her hand on the cell door, and she was the last person he wanted to see at that moment.

"I thought I told you to stay with Ruby. Why the hell can't anyone do as ordered?"

"She's fine," said Linette. "The healer was just finishing up and Ascilia is on her way to the room so Ruby won't be alone."

"Who do think poisoned him?" asked Locke.

Nyle just shook his head. Once again, a murder had taken place right under his nose, and someone was always one step ahead of him. He'd never felt such rage within as he did right now.

"Who brought him the food?" he asked.

"One of the kitchen servants," said the guard. "A very young girl."

"And the wine too?" He got to his feet as he spoke.

"Oh no," said the guard. "That was brought by the old woman."

"Old woman?" He looked over to the guard. "Which old woman?"

"I don't know her name," said the guard, "but she is the one who came to the castle with your sister."

"Ascilia!" both Linette and Nyle said at the same time.

"Didn't you just say she was going to Ruby's room?" asked Nyle.

"Oh my God," said Linette. "I had no idea, or I never would have left to come question the falconer by Ruby's request."

"Damn, that girl," he said, not having had her upset him this much since the day she ripped his cape and threw it in the mud. "Let's go," he said, rushing out the door. "And I only hope we are not too late this time."

Chapter 20

Ruby was asleep, having taken an herbal concoction from the healer before he left. He said it would help her relax and heal, and she knew it was working. She'd tasted the chamomile in the elixir and it always made her sleepy.

The door to the room squeaked open, and the next thing she knew there was a hand on her shoulder shaking her. Pain shot through her shoulder and she bolted upright.

"Oh, Ascilia," she said, relieved to see the handmaiden and not another assassin. "I was sleeping. Why did you wake me?"

"Because I just saw the healer in the corridor and he told me you need to drink the rest of the potion in order for it to work."

Ascilia seemed to be swirling the contents in the cup before she handed it to her.

"Thank you," said Ruby, sitting up and taking the cup in her hand. She brought it to her mouth but stopped when she saw the eyes of the handmaiden watching her intently.

"Sit on the bed and talk to me," said Ruby. When the

woman didn't do it, Ruby put the cup on the bedside table and held out her hand. "Please," she said. "I feel I need to talk to you."

The woman reached out slowly, taking Ruby's hand and settling herself upon the bed.

"What do you want?" she asked.

"I just wanted to say that I noticed the way you looked at the baby the other day when I handed him to you."

"It meant nothing." She jumped up and grasped the bedpost.

"Have you ever been in love?" she asked the woman.

"Why do you want to know?"

"Because I see such a loneliness in your eyes that it makes me want to cry. I think you have once loved and lost that love and that is why you are sad."

"Nay, that's not true."

"Isn't it?"

The woman didn't answer at first, but then she spoke in a soft voice. "I did love someone once, but it was long ago. And I didn't really know it until it was too late."

"What happened to him?" Ruby asked.

"I made a mistake or two and before I knew it, he wanted naught to do with me."

"I know the feeling. That sounds just like Nyle and myself lately. Was your lover anything like Nyle?" she asked. "Was he as handsome as my wonderful husband?"

The woman's face clouded over and Ruby thought she saw a tear in her eye. She just stared into the air and slowly nodded.

"Why didn't you try to get him back?"

"He wouldn't want me, so it doesn't really matter."

"How would you know that?" she asked.

"Because I was once beautiful, but one day I fell into the fire and my face was so burned that I was no longer recognizable."

"If this man truly loved you, then he would see past that and to your inner beauty. Kind of like the way Nyle sees past my rough and unpolished exterior to the love I hold in my heart. I know little about being a lady nor about being his wife, though I am learning. I think that is why he tolerates me."

"I have no inner beauty," she said. "I am ugly both inside and out and I hate myself so much every day that I no longer want to live."

"Don't say that," said Ruby. "Life is a precious thing and to be cherished, not to be thrown away. Nyle was married three times before me and those innocent women all lost their lives by the hand of a crazed killer."

"Mayhap they deserved it." Her voice took on a hard edge that Ruby did not understand.

"No one deserves to die," she told her. "Not even that falconer who only tried to kill me because he cared so much for his family that he would do anything at all to help his wife and children."

"Nay! How can you say that?" the handmaid shouted. "He tried to kill you."

"He did, but I forgive him. And I am only happy that I did not die from my own foolishness, as I love my husband as well as that baby so much, that I am sure my death would have affected them both in horrible ways that I don't even want to imagine."

"What do you mean?" she asked.

Ruby smiled and sat up straighter, picking up the goblet with her medicine as she spoke. "If Nyle doesn't have a wife he can't have little Tibbar. And between you and me, I think that baby is really his, don't you? After all they look so much alike and he loves the boy so much. Even if Tibbar isn't his, I am sure he would love him and raise him as his own. He would take better care of that child than he would of himself."

"Do you really think so?" she asked softly.

"I know so," she said. "Nyle is a wonderful father and would treat any child he had like a king." She raised the cup to her mouth to drink, but the handmaid jumped forward and knocked it from her hand. The contents dumped onto the front of Ruby's gown and she took a sharp intake of breath. "Why did you do that?" she said, feeling angry with the woman.

"Because you would treat that baby like a king too, I can see that now. And you love Nyle, and I know by the look in his eyes he loves you too. You are right about everything you said. I knocked that cup from your hands because you don't deserve to die either."

"What do mean?" Ruby gasped, suddenly realizing that the words coming from Ascilia's mouth sounded as if she'd meant to kill her. She noticed an odd smell in the spilled liquid and the realization hit her that it must be poison. "You were trying to kill me," she said, scooting back on the bed hoping to make distance between them. "And you were the one to kill all those other people as well, weren't you?"

"I wish I could deny it, but I can't," said Ascilia. "And for what I've done, I am the one who doesn't deserve to live."

The door to the solar burst open just then and Nyle ran in with his sword drawn. Locke and Sir Godin were right behind them with their weapons at the ready as well. Linette followed behind them.

"Get away from my wife," Nyle ground out, taking a step forward, the tip of his sword just under Ascilia's throat. Nyle was relieved he had gotten there in time and that Ruby was still alive. "Don't drink anything, Ruby. This murderous bitch has just poisoned the falconer."

"Nay!" she said. "That man said he had a family and many children."

"Who are you, really? Nyle backed the woman toward the window with the tip of his sword. "And why are you trying to kill my wife?"

The handmaid stumbled and caught herself, grasping onto the table that held the basin of water. When she righted herself, Nyle noticed something he'd not noticed before this day. Her sleeve rode up and revealed a strawberry birthmark on her inner right arm. The only birthmark he'd ever seen like this, belonged to one woman. It couldn't be. He lowered the tip of his sword slightly, and cocked his head.

"Jocelyn?" he asked, feeling the name of his ex-lover lodged in his throat.

"Jocelyn? Your lover?" he heard Ruby ask in shock from the bed.

"Nay," said the handmaid, shaking her head and backing away from him toward the window. "Nay, it's not."

"Then let's just see who the hell you really are under all that, shall we?" Nyle threw down his sword and reached out and pulled her toward him. He ripped the wimple from her head and with it came a crop of fake black hair that looked like horse tail. Under it was hair of golden silk.

He shook his head, not wanting to believe it was her. He grabbed a hold of her hair in one hand and dunked her face in the basin of water, pulling it upward to reveal that the wrinkles and signs of old age had washed off.

Her face was unrecognizable, burned and scarred, as if she had been in a fire. But her eyes gave her away and he wondered why he hadn't realized it the first day he saw her arrive with his sister. Her bright blue eyes, so much like little Tibbar's bore into him and brought back with it all the memories and all the pain of the past.

"Nay!" he said, shaking his head and still not wanting to believe it. "Jocelyn, what happened to you?"

"I was burned in a fire and am hideous," she said, holding up her hand and turning her head to shield her face from him. "I am hideous both inside and out now, as you know I am the one behind all the murders."

"But why?" he asked her. "Why the hell would you do such a thing?"

"I did it for family," she said, for some reason looking over to Ruby when she said it. "I did it because I wanted my baby to have a good life. A life I could never give him. I knew the king could give him that life, and that's why your wives had to die, in order to keep the king from handing over the baby to you."

"You knew he ordered me to have a wife, and you tried to keep the baby from me? You never cared a bit about that baby," Nyle shouted. "You never held it nor paid it any attention at all. All you cared about was your looks and luring men to your bed. Especially me. I curse the day I ever let you lure me into your little trap. You had me so enamored that I fooled myself into thinking I loved you. But I never loved you, Jocelyn. I know that now, because I found out what love really is when I married my wonderful wife, Ruby."

"I made some mistakes," she said, backing away from him as he moved closer. "And I must admit, another reason I killed your wives was because I could not bear to see you married to anyone but me, and I had to stop it. I thought I was doing the right thing paying off people to carry out the results I needed, but now after talking with Ruby, I see that I was wrong."

"I'll say. And you will pay for those mistakes with your life, as I cannot allow you to live after what you've done."

"No, Nyle, please," Ruby begged him from the bed.

"Ruby, stay out of this. I mean it," he said over his shoulder. "You have no idea the life of hell this woman has put me through, as well as the families of the people she's murdered."

"You said you loved me once," said Jocelyn. "Can't you look past all this for what we had together?"

"I may have thought I loved you at one time, Jocelyn, but that was my mistake. We had nothing together, I tell you. Nothing! I despise you more than you'll ever know. And now I want to hear the truth from your damned mouth. Is the baby mine or is it the king's or perhaps someone else's?"

She just shook her head and backed up to the wall next to the window. "Ruby is a wonderful woman," she said. "I know you love the baby and will take care of him better than the king would," she said. "Ruby showed me that. She loves the baby as well, and she also loves you."

"Whose baby is it, Jocelyn? I am losing my patience."

"Thank you, Ruby, for helping me find the answers inside myself. I only wish I had known you years ago. Goodbye."

"Goodbye?" asked Ruby from next to him.

Nyle watched Jocelyn reach for the window and turn

quickly, and he knew what she intended to do.

"Nay!" he cried out, rushing forward and reaching for her, but all he could see were her troubled blue eyes disappearing over the edge of the window as she jumped out and plunged to her death.

He got to the window, grabbing for her, but his hand just came up empty. He looked over the edge and saw her gown fluttering in the breeze as her body plummeted to the ground and crashed against the rocks along the way.

"She's gone," he said, shaking his head, still not able to comprehend any of this.

Ruby turned him away from the window and wrapped her arms around him in a hug. Nyle clung to her and kissed her atop the head, feeling relieved that Ruby would not be threatened again. His past was gone now and his future was standing before him. He felt sad as well as the happiest man in the world all at the same time.

Chapter 21

Ruby stood over the graves of Nyle's father and mother, with little Tibbar sleeping in her arms against her chest. They had traveled for two full days to get to the church of St. Agnes where Nyle's family was buried. The traveling had been slow coming from Sheffield, as they had the baby along as well as Oralie with her injured leg, and had to take a wagon. A half dozen of Nyle's guards traveled with them for protection, but Ruby knew that there would be no one else trying to kill her now that Jocelyn was dead.

She felt sorry in a way for the girl even though she had done horrible things. But she could see in her eyes before she jumped from the ledge of the window that she had held love for Nyle somewhere in her black heart.

Nyle had been quiet on the journey here and she knew he needed time to himself to think things over. He'd been through a lot lately, and now he worried what was going to happen to Tibbar once he received his next missive from the king. He believed that he'd receive it any day now.

Linette stood next to Nyle wiping tears from her eyes as a priest from the church said a short prayer over the gravestones of their parents and brother. The church was atop a steep cliff that overlooked the sea. Ruby closed her eyes and held her face up to the sun and delighted in the fresh breeze that flowed past them. She was excited, as after this stop, Nyle had promised her that they would be able to spend some time with her sisters and her father. Since the gravesite was close to Blackpool, they were going to stop for a visit.

"Well, this is where we part," said Linette, coming to Ruby's side as soon as the priest had finished. "I am going back to the Highlands now, and can only say that I am so glad to have met my brother's wonderful wife." She ran a hand over the baby's back as he slept. "I only hope I'll have the opportunity of seeing Tibbar again some day as well."

"I hope things work out and Nyle will be able to keep him," said Ruby. "He has grown so fond of him, and I have too, that we already feel like a family."

"I wish you the best," Linette said, and Ruby already missed her as she had become her best friend.

"Are you sure you won't come with us to Blackpool to meet my family?" she asked. "You know you are welcome."

"Mayhap next time," said Linette with a sad smile. "My husband is hopefully coming home soon, and I miss him dearly."

"I understand," she said, smiling at her own husband. "I never thought I'd feel this way about a man I once despised."

"I never despised my husband," said Linette. "Nor could I ever have married someone I didn't love."

"Well, things don't always turn out the way you expect them to," said Ruby. "Just remember that, as some day it may help you to get through a hard time."

"I will, thank you."

"Sister, I will miss you dearly," said Nyle, embracing

Linette in a tight hug and kissing her upon the cheek.

"Take good care of Ruby and the baby," she said. "I'll expect to see you all again soon."

"I only hope the king will decide not to claim the baby," said Nyle.

"Would you keep him even without knowing if he were truly yours?" asked Linette.

"I was very upset when Jocelyn took her life without revealing to me the truth about who sired the baby," he admitted. "But in reality, she's had so many lovers in her bed she probably didn't even know. I decided I don't care one way or another, as I will fight to keep Tibbar with me always, as I already feel as if I am his father."

"You'd fight the king?" asked Linette. "Brother, you are addled."

"Well, I didn't actually mean that literally," he said with a smile.

"Well, hopefully it won't come to that," Ruby broke in. "You realize, sometimes things just end up working themselves out and it is for the best."

They said their goodbyes and Nyle put his arm around Ruby as they watched Linette and her small entourage head back for the Highlands.

"Can we go to Blackpool and see my family now?" Ruby asked anxiously, feeling her excitement growing. "They will be expecting us since we sent the messenger two days before we left."

"We will see them shortly," he said, guiding her toward the wagon. "But first we have a stop to make in town on the way there, as there is something I'd like to buy for my wife."

"Let me guess - a new dagger?" she asked with a smile.

"I need to know you will always have a way of

protecting yourself." He took the baby from her and handed him to Oralie inside the wagon. "I never want to go through the hell of thinking my wife is going to be killed again. I know you can protect yourself because I've seen you do it. So with a dagger at your side I can rest easier at night."

"You are right," she said. "But if you don't mind, I will stay in the cart with Oralie and the baby instead of helping you choose it. Because no dagger will ever suffice, or be able to compare to my ruby dagger that I had when I was a child.

* * *

Nyle walked through the streets of Blackpool with Locke at his side. He never thought it would be such a hard chore choosing a dagger for Ruby. But after what she'd told him, every dagger he'd been shown seemed inadequate for such a wonderful wife.

He adjusted his signet ring on his finger as he walked, also feeling like the devil for not even getting her a proper ring. But towns such as this would never have a ring suitable for her and he would just wait til the next time he went to London and hopefully have one of the finest quality rings constructed for her there.

"Are you going to get a dagger or walk around aimlessly until the sun sets?" asked Locke as they made their way towards Grope Street. Nyle knew this was the street of whores and thieves and beggars and not much more. He didn't want anything that they'd be selling down this alley.

"There's no need to go down Grope," he told Locke. "Let's just head back to the cart as I know Ruby is becoming impatient and is anxious to get to her father's castle."

"All right," said Locke, looking toward the back of the pub part way down the street. "But I need to piss, so give me a minute. I see a dark corner. I'll be right back."

"Hurry," he told him, wandering down the street while he waited, looking at nothing in particular.

"Can ye spare a coin milord?" came the voice of a little boy behind him.

Nyle turned to see a bedraggled young boy with messed hair and dirt streaked across his face. His eyes were sunken and his body thin, and he had no shoes upon his feet. Nyle reached into his pouch and gave him a shilling. Before he knew it, he was surrounded by beggars and he felt a tug on his pouch and knew they were trying to steal his money.

"Stop it, you thieves," he told them, then realized they were naught but children. He saw something in their eyes that he saw every time he looked into Tibbar's eyes as well. He wondered if these children knew who their parents were, or if their parents even took care of them, because it didn't seem like it. "What the hell," he said, reaching into his pouch and pulling out a fistful of coins. "Help yourselves," he said throwing the coins down the street. They hit the cobbled stones with a light tinkling noise and then started to roll as Grope Street was downhill. The beggar children squealed and chased after the coins, trying to catch them, but every time they reached down, the coins continued to roll.

"That'll keep them busy for awhile," he chuckled.

"That was kind of you, my lord," said a woman's old crackly voice from behind him. He turned to see a woman older than he'd ever seen in his life and with many wrinkles she looked like a prune. She tilted her cloudy eyes upward and as the last sunrays of the day reflected within them, he realized she was blind.

"I'm sorry I have no more coins in my pouch," he told her. "But if you come back to my wagon I'll gladly give you money as well."

"I am not begging," she said with a sharpness to her tone that made Nyle feel as though he'd insulted her.

"I apologize. 'Tis my mistake."

"I heard you say to your squire you were looking for a dagger for your wife."

"I am," he said, "but I can't find a suitable one at all."

"I have daggers," she said, holding up a pouch and shaking it so he could hear clanking from within.

"Oh, thank you, but I don't think you have what I'm looking for." He started to walk away, and heard her call out behind him.

"Sometimes things don't always turn out the way you expect them to."

He stopped in his tracks and turned around. "That is odd you should say that," he told her. "My wife, Ruby, just told that to my sister not an hour ago."

"Ruby?" she asked. "I have a dagger that would be suitable for your wife named Ruby."

"Oh, I don't think so," he said with a laugh. "She has one dagger only on her mind and that disappeared years ago. It had a jewel in the hilt and was very ornate and expensive. I don't think I'll find one of those in Grope alley."

She reached into her bag and felt around and then held one up for him to see. "This is a ruby, so she may like it."

Nyle was surprised that she knew it was a ruby though she was blind, or that she would even possess such a thing. "Let me see that," he said reaching out to take it, and when he did, her hand covered his and her fingers ran across his ring.

"That is a very expensive ring," she said as he flipped the dagger over inspecting it. His heart beat faster as he realized this sounded similar to the one Ruby had lost years ago. He wondered if it would please her.

"It was my father's ring," he said, still inspecting the dagger.

"Silver?"

"Nay, gold. How much for this dagger?" he asked. "This sounds like the one my wife lost as a child and I think she would like it."

"She lost it as a child?"

"Well, actually, her father discarded it after the death of her mother, but 'tis a long story. I'll take the dagger, so how much do I owe you?"

"I thought you just said you had no coin on you."

"I don't, but I have more back at the wagon, if you'll follow me."

"Nay," she said, reaching out and taking the dagger from his hand. "This dagger is not for sale."

"What do you mean?" he asked. "Why did you show it to me if you weren't going to let me have it?"

"Do you love this wife named Ruby?" the old woman asked him.

"Aye," he answered. "I do."

"And have you told her?"

He hadn't, but he was waiting for the right moment. He'd been thinking a lot on the trip here and realized that he'd been afraid to love because of what happened to him in the past. But he did love Ruby and would tell her soon.

"Look, old lady, this is none of your business."

"Oh, but it is. You see, this dagger can only be given to you if you are her true love."

Ruby

"I told you I love her, now are you going to sell it to me or not?"

"This dagger cannot be bought because it has already been sold."

"Sold? To whom?"

"That, too, is a long story," she told him. "But I will give you the dagger if you give me your ring in exchange."

"My ring?" He held his hand over his ring, knowing that he hadn't taken it off his finger since the day he'd come back to Sheffield. It was his last remembrance of his father. It meant a lot to him and he wasn't about to give it to a blind old woman. "Oh, no, I couldn't do that. Besides, this ring is worth much more than that dagger."

"You can't put a price on true love," she told him.

"What the hell does that mean?" he asked, but the old hag just smiled a broken-toothed smile.

"Lord Sheffield, I'm over here," Locke called out from behind him and Nyle saw him heading over from the wagon. "Lady Ruby would like to leave now as it is getting dark."

"Give me a second," he said, and turned back toward the hag. "Is there any way I can give you coin for the dagger, please?"

"Nay," she said. "The only thing I'll take is that ring which you love so much that you won't part with it for the woman you say you love."

"I do love her," he said. "And this ring means naught to me at all." The ring did mean a lot to him, but she didn't need to know. That was probably why she wanted it.

"Then prove your love for your wife and trade that ring for this dagger." She held it up in front of his face and he could see the ruby glittering in the setting sun.

"Lord Sheffield," Locke called from behind him, and

Nyle noticed him walking down the street toward him.

He turned back one last time toward the hag. "My wife, Ruby, means more to me than all the money in the world. Take the ring," he said, slipping it from his finger and putting it in the woman's palm. "But please give me the dagger as I think this would make her very happy."

"You've proved to me you really are her true love," she said and smiled. "Here is your dagger, and I know she will be happy to see it returned."

"Returned?"

"Lord Sheffield, who are you talking to?" Nyle spun around to see Locke standing there. "Oh, you found a dagger, that's beautiful. Where did you get it?" asked Locke.

"From this blind old hag," he said, turning around, but to his surprise the woman was nowhere to be found. He peered down the dark street wondering how she had moved so quickly in the dark.

"I don't see any old hag," said Locke. "Are you sure you are not feeling ill, my lord?"

"I am sure. I traded her my signet ring for the dagger as she would not let me buy it." He held up his bare hand to show him, already feeling naked without it.

"Not your ring," said Locke in disappointment. "That was worth much more than the dagger."

"No," he said, running a hand over the dagger, knowing how happy it would make Ruby. "I think this dagger is worth more than that ring after all. Now don't say anything to her yet, as I want to wait and surprise her after we get to her father's castle."

Chapter 22

Ruby was very excited when they rode over the drawbridge and through the gate into the courtyard of Blackpool Castle. So excited, that she rode ahead of the entourage and dismounted, seeing her sisters standing there waiting for her right inside the gate.

"Ruby!" Her sister Sapphire picked up her skirt and ran over to her. Their twin sisters, Amber and Amethyst followed right behind. Ruby threw herself into their arms and they all started crying.

"What kind of a happy homecoming is this if you are all going to stand there and cry?"

Ruby's head snapped up at the sound of her father's voice and she looked over to see him descending the steps of the battlement. She darted across the courtyard, throwing herself into him so hard that she almost knocked them both over.

"Papa!" she cried, shedding more tears of joy.

"Welcome home, daughter," said her father giving her a hug and a kiss.

"Earl Blackpool." Nyle acknowledged Ruby's father,

dismounting and walking over to greet him.

"Sheffield," he said with a nod, letting go of his daughter and clasping hands with the man. "I trust you are taking good care of my daughter?"

"She is my wife," he said, putting his arm around her, and reaching down to kiss her. "Of course I am taking good care of her as I would have it no other way."

"I've prepared a feast in honor of your homecoming, Ruby," said her father. "Even though it is late, I have made everyone wait for your arrival before they ate. And tomorrow you can tell me every single thing you've been doing since you've been gone."

Nyle cleared his throat. "Well mayhap not every single thing."

"You devil," said the earl, putting his arm around Nyle's shoulder. "With that attitude I'll have grandchildren in no time."

Just then, Locke walked up and placed the baby in Nyle's hands. "I think he's fussy because he wants you," he said.

"Sheffield, you already have a child?" The earl's disposition changed and he looked toward Ruby.

"We are on a mission from the king," Ruby told her father. "Come, let us go eat," she said, putting her arm around him as they headed to the great hall. "And afterwards Nyle will tell you all about it."

* * *

Nyle felt uncomfortable telling Ruby's father that Tibbar was the king's bastard and they were on a mission by watching him and pretending he was theirs. But it was the truth, and besides he didn't fancy telling the earl that the boy could be his. As it was, the earl warmed up to him again as soon as he heard the king mentioned.

"I wish we could have been at the wedding," said Amber, as the meal finished and Ruby's sisters crowded around her at the dais.

"I like this cute little baby," said Sapphire, having claimed the child as hers since she saw it and not put it down yet.

"Sapphire, don't get too excited to have babies," warned her father. "After all, you need to be married first."

"I know, Papa," she said with a smile. "I only hope that I will be as happily married as Ruby."

"Well, you will have your chance, Sapphire," her father told her, "as I have decided to betroth you to Lord Roe Sexton of Rye, as I think it is time you marry."

"I'm going to be betrothed?" asked Sapphire with wide eyes.

"Papa, you made a promise to Mother to let us choose our own husbands," said Ruby.

"You know I can no longer uphold that promise," said her father. "In order to protect my holdings I have to make alliances. Besides, I would like many grandchildren some day."

"I don't mind," said Sapphire with a smile.

"You don't?" asked her sister, Amber.

"As long as he is handsome like Ruby's husband," she said with a slight giggle.

"I cannot promise that," answered her father, "as I have never met him. But I have made the betrothal through his father, as Lord Roe Sexton is away fighting overseas."

"I will be happy like Ruby," said Sapphire. "I just know

I will."

"Ruby, you do look happy," said Amethyst in her ever so positive view, smiling at her newly married sister.

"I am the happiest girl in the world," Ruby said, looking over and smiling at Nyle.

"Sheffield, I've made a decision," said the earl standing at the dais and raising his hand to gain the attention of everyone there. Nyle had no idea what he meant until he made the announcement to the crowd. "Tomorrow we will have a celebration for my daughter and her new husband. We will also have a proper wedding since she has yet to have one worth mentioning."

"Oh, Papa," do you mean it?" Ruby asked excitedly.

"I do," he said. "And Sheffield, this time you'd better make it right, as I expect you to give my daughter a worthy wedding present as well."

"I think I have something she will like," he said, his hand going to the pouch at his side that held the dagger.

"You do?" Ruby smiled at him then looked over to her father. "Papa, whatever he gives me, I am sure it will be wonderful and I will love it. And I bet anything, that you will love it too."

Nyle just forced a smile thinking about the story of how her father had discarded the daggers blaming them for the death of his wife. Suddenly, he didn't feel so confident that the earl would like him as much on the morrow.

Chapter 23

Morning came, and Ruby and Nyle stood on the steps of St. Andrew's church with a crowd of onlookers present. They had just finished renewing their vows and Ruby felt so happy to be with all the people she loved that she couldn't stop smiling. The priest closed his book and then proceeded in giving them all a blessing.

Ruby had chosen to don the cream colored gown she'd worn the first day she'd left for Sheffield with Nyle. It was her favorite as 'twas the most beautiful of her gowns and also had the longest train.

Her sisters all stood beside her with bouquets of handpicked wildflowers in bright colors of pink, purple and blue. Balanced on one hip, her sister, Sapphire, proudly held little Tibbar. Her handmaid, Oralie, was wiping her eyes and crying, sitting at the base of the steps with her injured leg elevated. And next to Oralie stood Ruby's father. He looked ever so handsome, sporting his best tunic and a long ermine trimmed cloak for the occasion.

This is what she had wanted all along. Her family to help her celebrate her new marriage. Now, the only thing that would have made it perfect was if her mother and baby brother had been alive and also there with her on this happy occasion.

Nyle stood at her right side with Locke next to him. Nyle's squire had the biggest smile on his face she'd ever seen. She laughed inwardly when she realized he wasn't smiling at her, but rather at all three of her sisters instead.

"Ruby," said Nyle, taking her hands in his. "I still have not gotten you a proper wedding ring, and for this I apologize."

"I have a ring," she told him, proudly holding up her hand with the ruby ring that was once her mother's. "Thank you, but this is the only ring I want or need, Nyle."

"But I do have a wedding gift for you, sweetheart," he said, digging into the pouch at his side. "And I do believe 'twill go well alongside your mother's ring."

"What is it?" she asked excitedly, as this was a surprise to her.

"Something I think you will really like, and also something I want you to keep at your side for protection, always."

Ruby's eyes popped open wide as Nyle handed her a jeweled ruby dagger.

"Nyle," she said, her heart racing as she took it into her hands to inspect it. "I believe this is the exact dagger I had as a child. The one my mother gave me. Wherever did you get it?"

"From a blind old hag in town," he told her. "It was the oddest thing. One moment she was there, and the next, she'd disappeared."

"Let me see that," said her father, racing up the steps and pushing his way between them. His face turned ashen when he saw the dagger, and immediately Ruby knew she had not been mistaken that this was the one given to her so many years ago.

"Sheffield, I don't like it," he ground out. "I demand you take it back to where you got it."

"Papa, no!" Ruby held the dagger possessively, not willing to give it up for anything. "This was a present from Mother and my last remembrance of her. And now it is a present from my husband. I will not give it up."

Ruby's sisters crowded around, surveying it eagerly.

"That's it, all right," said Amethyst. "That's the dagger you had as a child, Ruby."

"I agree," chimed in Amber. "Though we were young, I do remember it well."

"Let me see," said Sapphire, crowding in with the baby in her arms. "It is!" she exclaimed. "I'm sure of it. And I remember mother telling us that those daggers would ensure that we all find our true loves in this lifetime."

"Well, I know I found mine," said Ruby, reaching up and kissing her husband upon the lips.

"I want to find my true love, too," complained Sapphire. "I want my dagger before I marry Lord Sexton."

"I want my dagger also," said Amethyst.

"Me too," added Amber."

"Well, I can see I have no choice but to let you keep it," said the earl with a sigh. He laid his hand on Ruby's shoulder. "I once thought those daggers to be evil, and because of them I lost my true love as well as my only son. But I see that it has made you very happy, Ruby, and you two do seem to be in love, so I will let you keep it."

"Papa, can you get the rest of our daggers for us?" asked Sapphire excitedly.

"Sheffield, I will pay for the return of the daggers. Where do I find them?" asked the earl.

"I couldn't tell you," said Nyle. "The old woman just up and disappeared, so I don't think 'twill be an easy feat to find her."

"I think you imagined the old hag," broke in Locke. "After all, I never saw her."

"You couldn't see the broad side of a barn," Nyle jested, "so I'm not surprised. Besides," he continued, "I don't know if she had more like this, or even if they'd be for sale. I had to trade for this one, and I paid dearly, but 'twas worth what I gave for it, because nothing is more important than my love for Ruby."

"What did you trade?" she asked. He held up his hand and she noticed his expensive signet ring was missing. "Oh, Nyle, you didn't. I know how much that ring meant to you."

"Nothing means more to me than you, wife. And I plan on keeping you around for a long time – forever. I love you, Ruby. I know I had a hard time saying it before, but I have let go of my past and want to live with you in my future. I'll say it again, I love you Ruby, and I really mean it."

"And I love you, too, Nyle." They embraced and kissed, then Ruby held up the dagger to admire it once again. "This is the best present you could have ever given me."

Just then, the baby reached out and tried to touch the tip of the blade. Nyle's hands shot out and took the baby from Sapphire and pulled him into his embrace protectively. "No you don't, you little rabbit," he said.

"Rabbit?" Ruby looked at him curiously. "Why did you call him that? Does it have something to do with that pet rabbit you lost as a child and why you can't eat rabbit to this day?"

Ruby

"Ah, so that is why you never eat the braised rabbit at the feasts," said Locke. "And I'm just going to guess, but I'd say that boy's odd name, Tibbar, sounds an awful lot like rabbit spelled backwards."

"It is!" exclaimed Ruby. "You named him after your pet rabbit."

Everyone laughed, and instead of getting angry, Nyle laughed along with them. Then he added to the explanation. "Not to mention, the day I first saw this baby he was sucking his thumb and his nose was wriggling like a damned rabbit."

"I'm going to miss the little fellow," said Ruby, running a hand across the boy's dark locks. "I only wish there was some way we could keep him." She looked down to her dagger and gripped it tightly. This little boy reminded her so much of her baby brother, that she didn't want to lose him too.

"Lord Sheffield? Lord Nyle Sheffield?" A messenger of the king rode up to the bottom of the church steps. He horse was draped with the king's color and coat of arms, as well as having it displayed proudly on his chest.

"I am Lord Sheffield." Nyle descended the steps with the boy in one arm, and Ruby quickly followed. Sapphire reached down and picked up the end of her long train and straightened it for her when she got to the bottom. Ruby had a servant to do that, but her sisters were doting over her ever since she'd returned. Everyone crowded around as the messenger reached into his pouch and pulled out a rolled up parchment stamped with the king's privy seal in wax.

"The king made an unannounced visit to your castle just two days ago, but you had left already."

"I am sorry," he announced. "Had I known he was coming, I would have been there."

"Your steward and knights told him where you went, and he sent me with this missive to find you."

Nyle handed the baby to Ruby, and she noticed tension lining the creases of Nyle's mouth. She knew he was expecting the worse in the missive and so was she. Her heart already ached, knowing how hard it was going to be for Nyle to give up little Tibbar and return him to the king. She would miss him as well, as she had grown fond of him and started to feel like 'twas their child. The three of them had started to feel like a family, and she didn't want to lose that after all they'd been through.

She watched as Nyle reached out to break the wax seal, his hands shaking in the process. She saw the bead of sweat on his brow and the way he clenched his jaw so tightly in anticipation that a muscle actually twitched in his neck. He slid off the band that bound it, and dropped it to the ground. Then he hesitated, his hand lingering, but yet doing naught to unroll the parchment.

"Do you want me to read it?" asked Ruby.

He looked at the scroll once again and ran a weary hand through his hair. "Nay," he told her. "I need to do this. And I need to accept whatever the king decides."

"What's this all about, Sheffield?" asked the earl, making his way to the front of the crowd. "Read the missive from the king aloud so we can all hear. After all, we are now all family."

"You don't have to," Ruby whispered, knowing how hard this already was for Nyle.

"Nay, he's right," said Nyle. "You are all part of my family now and you need to know."

He unrolled the scroll slowly, looking at Ruby and taking a deep breath. Then he released his breath, and looked at the words written on the parchment. He scanned the contents and shook his head, his eyes closing briefly for a second as he read the missive to himself.

"What's the matter?" asked Ruby, reaching out her hand to rub her husband's arm to comfort him. "What does the king say?"

"He opened his eyes and glanced at her. "It seems when he arrived at Sheffield they were in the process of burning Jocelyn's body."

"Oh no," she gasped. "Did he know it was her?"

"My steward, Lewis, told him everything. How Jocelyn hired people with the king's money to murder my wives so the baby would be ensured a good life with him raised as his bastard."

"How did Lewis even know?" asked Ruby. "I thought you kept that part a secret."

"There were only two people I'd told that story to," said Nyle, "and one of them must have had a wagging tongue."

"I didn't tell the steward," said Ruby. "I promise you I kept that to myself."

"I wasn't accusing you," he said, turning his head and looking directly at Locke.

Locke made a face and hung his head in shame. "I am sorry, my lord. I may have been a little excited and spilled a secret or two but I assure you I meant no harm."

"It doesn't matter," said Nyle, continuing to read the king's words. "It seems the king decided 'twould be better if he distanced himself from this whole scandal. He doesn't care to sully his name by it."

"What does that mean?" asked Ruby, suddenly feeling hopeful. She watched as Nyle's frown slowly turned upward into a grin. He finished reading the missive and rolled it back up and turned to face her.

"It means my squire's ability to gossip like an old alewife, actually worked in my favor this time."

"My lord?" asked Locke, looking up in question.

"The king said he wouldn't raise a bastard whose mother was a murderer, and so he wants naught to do with Tibbar."

"So . . . what happens to him, then?" Ruby asked.

Nyle reached out and took the child from her. "He wants me to raise the boy as my own and never mention any of this to the queen."

"Really?" Ruby felt a wave of elation and relief wash through her. "So we can keep Tibbar? Forever?"

"It seems so," he answered, kissing the baby atop the head. "It looks like we're going to be a family after all."

Ruby fell into Nyle's arms and the three of them were brought together as the family she knew they really were. Her sisters congratulated her and even her father accepted everything that had happened, and reached out and clasped arms with Nyle and leaned over to kiss Ruby on the cheek.

"Lord Sheffield," said the messenger, as his horse danced anxiously beneath him. "One last thing before I leave." The man reached into his pouch and pulled out something from within. "I stopped in town on the way here to ask where to find you, and an old, odd woman gave me directions. She also asked me to give this to you. When I saw what it was, I wanted to question her why she even had it, but when I looked up, she had disappeared."

"What is it?" asked Ruby, peering over to see the object the man had just handed her husband. Nyle opened his fingers, and there on his palm was his father's gold signet ring shining brightly in the morning sun.

"Well, Locke, can you see this?" chuckled Nyle. "I

guess I wasn't talking to myself in town after all, was I?"

"'Tis your ring, my lord," gasped Locke. "I can't believe it."

"I can," he said, looking down to Ruby and smiling. The baby picked up the ring and tried to put it in his mouth before Nyle took it away. "Nothing will surprise me from this day forward. After all, my life is going to be far from dull now that I've married one of the ***Daughters of the Dagger – Ruby.***"

From the Author:

I hope you enjoyed Ruby and Nyle's story. Through my research I discovered that almost every medieval king had mistresses and bastards, as it was not at all uncommon. King Edward III did take a mistress later in life that happened to be his wife's young lady-in-waiting, Alice Perrers. And though he had a dozen legitimate children with his wife, (some died), he had three bastards with his mistress Alice.

The second book in the ***Daughters of the Dagger Series***, ***Sapphire***, addresses the issue of wool smugglers in medieval England, so please continue your journey through this series.

The books in the ***Daughters of the Dagger Series*** are:
Ruby – Book 1
Sapphire – Book 2
Amber – Book 3
Amethyst – Book 4

And following this series is my Scottish ***MadMan MacKeefe*** series that starts with the story of their brother, **Onyx** - Book 1, - a man thought to be dead. It is followed by **Aidan** – Book 2, and **Ian** – Book 3.

Please visit my website at **elizabethrosenovels.com** and subscribe to my blog to receive updates on new releases. You can also read excerpts from any of my novels on my website as well as get sneak peeks at covers of upcoming books. And please remember that there are other authors by the same name, but my novels can be identified by the rose on every cover. Be sure to also take a look at my new book trailer videos.

Elizabeth Rose

<u>Excerpt from Sapphire – Book 2</u>
(Daughters of the Dagger Series)

Lady Sapphire pulled the hood of her mantle lower to hide her face as she entered the *Bucket of Blood* behind her stable boy, Dugald. She knew she shouldn't be in town this late at night and amongst commoners, but she was trying to escape her husband, Lord Wretched. That is, the baron. People had no idea what a horrible man he really was. If he found out she'd ever been here, he'd take his fist to her, she was sure.

She only wished the marriage had not been so rushed, and that her father and sisters would have been present. Perhaps her father would have stopped the marriage, since the baron was not an original part of the negotiations he'd made with Roe Sexton's late father, Robert, who died just before her arrival. But she'd been convinced by her dead betrothed's uncle who was also Robert's brother, Lord Henry Sexton, that this was the proper thing to do and not to jeopardize the alliance between Blackpool and Rye. So she'd done the deed to ensure safety to her father's lands, and especially her younger twin sisters, Amber and Amethyst back home.

Sapphire didn't regret for a moment coming to the Bucket of Blood pub, searching for answers. After all, there was nowhere else to go since her own bed was occupied with one of her husband's latest women. Since he found her body not planted with his seed, his impatience won out and he went on to sample any woman in the castle he could get his hands on. Still, none of them had been impregnated by him.

She was grateful he hadn't touched her now in over two

months, as she wanted nothing to do with the vile man ever again. No woman would ever bear him an heir no matter how many he sampled. God was obviously punishing him for not only bedding every woman in the castle - be she a noble or merely a servant - but also for beating the women when they did not conceive. She'd had her share of bruises from his punishing hand, and knew this is not what she should encounter in a marriage or coupling.

She stopped in the doorway, glancing at the patrons in the dimly lit pub. The Bucket of Blood was a favorite gathering place for sailors and fishermen since it was so close to port. And with Rye being one of the Cinque Ports, she knew she'd find many honorable men here who had vowed to protect the channel for their king. Men of the sea filled the tables and wooden benches, and stood at the drink board that served as a counter. The innkeeper handed them ale, wine, brandy, and drinks of many kinds in large tankards made of metal or wood with curved handles on the side. Women of the night clung to the men, wearing their low-cut-bodice gowns, working the room, and trying to earn a living.

The large burly man guarding the door, the bouncer, held out his hand and growled in a low voice. "

"Ye know the charge. A hay-p'ny for each o' ye. Now pay up."

Like most pubs, there was a petty charge at the door to cover any damages of broken bottles or benches should a patron get rough. And in a place like this, chaos was always evident.

Sapphire slipped two halfpennies to the boy, and Dugald handed them over to the bouncer. The man held out his board of wet wood and one at a time bounced the coins atop it to make sure they were real and not made of lead.

Satisfied, he nodded and grunted.

"Go ahead," he said, stepping to the side, enabling them to enter.

She followed Dugald forward into the room, stepping carefully atop the dirty rushes spewed across the floor that looked and smelled as if they hadn't been changed in years. She wondered what rancid scraps of food or how much spittle lay hidden beneath them.

Sapphire felt nervous, yet excited at the same time. She knew 'twas far from proper to be sneaking out of the castle and coming here in disguise, but she just had to feel alive outside the clutches of her doomed fate. She'd convinced the stableboy to help her sneak away and to bring her to the pub that also served as an inn. He'd even supplied the commoner's gown she now donned to protect her identity.

Dugald fancied the innkeeper's daughter, Erin, so when Sapphire offered to pay his entry fee, he'd been more than happy to help her. She'd been here half a dozen times in the past two months, always staying in the shadows and just watching, and letting Dugald talk to the girl who was his own age of six and ten years. While Sapphire was only a few years older than them, she'd always had the nurturing aspect of a mother. While she wasn't the eldest of her siblings, she'd still acted the part of mother to each of her three sisters through the years.

She enjoyed getting away from the castle and out amongst people who were more interesting in her opinion. She needed this in her life right now. So Dugald kept Sapphire's secret and she kept his.

Sapphire wandered over to the side of the room and slipped into the shadows, trying not to be noticed. She surveyed everyone having a good time, and only wished she could join in on the merrymaking. A minstrel played a lute in the corner with a bard singing out the stories of his travels. Men played cards and gambled coins atop the trestle tables. And they all drank. There was laughing, lots of laughing, as the girls teased the men and the men grabbed them for a kiss or just pinched their bottoms. She watched the lovers disappear one after another up the stairs to the second level, sneaking away to have a tryst. They were coupling, and though the girls did it for coin, at least they seemed to enjoy it, as they always had smiles on their faces. So did the men.

She felt an emptiness gnawing deep inside her heart, wanting to know enjoyment and pleasure from coupling with a man. But Sapphire's marriage to the baron had proved to be uneventful and unfulfilling in every way. Somewhere along the way in the past few months, she'd started to lose her dream of being happily married to her true love and having a large family, and this bothered her more than anything. She wasn't one to give up her dreams easily, even when times got rough.

She wondered what it would have been like if her original betrothed, Roe Sexton, had not died overseas. Mayhap she could have enjoyed being married and making love then. And mayhap she could have had children, the thing that meant the most to her in all the world.

"There she is." Dugald's green eyes lit up as he spied Erin wiping a rag over the counter at the back of the room. Sapphire felt a certain sadness inside her soul, pitying herself, but yet was happy for the young boy. He had been a good friend to her ever since she arrived in Rye. Just in the past few months she'd witnessed his growth spurt, and now he was even taller than her. He had beautiful red hair and his face was covered in freckles. He was a nice boy, and any young girl should be happy to be in his presence.

"Go to her." Sapphire smiled, knowing Dugald wanted to be with Erin yet felt it his duty to stay and protect the lady of the castle. Never before had he left her out of his sight on these visits, but tonight would be different. The boy deserved some time alone with the girl. Everyone deserved some tiny bit of happiness once in a while. Dugald was more than a boy, as he was a man now. She would give him the opportunity he needed. Hopefully, at least he would have the chance of finding true love, even if she would never know it in this lifetime.

"I'll be fine, Dugald. Go." She turned him gently toward the girl. "Just take your time with her, don't hurry."

"But m'lady –"

Sapphire hushed him with a finger to her lips. "Please, Dugald, don't call me that here." Her eyes scanned the room to make sure no one heard him. "Tonight I'm just another commoner," she reminded him softly.

"Of course, I forgot, my la-" Dugald stopped himself from using her title and Sapphire smiled.

"I'll be waiting for you out in the stable. I'll go check on our horses," she told him.

Dugald nodded his head and disappeared into the crowd. Sapphire pulled her cloak closer around her as she felt some of the patrons' eyes upon her. There was no one here for her, she sadly realized. No one that was any different than what she'd left back at the castle. These men were all looking for a whore to satisfy their itch. And satisfied they'd be, and she was happy for each and every one. But she knew not a one of them would ever be able to tell her anything about true love.

"Wench, come give me a kiss."

She saw one of the dockmen well in his cups looking in her direction, and knew 'twas time for her to leave. The men hadn't bothered her before now because she'd always been with Dugald. But tonight was different. She was alone and fair game for any sex-starved man that saw her as a cure to his problem. Though she wanted to feel the ecstasy of making love, it would not be here and with one of these men.

She was headed for the door when one of the drunken patrons grabbed her by the sleeve and spun her around.

"Where are ye goin' so fast?" the man asked.

Her eyes frantically scanned the room for Dugald. She saw him disappearing out the back with Erin on his arm. It was too late for her to call out to him to help her. Besides, he would never hear her in this madness.

"Let go of me, you swine."

She tried to shake the man's grip from her sleeve when one of his friends came up and grabbed her from behind. His hands snaked around her hips as he pulled her closer.

"Stop it!" she screamed, jumping away from him, but the men only laughed.

"Tryin' ta play hard to get, whore? Well, how bout three on one? I think the French have a name for this game."

Just then another filthy man with blackened teeth and rotten breath stepped in front of her and started to undo the tie on his hose. Her heart beat furiously and her eyes opened wide, and once again the other two men decided to grab her by the wrists, not enabling her to move. She knew now she was wrong in allowing Dugald to leave her side in a place like this. If only she had her sapphire dagger that her mother had given her as a child. If so, she could protect herself the way her sister Ruby had done, by killing a man in self-defense. She hadn't even her regular dagger or eating knife at her waist, as she'd changed in such a hurry, she'd forgotten them back in the stable at Rye.

The door swung open at that moment and a group of boisterous, noisy knights entered, cheering and shouting and sounding very drunk.

"Go on in, Sirs," said the bouncer. "No charge fer the nobility, as always."

"We beat those damned French at Poitiers," one called out, handing the bouncer a handful of coins anyway. The man greedily shoved them into a pouch at his side without bothering to bounce them on his board.

"Ground them into the dust, we did," shouted another knight to the crowd. "You should have seen it, as we were drastically outnumbered, and still managed to come out victorious in the end."

"Let's hear it for the longbow," shouted an archer who'd entered with them, his hand raised in the air with a longbow held high for all to see. The crowd cheered and shouted their praises.

"Hold on," said another, raising his hand to silence the crowd and regain their attention. "The best part is that the Black Prince captured their king and his son, and is holding them for ransom. King John the Good is not faring so good any more, I should say."

That sent everyone in the room into a joyous frenzy, and they whistled and shouted. Much back-slapping and playful shoving followed as the knights congratulated each other. Several of them tossed coins atop a table and emptied their pouches to display jewelry - some of the great bounty they'd plundered when they'd defeated their enemy across the channel.

A tall, dark, handsome knight wearing a torn and dirtied

tunic beyond recognition over a covering of chain mail, stopped just inside the doorway. He was one of the victorious warriors who'd just helped win the battle at Poitiers for King Edward III. He looked weary, yet still held an air of importance about him. He had a mustache and beard and long black hair that lifted with the autumn breeze as his blue eyes swept the room and settled upon her. He was a very handsome man indeed.

She pulled once more against the hold of the men detaining her, trying to free herself and make it to the stable. "Let me go," she shouted.

"Release her," ordered the dark knight standing in the doorway. It was only two words, but words that had her captors obeying. The men took their filthy hands off of her and went back to their prospective whores who awaited them in every corner.

She looked up to her mysterious savior, their eyes interlocking, and she smiled and nodded slightly to show her thanks.

"Welcome back, milord." The innkeeper rushed to the door with a tankard of ale in his hand. He handed it to the knight and half bowed before him. "We thought ye been killed campaigning in France. Ye've been gone a long time and we all thought –"

"Well I'm back now, so stop with the idle chatter. I want a room and a whore for the night. Do you have what I need?"

"Aye, milord. The room at the top of the stairs is free," said the innkeeper with a nod of his head toward the stairway. "And ye know yer always apt ta pick any of m'girls that ye take a fancy to."

His eyes scanned the room and Sapphire just stood and

stared, mesmerized by his domineering presence. He was rugged and handsome. Exciting in a raw sort of way. Yet he held a regal air of nobility. He was a warrior and a protector of her country. He was a brave man who risked his life for others and was well respected. And he also just protected her from her attackers. Why couldn't she be married to someone like this instead of what she'd gotten?

He walked over to her, several whores rushing up to try to gain his attention in the process. He ignored them, his eyes still fastened upon her. Sapphire felt a flush of heat surge through her body when she realized he was staring at her. She lowered her gaze and looked to the ground.

He stopped right in front of her, and she had no chance to even think of what to do. He reached up, and with a flip of his hand he pulled the hood from her head, causing her long brown hair to spill forth in the process. She gasped and her hand flew to her hood to try to once again mask her identity, but he grabbed her wrist and looked her in the eye.

"I'll take her," he said in a low voice, still holding on to her. The whores grumbled their disappointment and hurried over to the other men who'd just returned from war. The knight started for the stairs, pulling her along with him before she could even react.

"I'm not available, my lord," she told him, using her free hand to pick up the end of her cloak so she wouldn't trip, moving so quickly through the crowd.

"I pay twice as much as anyone here," he said without even looking back at her. He made his way up the stairs with her in tow, his tankard of ale gripped tightly in his other hand.

Elizabeth Rose

Series by Elizabeth Rose:

Daughters of the Dagger Series
Legacy of the Blade Series
Elemental Series
MadMan MacKeefe Series
Greek Myth Fantasy Series
Tarnished Saints Series

Follow Elizabeth at:
Twitter: ElizRoseNovels
Facebook: Elizabeth Rose - Author
Goodreads
Website: http://elizabethrosenovels.com

Made in the USA
Columbia, SC
29 May 2018